# REILLY'S LUCK

# REILLY'S LUCK
## LOUIS L'AMOUR

BANTAM BOOKS
NEW YORK · TORONTO · LONDON · SYDNEY · AUCKLAND

REILLY'S LUCK
Bantam edition / October 1980
The Louis L'Amour Collection / September 1981

If you would be interested in receiving bookends for The Louis
L'Amour Collection, please write to this address for
information:

The Louis L'Amour Collection
Bantam Books
P.O. Box 956
Hicksville, New York 11801

ISBN 0-553-06208-5

Published simultaneously in the United States and Canada

Bantam Books are published by Bantam Books, a division of
Bantam Doubleday Dell Publishing Group, Inc. Its trademark,
consisting of the words "Bantam Books" and the portrayal of a
rooster, is Registered in U.S. Patent and Trademark Office and in
other countries. Marca Registrada. Bantam Books, 666 Fifth
Avenue, New York, New York 10103.

PRINTED IN THE UNITED STATES OF AMERICA

11   10   9   8   7   6   5   4   3

# REILLY'S
# LUCK

**EASTERN AUSTRIA**

0    MILES    25

**WESTERN UNITED STATES**

MILES

0   50   100   150   200   250

Inn River

Gries   Sellrainer   Innsbruck

A U S T R I A

Melach

Otz River

STUBAIER ALPS

Brenner Pass

SWITZERLAND

I T A L Y

Merano

Missouri River   St. Louis

ri River

Kansas City   MISSOURI

KANSAS

vs

Newton

Wichita

Dodge

INDIAN TERRITORY

Arkansas River

be Walls

Mobeetie   Canadian River

ARKANSAS

MISS.

Mississippi River

LOUISIANA

TEXAS

Fort Griffin

Brazos R.

New Orleans

Fredericksburg

Pedernales R.

San Antonio

Map by Alan McKnight

# ONE

It was dark and cold, the only light coming from the crack under the ill-fitting door. The boy huddled in the bed, shivered against the cold, listening to the low mutter of voices from the adjoining room.

Outside everything was buried in snow. The window was thick with frost, shutting out what light there might have been. Once he heard boots crunch on the snow as a man walked back from the street.

Suddenly Ma's voice lifted, strident and impatient. "I've got no time for the kid! Now you get rid of him! Let one of those farmers have him. They all seem to want kids. Lord knows they have enough of them."

Then Van's voice, quiet, even-tempered as always. "Myra, you can't do that! He's your son. Your own flesh and blood."

"Don't be a fool! There's no place in my life for a kid." After a moment of silence, she added, "What kind of a life could I give him? Batting around from cow town to mining camp? Get rid of him, Van." Her voice rose sharply. "You get rid of him, or I'll get rid of you."

"Is that all it means, then? I knew you were a hard woman, Myra, but I thought I meant more to you than that."

1

"You're a fool, Van. Without me, you'd be cadging for drinks around the saloons. You take him out of here right now, and get rid of him. I don't care how you do it."

The boy tried to huddle into a tighter ball, tried to shut his ears against the voices, to close out the growing terror.

"All right, Myra. I'll see to it."

There was a mutter of voices again, and then he heard Ma go out, listened to her retreating steps as she walked along the path toward the street. For a few moments there was silence, then the faint clink of glass in the next room; the door opened, letting a rectangle of light fall upon the bare plank floor.

"Val? Are you awake? We've got to get you dressed."

"All right."

Anything was better than the cold bed, but he dreaded going out into the night, and dreaded more whatever was to come. He liked Van, and he trusted him. Sometimes when they talked Van referred to themselves as the two V's.

Van was slim and tall, with a sort of faded elegance; there was a puffiness around the cheeks, and an ever-present smell of whiskey; but his easy good manners never failed him, and Val admired him for that, and for the stories of his boyhood that he often told Val when Ma was not around. She detested hearing Van talk about anything that had happened before they met, and would not tolerate any mention of his family or the schools he had gone to. His family had been wealthy, and the schools had been good schools.

Van struck a match and lighted the lamp. In the light, the bare room looked even more bleak and empty, even emptier than the rooms on the farm where he had stayed until a few weeks ago.

It had been cold there, too, although there was usually a fire in the fireplace, and the farmer and his wife had been kind. Then the farmer's wife had become ill and nobody had any time for Val.

When he was dressed, Van took him into the other room. The boy rubbed his eyes against the stronger light, and then the outer door opened again and Myra came in. She did not look at him or speak to him. All she said was, "Get him out of here."

Van shrugged into his buffalo coat, and then he picked up Val and carried him to the door.

There Van hesitated. "He's only four years old, Myra. Can't you—?"

"Get out!" her voice was shrill. "And close the door after you!"

"Myra, I'll say he's mine. Nobody will know—"

"Get out."

It was icy cold in the barn. Van saddled his horse, lifted the boy to the saddle, and mounted behind him. He hesitated again, holding the boy to him and waiting while Val wondered when he would start. At last he touched his heels to the horse and they moved out of the barn. Van turned the horse to reach over and push the door shut, then they moved away toward open country.

Wondering, Val snuggled down inside Van's buffalo coat. Why were they going that way? There was nothing out there but open plains, but he trusted Van, and in the warmth against him he closed his eyes.

They had been riding for several minutes when suddenly Van swore, and wrenching the horse's head around, he turned back upon their trail. Snow was already covering their tracks, and it was bitterly cold.

"Are we going back, Van?"

"No, Val, we can't go back. At least you can't. We're going visiting."

When the lights of the town could again be seen, Van said, "Do you remember Will Reilly! I think you'll be staying with him tonight."

Val did remember him, a tall, wide-shouldered young man, not much older than Van, but somehow stronger, more forceful. He was a man who rarely smiled, but when he did his whole face seemed to light up. Val not only remembered him, he liked him. Maybe more than anybody, but he could not have said why that was so.

By the time they reached the hotel Val was chilled to the bone. Not even the heavy buffalo coat could keep out the bitter cold. Van tied the horse to the hitch rail, and carried Val inside to the stairs.

The clerk looked up. "Mister, you'd better not leave that horse out there. It's forty below."

"I'll only be a minute."

They went up the stairs and down the carpeted hall. Van stopped and rapped at the door. When the door opened a wonderful warmth came out.

"Will, I've got to ask a favor."

Will Reilly stepped back and let them come in, closing the door behind them. The chimney from the huge fireplace in the lobby came right through this room, accounting for the heat.

Reilly was in shirtsleeves and vest, and a gold watchchain draped from pocket to pocket of the vest. "What is it, Van? You know I'm expected downstairs. Couldn't this wait?"

"It's the kid, Will. Myra told me to get rid of him. He's cost her plenty in the past few days, and she told me to get rid of him or not come back."

"All right, take my advice and don't go back. If you need a stake I'll give you the stage fare to Denver and enough to make a start."

"At what? Thanks, Will, but no . . . no."

"Well? What do you want me to do?"

"Keep the boy until morning, will you? I couldn't think of any other place to take him, and the boy likes you."

"What do you think I am, a nurse? All right, put him down on the bed, but you be almighty sure you come back to get him in the morning, d' you hear?" Then more quietly he added, "She's a fool. That's a mighty fine boy there."

Van put Val down on the bed and helped him undress; then he covered him up. The warmth of the room after the cold Montana night made him very sleepy. It seemed as if he had been cold as long as he could remember.

There was a moment or two of subdued talking, then the door closed and Val heard the sound of footsteps going away.

Val opened his eyes and peeked at Will Reilly as the gambler combed his black hair, and buckled on his gun belt and holster. He caught Will's eyes in the mirror and quickly closed his own.

"All right, Val. Quit faking. I know you're awake."

Val opened his eyes and Will grinned at him in the mirror. Then Will came over to him and gently ruffled his hair. "You go to sleep, boy. You'll be all right here."

Reilly picked up a small holster with a derringer in it and buttoned it at a special place inside his belt. "A bit of insurance, Val, boy. We live in a harsh world.

"Always give yourself an edge, boy. You may never need it, but it saves a lot of worry. Learn to depend on yourself, and if you expect nothing from anybody else you will never be disappointed."

He sat down on the bed beside Val. "Remember this, son. *You*

are all you have. Learn . . . learn everything you can, then you
will always know a little more than they think you know. Most
people in this world are out to take you. It isn't always their fault,
but it is the way they live. If you know that, and make allowances
for it, you won't go far wrong."

He got up and reached for his coat. "I am a gambler, Val, and
I'll be gone most of the night. If you want a drink there's water in
the pitcher and a glass beside it. But you can rest easy—nobody
will bother you here."

After Will left the room, Val lay awake only a few minutes,
studying the flowered wallpaper. A dresser with an oval mirror
stood against one wall, and there was a huge old wardrobe filled
with clothes . . . Val had never seen so many. Will Reilly had
more clothes than Ma. Several pairs of polished boots and shoes
were on the floor of the wardrobe.

There was a Winchester standing in the corner, a rifle that had
seen much use, by the look of it, but a rifle that had been cleaned
and cared for. There was a big black trunk against another wall.

It was broad daylight when Val opened his eyes, and Will
Reilly was sleeping in the bed beside him. Will lay on his side
with the holster near his hand, the pistol grip only inches away.
Carefully, Val eased from the bed so as not to disturb the gambler.

On a stand near the window were six books, all much worn. Val
picked up one of them and turned the pages, but he was disappointed to find no pictures. Then he went to the window and
looked out.

He had walked that street several times with Van, but never
with Myra. She had not wanted anyone to know he was hers . . .
if he was. Val had never been sure about that, but it might be
that he just did not want to believe she was his real mother.

From up here the street looked very different. He could look
right down into the wagons, and if they were not covered by
canvas tarps he could see what was in them. He had never been
able to do that before.

The men standing in front of the stage station wore buffalo
coats or mackinaws, and most of them had ear-flaps. He could see
their breath in the still, cold air. One of the men turned his face
toward Val—it was Van. Just as Val saw him, Ma came from the
stage station and got on the stage, scarcely waiting for Van to help

her in. Van gave one quick look toward the hotel, then followed her into the stage.

The door closed, the driver cracked his whip, and the horses lunged into the harness and went down the street with a rush, turning the corner at the bottom of the street and disappearing from sight.

Val stood staring after it, feeling queer. They were gone. Van had left him behind.

Until a few days ago he had seen Ma only a few times. He had lived with the people on the farm, and once in a while Ma came out to visit, and once she brought him some candy. She would sometimes pat him on the head, but she would never listen to anything he wanted to tell her. Then she would leave again, very quickly. He seemed to remember other people in other towns.

Then a few days ago a black shiny carriage had come to get the lady where he lived, and there were other people too, all wearing black, and after they had all gone away the man brought Val into town and left him with his mother.

He was standing at the window now, staring after the stage, when he felt eyes upon him, and turned around.

Will Reilly was lying awake, hands clasped behind his head, watching him. "What do you see, Val?"

"Wagons. Lots of wagons. I can see right down into them."

Will indicated the book Val had taken. "Did you like it?"

"There weren't any pictures."

Will smiled. "I suppose pictures are pretty important in a book."

"Anyway, I liked to hold it."

Will Reilly gave him a thoughtful look. "Now, that's interesting. So do I. I have always liked the feel of a good book. It's like a gun," he added. "When a man opens a book or fires a gun he has no idea what the effect will be, or how far the shot will travel."

He sat up. "I'll get dressed and we'll go downstairs for breakfast. Van will be coming for you."

"They aren't coming."

Will Reilly glanced at him sharply. "What do you mean?"

"They went away. I saw them."

"Oh?" Then, realizing the boy's position at the window, he said, "You saw the stage leave?"

"Yes, sir."

"Well, I'll be damned."

Will Reilly dressed slowly and with care, trying to hide his anger. That would be like Myra. Like Van, too. Van had been dodging responsibility all his life.

He looked at the boy, who was dressing slowly, clumsily. "Did you go anywhere before you came here last night? I mean, did Van take you anywhere else?"

Val pointed toward the wide-open plain. "We rode out there, a long way out."

Out *there?* In this kind of cold? Could the first idea have been to abandon the boy, leave him to die in the cold? At forty below that would not have taken long.

Did Myra know he was alive, then? Will considered that, and doubted it. If Myra had planned for the boy to be abandoned— and she was just the woman who could do it—Van would never dare tell her what he had actually done.

Will Reilly swung his gun-belt around his lean hips. His anger at being left with the boy was gone. It was far better that they had brought the youngster here than to leave him out there to die. But was it, really? What kind of a chance did the boy have?

Will Reilly's own beginning was scarcely better, and he had survived. How he had done it was not pleasant to remember, but he had survived. Did this boy have the guts it would take? Could he be tough enough, resilient enough, and wily enough to make his way? Will turned and looked thoughtfully at him.

There was a lost and wistful look about him, but there had been no tears, at least there were no traces of any now. He looked— well, he looked pretty much as Will Reilly might have looked at that age.

Will Reilly was an immaculate and coldly handsome young man who had the reputation of being an honest gambler—and no man to trifle with. He had had his bad times and his good, but he knew cards and he knew men, and he won much more often than he lost.

His father had been killed in a boiler explosion in Pennsylvania when Will was fourteen, and for the next six years he had worked as a common laborer, moving from job to job until he discovered he could do better playing poker. He had begun it on the jobs where he worked, moved from them to the river ports, and finally to the cities, and on to the Isthmus of Panama, South America, and then California and the mining camps.

"We will have breakfast, Val, and then we will decide what to do." He put on his coat and straightened it. "What's your name, Val? I don't believe it was ever mentioned."

"Valentine. Ma said my pa's name was Darrant."

"Darrant? Yes, that could be. Well, you've got some good blood in your veins. I knew Darrant, and.he was a good man, a brave man."

Will straightened his cravat, trying to remember what he knew of Darrant. He had been a French-Canadian of good background, an educated man, to judge by his conversation, and a traveled one. He had been a soldier, but Reilly had no idea when or where, and briefly he had operated a newspaper. Like many another man in the mining camps, Darrant was looking for a rich strike, but somewhere along the line he had vanished from the picture. It was unlikely he knew he had a son.

Val was quiet at breakfast. He liked the tall, easy young man who talked so readily yet took the time to listen to him, too. Reilly talked of his steamboat days on the Mississippi and the Missouri, and Val listened with rapt attention.

There were few people in the dining room. Several of them spoke to Reilly and all looked curiously at Val.

Reilly presently fell silent, thinking of the problem. He was a gambling man, drifting from town to town as the occasion demanded, and he had no idea what to do with a small boy, but he had no idea of shirking the responsibility that was suddenly his.

His anger at Van had departed quickly. Undoubtedly the man had shrunk from abandoning the boy, and he had brought him to the one strong person he knew that he felt he could depend on.

Myra was a tough-minded, hard-souled wench who had chosen her life's work from preference, and neither of them should have anything to do with rearing a child, especially a sensitive boy like this.

Reilly considered the people he knew who might perhaps be equipped for the job, but he came up empty. The local minister was a fire-and-brimstone gospel-shouter who saw evil in all things, and who would never allow the boy to forget who his mother had been.

Ed Kelley, a good man with three children, had a wife who was ailing.

After three days had passed, Will Reilly was no closer to a solution. The boy had the run of the hotel, and was liked by everyone. And a curious fact brought itself to Reilly's attention. The arrival of the boy coincided with a consistent run of luck that left him a substantial winner. The pots he had been winning had not been large, but they had been several percentage points higher than was reasonable.

He was a gambler who knew to perfection the odds on filling any hand he might pick up, and he played according to those odds, so when anything unusual happened he was aware of it at once. Will Reilly was not a superstitious man, but neither was he one to fly in the face of providence.

On the morning of the fourth day, Loomis, who operated the hotel, stopped him on his way to breakfast. "Will, the Reverend was inquiring after the youngster. He declared you were no fit man to have a child, and I think they're fixing to take him from you."

Will Reilly was nothing if not a man of quick decision.

"Thanks, Art. Now about that buckboard of Bronson's? Did you ever find anyone to drive it back?"

Art Loomis was not slow. "I can have it hitched up and out back waiting, Will. I'll even pack for you."

"I'll pack. You get the buckboard hitched, and while you're at it, stop by Ferguson's and buy a couple of bedrolls for me and about a hundred rounds of .44's. I'll also need a camp outfit."

Dunker would know all about the boy. The Reverend had preached the funeral sermon for Mrs. Schmitt. The Reverend Dunker's allies would be Mrs. Purdy, and probably the wife of Elkins, who operated the Ferguson Store. Elkins himself was a good man, but Reilly had no use for the Purdys, for Mrs. Elkins, or for Dunker. There was little of the milk of human kindness in any of them.

He stepped out into the brisk morning air and paused briefly in front of the hotel. Because of the early hour, there were few people about. He turned abruptly toward the store.

Jess Elkins got up when Reilly walked in, and from the expression on his face Reilly knew that he himself had lately been under discussion.

"I'll need some warm clothes for the boy," he told Elkins. "You have a nice town here, but it is cold this time of year."

"Yes, sir. He's about four, isn't he?"

"He's about five. Give me four sets, complete. And he'll need a warm coat and a cap."

Elkins glanced up at him. "You sure you want to spend that much? After all, he isn't your boy."

"In a sense he is." Will Reilly was not one to hesitate over lying in a good cause, and it would give them something to worry about, something that might keep them in doubt until he could get away. "The boy is my nephew."

"*Nephew?*" Elkins was surprised. "But I thought—?"

"You thought he was Myra Cord's boy? He is, of course, but his father was Andy Darrant, my half-brother. Andy asked me to care for the boy. That was why Van Clevern brought him to me."

He paid out the money, and gathered up the parcel and started for the door.

"You're Darrant's half-brother? Why, I never—"

"Be in tomorrow," Reilly said. "There's some other things I need for him. Tablets, pencils, and such."

He walked quickly back to the hotel, his boots crunching in the snow.

It was very cold, too cold to be starting out in the snow on a long drive. And if it snowed any more the buckboard would be a handicap. But he had his own ideas about that, and when he reached the lobby he glanced around. It was empty, and there was no one at the desk. He walked right through to the back door.

Art Loomis was coming in from the back. "Everything is ready, Will, but if I was you I'd hole up right here. It looks like more snow."

"Can't be helped. The wolves are breathing down the back of my neck, Art."

"Ain't you even waitin' until dark?"

"No. As you say, it may begin to snow. Art, if they come around asking questions tell them I said something about driving out to Schmitt's to pick up some clothes for the boy."

It required only a few minutes to pack, and Loomis took the trunk down the back stairs himself. Then Reilly bundled Val into the seat and tucked a buffalo robe around him.

"Good luck, Will," Loomis said. "You'd better look sharp until you're over the pass."

"Thanks."

"Will?" Art Loomis was staring at him. "*Why,* Will? Will you just tell me why?"

Will Reilly looked at the horses' backs for a moment and then he told the truth. "Art, I never had a kid. I never had anybody, never in my whole life. This is a fine boy, Art, and I figure he came to me for a reason."

He slapped the reins on the horses' backs and the buckboard started off fast.

He did not turn down the main street, but circled the livery barns and left by the back way. It was bitterly cold, and it was thirty miles to the nearest shelter of any kind.

# TWO

The horses were grain-fed and strong, and in the intense cold they moved off at a good clip. Reilly glanced back only once. Somebody was standing in the street looking after them as they mounted the rise outside of town. When he had put three miles behind them, he drew up and broke open the package containing the boy's clothing.

"Put these on, Val. No, put them on right over what you're wearing. Then get into this sheepskin coat."

It was wide-open country, without landmarks except for the trail left by the stage and several freight wagons. The ground was covered by only an inch or two of snow, but the temperature was hovering around ten below zero.

He trotted the horses, walked them, trotted them again. From time to time as they went on he glanced back.

Dunker was the kind of man to organize a pursuit, and the sheriff was under his thumb, but the sheriff was also a very lazy man who would have no desire to get out in the cold.

Three hours, and perhaps twelve miles out of town, it began to snow. Only a few fine flakes at first, drifting slowly down. Then it began to fall faster and faster, and soon the horses were white with it.

He was not more than fifteen miles out when the snow became so thick he could scarcely see. The going was heavier, and the horses slowed down. For some time they had been climbing steadily, and now they had left the flat land behind them and were in the low foothills.

Reilly looked down at the boy. Val was awake and sitting up, peering into the snow.

"Cold, Val?"

"No, sir."

"We're in trouble, Val. The snow is getting too deep for the buckboard, and the horses are tired. We'll have to find a place to hole up until the storm is over."

"Is there a place?"

"There's an old cabin, if I can find it. It was off the road to the right, and among the trees. But that's a few miles further on, almost at the top of the pass."

Val huddled in his warm clothes and the buffalo robe. Only his nose was cold, but he succeeded in keeping it back of the sheep-skin collar most of the time. The horses were making hard work of it now. Several times they stopped and had to be whipped to make them move.

"Have to do it, Val. If they stop here they'll freeze, but they don't know any better."

They were almost to the crest of the ridge and the wind was rising when the horses stopped again. Will Reilly got down from the buckboard and, taking them by the bridles, he led them on.

Once, screened from the worst of the wind and snow by a wall of pines, he came back to the buckboard.

"How are you making it, boy?" he asked. "Are you all right?"

"Yes, sir. Can I help?"

"Just stay warm. And Val, remember this. If you stop pushing on, you lose. If we keep going, there will be shelter. It is always a little further to the top than you think."

For what seemed like a long while they plodded on. They seemed to be lost in time; in the blowing snow there was no perspective, no way of judging time or space, for they moved inside a whirl of blowing snow in a white world where most of the time Val could not even see Will Reilly.

Finally Reilly took an abrupt turn. For a moment the buck-board canted sharply and Val hung on, wildly afraid that it would tumble over. But the buckboard righted itself and they were out of the wind behind a shoulder of the mountain.

For thirty or forty yards they had clear going on a ridge that fell away on both sides and was blown free of snow. Then they were under the trees, in a thick stand of timber.

Reilly came back to Val. "You'll have to sit tight. If you see me go on ahead, you stay right in the seat. The old Ebbens' cabin is just up ahead, but if we don't make it soon the trail will be blocked.

Reilly moved back and forth across the road, trampling down the snow where it was too deep, then leading the horses on.

Suddenly a black bulk of rock showed before them, and close to it a slanting roof and a doorway. Surprisingly, a thin trail of smoke rose from the chimney.

Will Reilly stared at it, then with numbed fingers he unbuttoned his coat. Tucking his right hand into his armpit, he warmed his fingers while Val watched curiously.

Why didn't they go on, he thought. It would be warm inside the house, and he was cold now, especially his toes. After a few minutes Reilly walked on. He did not go right to the door, but veered off along a beaten path that led to a stable. He opened the door and went inside. When he came out he walked back to the buckboard.

"Val," he spoke quietly, "I don't want you to be afraid now. There are some men in there, and they may be outlaws. No matter what happens to me, you be friendly with them and they will take care of you. There are mighty few men who wouldn't be good to a little boy.

"There are three of them. Probably I will know them when I see them. They may even try to rob me, but you'll be in a warm place, and we haven't any choice. I'll put the horses up first." He started off, but paused and looked back. "Don't worry too much, Val," he said. He slapped his waistband. "I can handle this sort of thing pretty good."

He drove on to the stable through the steadily falling snow, and Val watched as Reilly stripped the harness from the horses, and then rubbed them down with care.

"Always take care of your horses first, Val," he said. "You never know when you may need them in their best shape."

He flexed his fingers a few times. "All right, let's go see what kind of a hand we've drawn."

Their arrival had been muffled by the snow, which covered and banked the cabin. Reilly's knock brought sudden silence within. He pounded on the door. "Open up in there! It's cold! I've got a boy out here."

There was the sound of a bar being removed, then the door swung inward. Will Reilly pushed the door back further and walked in, holding Val's hand in his left one, then releasing it.

He pushed the door shut behind him, still facing the three men who sat around the room. They stared at Reilly, then at Val.

"Looks like I drew a pat hand," Reilly said quietly. "Val, this is the Tensleep Kid. He's one half Irish, one quarter Dutch, one quarter Sioux Indian, and he's four quarters bad. But he's a strong man and he's honest with his friends."

Tensleep chuckled. "I'm not all bad, kid. I got a liking for kids and gamblers." He looked up at Reilly. "How'd you find this place, Will?"

"I grubstaked Ebbens a couple of times."

"Anybody else know of it?"

"I doubt it. Ebbens wasn't a talking man, you'll recall."

"It's mighty cold to be travelin'," one of the others said. "Maybe you'd like to tell us how come?"

"This is Myra's boy. Van left him with me when they skipped town, and the sky pilot down there was going to take him away from me. I like the boy, and I don't like Dunker."

The man was heavy-set, with powerful shoulders. "I don't buy it," he said, looking hard at Reilly, "and I don't like you."

"Your privilege, Sonnenberg. I don't like you, either."

"Then get out."

"No." Val was afraid of that thick, bearded man, but when he looked at Will he saw his friend was smiling. Will Reilly was not afraid. "We're staying, Henry."

Sonnenberg started to rise, but Tensleep's voice cut the movement short. "Let him stay, Hank. We'd put no man out on a night like this, would we, Tom?"

The third man was tall and lank. He looked around lazily, "No, we wouldn't. Forget it, Hank."

Sonnenberg swore. "How do we know he ain't a spy?"

"Reilly?" Tensleep chuckled. "Reilly's a gambler."

There were bunks enough. The outlaws had added bunks when they chose the place, and Ebbens had had several in the beginning. He had always planned to hire help.

"We'll leave when the storm is over," Reilly said. "I'll make some runners for the buckboard."

"I don't like you, Reilly," Sonnenberg said again. "I never did."

"Nobody asked you to, Henry. I'll try to keep out of your way, and you keep out of mine."

"Or . . . ?"

Will Reilly smiled. "I can shoot as quick and as accurately as any man in this room . . . and it's a small room."

"He's right, Hank," Tensleep said. "I've seen him shoot. I've also seen him use a bowie. I saw him carve three men into ribbons before they could get off a shot . . . and they were sent to the table to get him."

Henry Sonnenberg looked thoughtfully at Reilly. "Well, now, maybe I underrated you. Maybe you're better than I thought."

"It's kind of close in here," Reilly said. "I think we'd both get hurt, Henry."

The heavy man stared at him with reluctant admiration. "All right. You got nerve. Only don't cross me."

Val had edged close to the fire. He was beginning to get warm all the way through. Though he had not admitted it to Will Reilly, he had been cold for hours. He was still afraid of these men, although Tensleep smiled at him.

"I didn't know Myra had a kid," Tom said suddenly.

"Nobody did. She kept still about it and the Schmitts cared for him until Emma died. Then Myra told Van to get rid of him."

They were shocked, and showed it.

"That's right," Reilly continued, "only Van wasn't up to it. So he brought him to me to keep overnight, then they skipped out."

"I knew Myra had a streak of mean," Tensleep said, "but a *kid!* She'd do that to a kid?"

"She's a strange one," Tom said, and added, surprisingly, "I knew her family."

Reilly glanced at him. "Where was this?"

"Back east. She came of good people . . . well-off. But she was always a mean one. She skipped out and never did go back."

When Val woke up the cabin was light and he was lying on a bunk with blankets tucked around him. Tensleep was sitting by the fire with his feet propped up on a stump that did duty for a chair. He glanced over when Val moved. "Mornin', boy. When you get right down to it you're an almighty good sleeper, you know that?"

"Yes, sir."

"Sir. Now that's right nice. Who taught you manners, boy?"

"Mr. Van did, sir."

"Well, I reckon he was good for something, after all. But a pleasant man, too, a right pleasant man. I never did talk to anyone who was easier with words . . . unless it was Will Reilly. You got a friend there, boy. You stick to him. A man never has many friends in this life and he had better hold onto them."

"You have friends."

Tensleep chuckled dryly, and gave Val a quick, sidelong glance tinged with ironic humor. "Yeah? You might call 'em that. We work together, boy, and they're good at what they do, but I was talkin' of friends you can turn your back on."

"Mr. Reilly likes you."

"Reilly does? Now, why do you say that, boy?"

"I can tell by the way he talks to you and looks at you. He likes you, all right."

"I'm honored. Will Reilly is a man sparing of his likes. And what about you, boy?"

"Yes, sir. I like you."

"How about Hank? An' Tom?"

"I don't like Hank . . . Henry. I don't think he likes me, either. I don't know about Tom."

"Nobody knows about Tom. Not even Tom." He got up and added wood to the fire. "You keep shet about your likes an' dislikes, boy. Though I don't s'pose it will make much dif'rence, one way or t'other."

The snow had stopped, but outside the window, which he could scarcely see through because of the frost, everything was white and still. He could hear an axe being used, and from time to time the sound of voices. He could see big chips lying on the snow, and a couple of long poles, curved on one end. Will Reilly had chosen young saplings with a slight curvature for the runners. Now he was trimming them to smooth the surface that would ride on the snow.

Sonnenberg, Tom, and Reilly wheeled the buckboard into view

and Reilly went to work to remove the wheels. The buckboard had been built so that runners could be mounted for winter use.

After a while they all came in. Tom went to work preparing a meal, and Reilly tilted his chair back against the wall. "I've got some extra grub," he said, "and we're obliged for your help. If you stay here until you get a chinook, or spring comes, you'll need more than you've got."

"It would help," Tensleep agreed.

"I can leave you a couple of slabs of bacon, some frozen beef, maybe half a dozen cans of beans. We didn't pack flour because we didn't figure to have any place to bake."

"See?" Tensleep said. "I told you he was all right. You never lose anything if you stand by Will Reilly."

Reilly drank coffee, and then nodded to Val. "Get bundled up, Val. We're pulling out."

"You got a long drive." Sonnenberg studied him warily. "How do we know you ain't just goin' out to meet the sheriff some place?"

"If you knew Daily Benson," Reilly answered, "you wouldn't worry. You couldn't get him three miles from town in this weather for twenty thousand dollars. He's a warm-weather sheriff . . . and he isn't looking for you boys, anyhow."

Reilly put down his cup and got to his feet. "Come on out, a couple of you, and I'll give you what I can."

Outside he loaded Sonnenberg down with the bacon and beans, and while the outlaw went inside, Reilly said, "Thanks, Tensleep, I'll remember this." He dug into the buckboard and came up with a ten-pound sack of dried apples. "Take this for an added benefit."

"Thanks." Tensleep started to turn away, then came back. "I just recalled, Will. You be careful down to Helena. The Gorman boys are down there."

Henry Sonnenberg stood by sullenly, but Tom stepped forward and picking up Val, placed him in the buckboard, and tucked the buffalo robe around him. "You ride warm, son. You've got a cold drive ahead of you."

"Thank you, Tom," Val said. "Thank you very much."

Will Reilly stepped up into the buckboard and sat down, then he clucked to the horses and slapped them with the reins. "You boys take care," he said. "And scatter some snow after I'm gone."

He drove down the trail toward the main road, and Val saw his coat was still unbuttoned and the flap loose on Reilly's holster. Will Reilly was a gambler, they said, but he did not gamble in every sense, and it was only when they had put two good miles behind them that he buttoned his coat.

For a few miles they rode in silence, and then Will glanced down at the boy. "Are you cold?" he asked.

"A little."

"Did you watch what happened back there, Val? It is always important to watch . . . and listen."

"Yes, sir."

"Do you know why we're alive now, Val?"

"They were afraid of you."

"No, they weren't. Especially, Tensleep wasn't. But neither were the others. What was important was that they knew I wasn't afraid of them, and that they couldn't injure me without being injured themselves.

"And there was something else, Val. A man who is strong has to know when to use his strength. I did not challenge Henry Sonnenberg. If I had challenged him he would have felt he had to prove me wrong. There would have been a fight, and some of us would have been hurt. In such a case it is a fine line one must draw, Val. I accepted Sonnenberg as a dangerous man, while not yielding in the least."

"Yes, sir."

"Of those men back there, Val, Sonnenberg is the toughest and meanest. Tensleep is the best with a gun, and by far the most cunning, but Tom is the most dangerous."

"Why?"

"Because he is not right in his mind. He looks all right, and most of the time he acts all right, but you can't count on what he will do under strain when it comes to a tight spot. He could very easily go wild and kill everybody around him. Afterward he might be sorry for a little while, but more than likely he would forget all about it."

After that they rode in silence again, but presently Reilly said, "Val, you are alone in the world. Don't ever forget that, and don't forget that he who stands alone is the strongest. It is a wonderful thing to have friends, but you must know who your friends are. Learn to judge men, Val. If you do, you will live longer . . . and better."

The air was crisp and clear, and the horses moved briskly. Val burrowed down in his warm clothes and watched the ears of the horses. From time to time Will Reilly talked of one thing or another.

This was only the first of many rides, in buckboards, on trains, on steamboats, and on horseback, and on every occasion Will Reilly talked. He liked to talk, and Val was a good listener.

It was only a long time later that Val began to realize that Will Reilly was doing his best in his own way to teach him the things that he himself valued. Among these things were to have responsibility and courage, to be a gentleman always, and to realize that a man's word is his bond. There were many other things, too, little things about working at various jobs, getting along with people, noticing the mannerisms that men develop, the tricks of expression or gesture that may indicate when they were lying, or when they are uncertain or afraid. In the hit-or-miss way of the gambling table, the steamboat and the mining camp, Will Reilly's own education had been gained the hard way.

On that first night in the strange hotel in Helena, Will Reilly dressed to go out. As he turned away from the dresser he opened a fresh pack of cards and handed them to Val.

"Take these. Shuffle them a hundred times tonight. Learn the feel of them, learn how to handle them easily. Even if you never play cards it will make your fingers more agile, your eyes quicker." Reilly went out then, and Val was alone.

He went to the window and listened to the crunch of footsteps on the snow, remembering what Tensleep had said about the Gormans. Would they find Will? Would they kill him? Would he never come back?

He watched the lights on the snow, and he thought of all that had happened—of Myra and Van, of Tensleep, Henry Sonnenberg, and Tom . . . did Tom have another name?

Then he began to shuffle the cards. He shuffled, dealt, gathered them up again . . . a hundred times, and a few more.

And so it was to be, night after night. He learned to handle the cards smoothly and with dexterity, to deal, second-deal, to deal off the bottom. He learned to cut cards and shift the cut, to build up a top stock or a bottom stock from which the hands he wanted could be dealt.

"A gentleman never cheats, Val," Will Reilly told him the next night while brushing his hair, "but you will not always play with gentlemen, and it is well to know when you are being cheated; and to know that, you must know what it is possible to do.

"If you suspect a game of being crooked, get out. Use any excuse, but leave it. Don't call a man on cheating, because if you do you'll have to kill him, and a dead man doesn't rest easy on your mind.

"Train your memory . . . and observe. Learn to know and recall every card that has been played, and who played it; but above all, notice people, places, things."

Will Reilly had turned from his hair brushing. "Go to the window, Val, and look out."

When the boy had stood looking out for a minute, Will called him back and said, "All right, how many buildings are there across the street? That you can see from that window?"

"I don't know. I think . . ."

"There are seven that front on this street. Three of them are two-storied, two have balconies."

Will Reilly put on his coat, straightened his tie. "Don't just look out the window, Val. You must learn to *see*, and to remember.

"Now let's go to dinner."

# THREE

By the time he was eight years old, Valentine Darrant knew everything there was to know about a deck of cards. He knew that, in draw poker, when holding a pair and drawing three cards, his chances of making three of a kind were eight to one, his chances of four of a kind, three hundred and fifty-nine to one. He knew all about check-cop and hideouts, and he could detect the whisper of a bottom deal as well as Will Reilly himself.

He had ridden horseback more than a thousand miles over the roughest kind of country, and he had ridden the stage three times that far. He had ridden steamboats from New Orleans on the Mississippi to Fort Benton on the Missouri.

He had followed a dozen rushes to boom towns, had seen those towns born and had seen them die. He knew hundreds of the professionals of the frontier, the gamblers, the bartenders, the shady ladies, and the law officers who drifted from town to town.

Will Reilly liked to sing, and Val had learned dozens of songs which they sang while riding across country, and he knew as many poems, some of them fairly long, that Will was given to reciting to pass away the long hours of travel. Will had read a lot, from anything available, and he had a ready memory for facts gleaned from histories and almanacs. This had begun as a pleasure, but had developed into another source of gambling income, for he had learned very early that men will back their opinions with money, and that the memories of most men were hazy as far as historical facts were concerned. He was also a fine athlete, and an extremely fast foot-racer.

Foot-racing was a favorite frontier sport, and such races could be set up at a moment's notice, and they were features of every frontier celebration. Will Reilly kept a small black book in which he listed the vital facts about the racing and fistic abilities of hundreds of men.

"Percentages, that's the important thing," he told Val. "Always play on the percentages; and never be enticed into a bet when you're angry. Don't ever risk money on sympathy or anger.

"Now you take Ray"—he indicated a stocky man who sat across the room, a dead cigar in his teeth—"Ray is one of the fastest men on his feet west of the Mississippi. He isn't smoking that cigar. He never smoked or drank in his life. It's all for show. He looks fat, but he isn't really. And he can run like a bullet out of a gun—for a hundred to two hundred yards. Beyond that he's no good. For him, the short distances are best."

The black book also listed the speed of known horses, many of which were taken around the country and brought into town hitched to a buckboard or a farm wagon to fool those who might be led into betting.

"Never buck the other man's game, Val," Reilly said, "but watch the percentages. It is not one or two pots that make a poker player, but the consistency with which he plays. Winning big pots, while it can be spectacular, can also attract unfavorable attention. Thieves may decide you're fair game, or some may get the idea that you are cheating."

By this time Val had noticed that Will usually won several small pots during several days of play, and often would seem to let the big ones go by. "The secret of gambling, Val, is to gamble as little as possible. Nobody has to be dishonest to win. It is a matter of card sense, good memory, knowledge of people, and just a shading of luck."

Will Reilly was strict, too, with Val. He demanded cleanliness, neatness, and gentlemanly conduct from him, and he made sure that he got them. What schooling Val got, he received from Will himself, for they rarely stayed anywhere long enough for the boy to enter a school.

Will taught him how to read, although he had already begun to learn, when he came to him, and how to cipher, and to make quick, accurate calculations of probabilities and percentages. And always there were the lessons in observation. Rarely a day passed when Val was not suddenly called on to describe country they had passed through, the clothing of a man, or the location of articles in a store.

"I don't want you to be a gambler," Will commented, "but the handling of cards will give dexterity to your fingers, improve your memory, and give you a quick grasp of a situation."

Will never mentioned Myra, and Val did not ask about her. Actually, it was Van he remembered best, because Van had been kind when no one else had been.

Will Reilly had an Irishman's addiction to eloquence, and a natural love of politics. He had memorized passages from dozens of speeches, and on their long rides they often recited together, or one of them would begin a poem, the other would complete it.

They were eating in a restaurant and talking of poetry when a bearded man at the next table turned around in his chair. "What you tryin' to do, make a mollycoddle out of the boy? Teachin' him all that sissy stuff?"

Will Reilly looked at him coldly for several seconds. Then he took the cigar from his mouth and placed it on the edge of a saucer.

"My friend"—his voice was cold—"I read poetry, I like poetry. Do you wish to call me a mollycoddle?"

The bearded man started to speak, and his companion kicked him under the table. "*Jeff!*" he said warningly, but Jeff was not listening.

"Now maybe I might. Just what would you do about it?"

"I will tell you what I'd do about it," Reilly replied coolly. "If you had a gun, I would kill you. If you did not have a gun, I'd whip you within an inch of your life."

The big man had been drinking, which destroyed any natural caution he might have possessed. Suddenly he dropped his hand to his boot and flashed his knife.

Val never saw Will's own hand move, but suddenly his blade was out and the big man's hand was pinned to the table. The bearded man gave a choking cry of pain, and a trickle of blood ran from his hand.

"Val," Will Reilly spoke calmly, "hand me that copy of Tennyson, will you? I believe this gentleman should have his education improved."

Taking up the bottle on his table, he filled a glass and handed it to the bearded man. "Use your free hand, and drink that," he said, "then listen."

Val never forgot those next few minutes. With the man's hand pinned to the table, Will Reilly leafed through the pages of Tennyson, one volume of a two-volume set he had recently acquired, and then read slowly, in a strong, beautiful voice:

> It little profits that an idle king,
> By this still hearth, among these barren crags,
> Matched with an aged wife I—

Slowly, while men gathered around and watched in awe, Will Reilly read the whole of Tennyson's "Ulysses."

Then he reached over and grasped the hilt of his knife and said, "Let that be a lesson to you, my friend, and if I were you I would cultivate the study of poetry. There is much to be learned, and poetry can be a companion for your lonely hours."

He lifted the knife clean from the man's hand and the table and, reaching over, wiped the blade clean on the big man's beard. "I am a quiet man," he said, "and prefer to eat and talk in peace."

He got up. "Come, Val. And bring the book."

They went outside. Val felt sick at his stomach, and he was trembling.

"I am sorry, Val, that you had to see that, but the man was a trouble-hunter and he might have forced me to kill him, which I would not want to do."

They walked slowly down the street together. "I do not like violence, but ours is a time of violence, and there are some men who understand nothing else."

At daybreak they were on the stage to Silver City.

The driver had walked to the station with them when the last stars were fading. "You won't be crowded none, Will," he commented. "Not many riding the stage these days. Skeered of the 'Paches."

"I put my faith in you, Pete," Will said, smiling. "If you can't outrun them, you can outfight them."

"Me? You're funnin'." He glanced at Reilly. "That true, about you an' Jeff Reinert?"

"I met somebody called Jeff last night," Will admitted. "He didn't tell me his other name, and I didn't ask."

"Heard you pinned him with a blade and then read poetry to him."

"Something like that."

"You're a hard man, Reilly." They walked a few steps further. "You come close. Reinert killed a man over to Tubac a few weeks back, an' they do say he cut up somebody over to Yuma."

"He was a reckless man." They had reached the station. "It is never a good idea to call unless you have some idea of what the other man is holding."

The driver glanced at Val. "You want to ride topside with me, young feller? Glad to have the company."

"Nobody riding shotgun?"

"Later. We'll have two good fightin' men, at least, an' goin' through the Pass we'll need them."

Val was swung up to the box, and he looked back, watching Will Reilly get in. Whenever they were apart, Val waited in a kind of fear, worrying that Will might be separated from him and not come back.

He thought back to Van, who had left him, and he wondered why he had done it. Was there something about him that people did not like? Why didn't his mother like him? But Will Reilly liked him, he knew, and seemed to enjoy having him with him.

The horses were restless, and when the driver swung up to the box, Val clutched the handrail excitedly. He had never ridden on top of a stage before, but he knew it was considered a privileged position. Pete gathered the lines and took up his whip. The whip cracked, the driver shouted at his team, and they were away, at a fast pace. After a short run they might slow down, but most drivers liked to leave town with a rush.

The air was clear, the day cool. It was early autumn, with occasional cloudy days, but today the clouds were far away, and one could see for miles upon miles.

"You're travelin' with quite a man there," the driver said to Val. "He kin o' yours?"

"He's my uncle." They had agreed on this story, and it satisfied people they met. Then Val added, "I like him."

"Reckon you do. I like him myself. He don't bother nobody, but he can sure take care of hisself when trouble comes. He's a well-thought-of man, and you can bet it gives me comfort to have him riding inside there in Indian country."

"Why?"

"Will Reilly? Ain't a better rifle or pistol shot in the country, boy. You look at him now, a-settin' back there like he was goin' to meet the queen, an' you'd never guess that out in rough country he could out-Injun the Injuns. Reminds me of stories my pa used to tell of Colonel Jim Bowie."

It was thirty miles to Cienaga, the first stop on the way east, and when they drew up at the stage station Val marveled at the speed with which they changed horses. It was there two riflemen emerged from the stage station and strolled out to watch the hitching of the fresh team.

Will Reilly and Val had gone inside, and then paused under the overhang to get a cool drink from the olla that hung there. The water was cold, delightfully so, for it was cooled by even the slightest of passing breezes.

Pete talked a moment to the two riflemen, and to another man who looked like a miner.

Inside the low-ceilinged room there were two tables, some benches, and a short bar. A man in a business suit, with a linen duster over his arm, stood at the bar, while a woman and a small boy sat at the table. Evidently they had just finished eating. The boy looked curiously at Val.

"You ridin' the stage?" he asked.

"Yes." Val was hesitant, but curious. He had rarely talked to anyone near his own age; this boy might be a year older.

"Those are kind of sissy clothes. You a sissy?"

Val glanced at Will, who did not appear to be listening, but Val knew very well that he was hearing every word. The realization gave him confidence. "No, I'm not. You don't judge a man by his clothes."

The words were right out of Will's mouth, but Val had the feeling they were good words for him to use.

The boy had gotten up and walked over to Val, who was standing by himself. He was half a head taller than Val, and sun-browned and tough-looking. Val felt vaguely uneasy, but he did not know why.

"I think you're a sissy, and I'm going to wallop you in the dust."

Now, one of the things Val had learned from Will Reilly was not to talk in such a situation. If you were going to fight, you must land the first blow.

He doubled his fist and swung hard. The blow was quick and it was totally unexpected. It landed on the bigger boy's cheekbone, and then Val threw a second punch, which was to the body. The bigger boy backed up and sat down hard.

Will Reilly stepped over and caught Val by the arm. "That's enough now. Let him alone."

The other boy was up, his eyes blazing. "You turn him loose, mister. I'll show him!"

"You just be glad that I don't turn him loose," Will said. Then he tipped his hat to the woman at the table. "I am sorry, ma'am, but boys will be boys."

With a hand on Val's shoulder, he walked him outside and to the end of the overhang, away from the others.

"I suppose you think you won that fight?" he queried, giving Val a quizzical look.

"Yes, sir. I knocked him down, sir."

"You did put him down, but he was surprised and off balance. You did not win the fight. I won it for you."

Val stared at him.

"He would have whipped you, Val. He is a little older, a little bigger, and a whole lot tougher. That boy has worked hard all his life, and he has nerve. I could see that as he started to get up.

"Understand, you did the right thing. He was pushing you. He was hunting trouble. You hit him right, but not hard enough, and the first punch should have been in the belly. The second blow was not hard enough to hurt him. He would have whipped you, Val."

Val was unconvinced.

"The time will come when you have to take a licking, Val, so just see that you take it like a man. No whimpering, no crying—at least, not until you're alone.

"I did not want you to take that licking now, so I stopped it. I've only taught you a little, and in not a very serious way, but I see the time has come. The next town where we stop will be the beginning of some real training."

The stage was loading. Val walked out and got on with Will. There was a moment before they got into the stage when one of the riflemen nodded, "Howdy, Will."

Reilly glanced at him, then nodded, "How are you, Bridger. Been a long time."

"Long time, Will." He gestured to the lean, slope-shouldered man with him. "This here's Bob Sponseller. He's from Australia."

They shook hands, and Sponseller measured him with cool gray eyes. "You ever been in Sydney, Mr. Reilly?"

Will Reilly smiled. "Why, that's a possibility, Mr. Sponseller, it is indeed; but then there are a lot of Reillys in Australia, no doubt."

"Aye, but there was one a few years back had himself a fuss with the Larrikins down in Argyll Cut when the Cut was a new thing."

"What's the Larrikins?" Bridger asked.

"It was a name for the street gangs," Sponseller said, "and they had a running feud with the sailors ashore from the ships. There was this young chap named Reilly who set his cap for a girl on Playfair Street, a girl one of the Larrikin chiefs had a preference for. There was a brawl, they say, that started with the two of them, and ended with half of Sydney fighting."

"That is quite a story," Reilly said. "Has that man Reilly been back again?"

"He daren't go back. That's one man they have their eyes ready for, and after their eyes, their fists and clubs."

Will chuckled. "Then if he goes back he had better carry a gun."

Sponseller smiled grimly. "Now, that would be a likely thing to do."

Sponseller mounted the box with the driver, and Bridger Downs got inside. The whip cracked and the stage started to move. The boy Val had fought and his mother rode on the seat facing Will and Val. Bridger rode beside Val, while the miner and the man in the business suit sat on the seat in the middle.

It was twenty miles to Tres Alamos, where they had scarcely

time to stretch their legs before the stage was rolling on toward Steel's Ranch, the last stop before the dreaded Apache Pass.

It was quiet inside the stage. Val dozed, woke up, dozed again. Once he woke up and saw the other boy staring at him. "My name is Val," he said.

"I don't care." Then after a minute, and rather sullenly, the boy said, "I'm Dobie Grant."

His mother was sleeping, and so, apparently, was Will Reilly. The miner looked over at Val. "Boy, would you like to swap seats? I'd surely admire to lean back and catch some shut-eye."

"Sure," Val said, and moved.

The miner sat down where Val had been and leaned back. Almost at once he was asleep.

"That was a nice thing to do," the businessman said. "Are you traveling far, you and your uncle?"

"To Silver City, then El Paso."

The man glanced at Will Reilly again, started to speak, but subsided. After a moment he looked over at Bridger, who was watching out the window, his Winchester between his knees. "Where you going?" the man asked.

"Through the Pass . . . I hope."

"Is it as bad as they say?"

"Worse. Maybe we'll be lucky. It's a narrow trail and built for ambush. If they want us bad enough, they'll take us."

"I can shoot," Val offered.

"No better than me," Dobie declared belligerently.

"You may have to shoot, both of you," Bridger said.

"One thing," the businessman said, "we've plenty of guns and ammunition."

Bridger Downs did not reply. Maybe that fellow thought so, but with Apaches you never knew.

They rolled into Steel's Ranch as dawn was breaking, and got stiffly down from the stage, standing in the chill air of morning to stretch their muscles. Val trudged sleepily after Will Reilly as they went inside.

A coal-oil lamp with a reflector behind it was burning on the wall, and a lantern stood on the table where the hostler had left it when he came from the stable.

"Breakfast'll be on soon," he said, and then added, "It gets right cold of a morning here."

Bridger Downs lounged by the door, watching outside, for this was Apache country, and they might not wait for the Pass. Sponseller was standing under a paloverde tree, watching the changing of the teams.

The driver strolled over to the Australian. "Did you know Reilly before?"

Sponseller shrugged. "There was a Reilly came ashore from a Frisco bark, and he made a play for a girl . . . or she made it for him . . . and her bloke took exception. There was a pretty bit of a brawl, and Reilly won, which nobody thought he could do, and then the Larrikins took after him."

"What happened?"

"Some of them caught him . . . the worse for them."

"He got away?"

"Oh, they'd have fixed his tripe if he hadn't, but the girl smuggled him aboard a China clipper that left whilst they watched the bark he'd come in. The story's often told down along the Cut and in the dives around Circular Quay. I don't know if it was him, but they've the same look."

"He's a good man to have along, going through the Pass," said the driver.

"What's the fat feller got in that bunch of long boxes?"

Pete shrugged. "I wouldn't know. They're heavy."

"Gold?" Sponseller speculated.

"Doubt it. Hasn't the feel of it, somehow. Gold is heavy, all of a chunk. You know when you pick it up. This hasn't the same feel."

The sun came gingerly over the mountains, and the sky and the ranch yard were pale yellow. Pete looked at the mountains for smoke, but saw none.

He looked around again. With Reilly, Sponseller, Bridger Downs, and himself, there were four good rifles. The miner was a likely shot, and as for the fat businessman with the mutton-chop whiskers—there was no telling, although he had a keen eye and did not, somehow, have the look of a tenderfoot.

The horses pawed earth, and Pete went over to take the lines from the hostler. Reilly walked outside and lit a thin cigar and squinted at the mountains. He was wearing a black broadcloth suit, a white planter's-style hat, highly polished boots, now somewhat dusty, and a dove-gray vest.

"If they're riding, Val, you have to lead them a little. And if they're up in the rocks, aim a little high and watch your bullet strike. There's a tendency to shoot low."

"Yes, sir. Do you think there will be a fight?"

Will Reilly shrugged. He glanced at Sponseller, who had taken off his hat to run his fingers through his curly blond hair. "Do you still favor red shirts?" Reilly asked, and he walked to the stage.

Sponseller swore softly, then grinned. "I'll be blowed," he said.

"What did that mean?" Bridger asked.

"He was the one," Sponseller said. "I was wearing a red shirt all the time in those days. I was one of the Larrikins. It was our chief that he whipped . . . whipped him fairly, too."

They mounted up. The driver glanced once at the station, touched the brim of his hat with his whipstock, and they left the station at a brisk trot.

With the horses occasionally walking, then trotting, the stage moved toward Apache Pass. Val now sat by a window, with the words ringing in his ears: "If you see an Indian, or anybody else does, you get out of the way, and fast!"

He liked looking at the desert and the mountains. A roadrunner kept pace with them for some distance, seemingly amused by racing along; sometimes it ran ahead of the stage, sometimes beside it.

The air was cool; the dust stayed behind them. There was a faint smell of horse and leather, and the hot, baking smell one sometimes gets from old painted wood in the sunlight.

Quail flew up . . . a buzzard swung wide circles in the sky. The rocks of the pass began to take on detail. The trail dipped into a hollow, emerged suddenly, and wound among boulders and brush.

"All right," Will said, "we'll change places." He had moved to sit by the window when the stage suddenly gave a lurch and they heard the driver's wild yell, "Hi-yah! Hi-yah!" And almost simultaneously the boom of a rifle sounded right over their heads.

Crouched near the floor, Val could see nothing, but he could feel the grind of the wheels over gravel and stones, and hear the rattle and creak of the stage as the horses fled eastwards.

Suddenly Bridger Downs fired, then fired again and again. Will was holding his fire, as was the miner. The drummer had drawn a pistol.

All at once there came a ripping sound, and there was a bullet hole in the side of the stage right above Will's head. At almost the same moment the stage gave a leap as though it were taking off to fly, and then it came down with a grinding crash, a wheel splintered, the stage plunged forward, and slowly fell on its side.

How he did it, Val never knew, but Will was suddenly outside. He had lost his grip on his rifle, but as the Apaches came charging down upon them he stood erect, and when Val scrambled through the door, now on the top side of the stage, he saw Will fire. An Indian, dashing toward them on horseback, was struck from his horse.

The Indian fell, hit the dust and slid, and then, surprisingly, started to get up. Coolly, Will shot him again.

The others in the stage were scrambling out. Will Reilly stepped over quickly and pushed Val to the ground among the rocks. "Stay there!" he said sternly.

Pete was sprawled in the dirt half a dozen yards from the stage, and he lay still.

Dobie and his mother were crouched close against the bottom of the overturned stage, and the boy's eyes were bright and hard. There was no fear in them, but rather curiosity and a sort of eagerness. Val wondered how he himself looked.

Turning his head, he picked out the men. Bridger Downs had quickly found himself a spot, and kneeling on one knee, he was waiting for a good shot. Sponseller, who had jumped clear when the stage started to go, was about fifty feet away among the rocks, in a somewhat higher position.

The miner, crouched near Val, was favoring an arm, and there was a slow staining of red on his coatsleeve, but he had his rifle in position, partly braced by the fork in a shrub.

The drummer had crawled to the back of the stage and was trying to get one of his long boxes off the roof of the stage.

He turned to Val. "Boy, can you help me? Crawl over here."

Val moved over toward him, and lying down, managed to crawl over and unlash the other end of the box without exposing himself to the Apaches' fire. He pushed the box, the drummer heaved, and it crashed to the ground. The drummer picked up a rock and began to pound on the edge of a slat.

Val crawled back and looked around again. The stage lay just off the trail, forming a partial wall on one side, while on the other side was a bank of rocks and brush. One of the stage horses lay dead almost under the stage, and it must have been his fall that sent the stage into its wild careening.

Val lay crouched close to the ground as the Indians worked closer. He could smell the dust and the powder smoke. Something splintered behind him; the long box broke open and the drummer began taking out rifles. He had twelve brand-new rifles, and from another box he began taking out ammunition.

"Come on, son, help me load these," he said. Val moved over to help, and Dobie joined him. As fast as they could load the rifles they passed them to Will, Bridger, and the miner.

Val kept one rifle himself, and so did Dobie. Filled with excitement, the boys waited for the next rush of the Indians.

"Ma'am," the drummer said, "if you can load these rifles for us, we'll teach those redskins a lesson."

Bridger, with his own rifle and two others beside him, suddenly opened fire. He was making a demonstration as much as anything else, deliberately firing rapidly to show the Apaches what they had run into.

When an Indian showed himself Bridger Downs fired six times as rapidly as he could work the lever, then spaced his shots until the magazine was empty. Then he picked up his second rifle and did the same thing.

Suddenly three Indians moved at once, and the drummer, firing with almost negligent ease, dropped two of them and dusted the third.

Then, very deliberately, he picked up a chunk of slate and tossed it into the air, smashed it with a bullet, and smashed one of the pieces before it could touch the ground.

Will Reilly chuckled, and picking up an empty bottle, tossed it into the air, smashed it, then smashed the neck while the drummer broke one of the fragments.

Sponseller called out: "What the hell you fellers doin', play-actin'?"

Hoping some Apache would understand what he said, Will Reilly yelled back in English, and repeated it in Spanish. "We've got forty rifles an' two thousand rounds of ammunition, so we might as well have some fun!"

One Indian, who lay in plain sight where he had fallen, suddenly leaped up, blood showing on his skull, and made a dive for shelter among the rocks.

Val shot . . . he never knew whether he hit the Indian or not, for four rifles spoke as one and the Indian threw up his hands and plunged forward against the slope, then rolled over twice and lay sprawled, arms flung wide.

Val turned. "I want a drink," he said to Will.

Reilly looked at him and was about to speak when Downs spoke from the corner of his mouth. "Boy, you forget it. That's the one thing we ain't got any of!"

# FOUR

T he sun was high, the few clouds disappeared, the heat in the
  bottom of the canyon grew oppressive. No Apache showed
along the rock walls. The five remaining horses stood in their
harness, heads drooping, unable to leave, for they were still hitched
to the overturned stage by one trace chain.

The Apaches evidently needed the horses, for they made no
attempt to kill them. Nor did they make any further attempt to
dare the fire power of the little group behind the stage.

But the Apaches knew they were out of water. Among the first
shots they had fired had been the ones at the waterbags sus-
pended beside the boot. So they had only to wait—and an Apache
can be as patient as a buzzard.

Pete was dead—there was now no doubt of that. The miner,
whose name turned out to be Egan Cates, had been wounded
twice.

Val loaded the miner's gun, and replaced it for him. "That's a
good lad," Cates said. Then he looked closely at Reilly. "You any
kind of an Injun, Reilly?"

"Why?"

"There's water yonder." He pointed north of their position.

36

"There's a spring over there, but there's a tank up yonder in the rocks."

"Don't try it." Bridger Downs was emphatic. "You'd never make it. Once it gets dark they'll draw the net tight around us. You wouldn't have a chance."

A slow hour passed, and then another. Only one shot was fired, and that was from the Apache side.

There was no sound from Sponseller, and from their position they could not see him. Whether he was alive or dead they had no way of knowing.

Slowly the day grew cooler. Shadows began to reach out from the rock walls. Val lay against the earth, feeling his heart beat, and listening to the sounds. Would they ever get out alive? He tried to remember the stories he had heard. There were not many who had escaped the Apaches . . . but there had been a few.

His mouth was dry, so dry he could scarcely swallow. Will picked a smooth pebble from the sand. "Put this in your mouth, Val. It will keep you from being so thirsty."

The pebble felt cool, almost cold. Saliva began to flow, and he did feel better.

A star came out, and the night air grew more chilly. Will glanced over at the woman. "Ma'am, did you have anything to eat with you?"

"Yes, there's some bread and coffee, and some jerky."

"There's some'at in my parcel in the boot," the miner offered. "You can get at it easier, but without water it won't help much."

Val thought of the olla back at the stage station, and its deliciously cool water. Then he tried to forget it and think about other things. He tried to remember Myra, but the only thing he could recall was her voice, how harsh it had sounded on that last night.

More stars came out, and they seemed like distant campfires on the field of the night sky, as though a vast army camped out there, far away.

Will Reilly sat up, wrapping his arms about his knees. "Don't worry, Val," he said easily. "I have been in worse spots. Although not many," he added, more grimly. "At least, they won't attack us in the night."

He added, "When this is over I think it will be time to go east again."

Val said suddenly, "I might be able to crawl to the water."

Will looked at him. "You'd try it, too, wouldn't you?"

"Yes, sir."

"Don't. That would be dangerous, even for an Indian."

"I'm small, sir. I take up less room than you, sir, or any of the others. When I lived with the Schmitts, we used to play Indian all the time. I could crawl and hide better than anybody."

"You just wait."

"We need water, sir. I know there'd be Indians there, but they wouldn't be looking for a boy."

"No," Will Reilly said firmly.

Then Val slept, and when he awoke it was very cold. He dug himself deeper into the sand and tried to turn his jacket collar higher. For a long time he lay awake, thinking about the rocks where Egan Cates had said the water was. They formed a steep wall, but they were very broken, with cracks and chimneys everywhere; there were fallen rocks all down the mountainside. A boy could hide where a man would have no chance.

Val would never forget that night. The stars seemed brighter and closer than they ever had, or ever would again. Presently he heard a vague stirring, and then what sounded like a scuffle.

After that there was somebody panting nearby, and he heard Bridger Downs's voice. "In the side . . . I don't think it's bad. He had the same idea I had."

"Did you kill him?"

"I killed him. Oh, he was tough and slippery. He got the knife into me slick as a whistle, but I grabbed his wrist and held on while I clobbered him with my fist. Then I got hold of his throat, dug my fingers in, and smashed his head against the rocks."

"How are the horses?"

"They seemed all right, but they'll be needin' water."

Finally Val slept again, and was awakened by the slam of a gunshot, and he saw Will holding one of the new rifles. The drummer was loading another. "I thought our little demonstration of shooting might scare them off," he said.

Will lit the stub of his cigar with his left hand. "Apaches don't scare worth a damn," he said. And he added, "Although they take notions."

"Notions?"

"Watch for their chief. If you kill their chief they'll back off until they've chosen another. They might leave altogether."

There was no attack, and no Apaches were seen. Val grew restless. He thought the Indians were probably gone. His mouth was parched and his skin was hot, but he did not complain. Nobody else was complaining, and he was determined not to be the first.

They waited, sleeping by turns. It was midafternoon before Will Reilly suddenly reached over and shook Downs awake. "They're coming."

"You sure?"

"I'm sure. They've been filtering down from the rocks, working closer and closer. I think they're going to try a rush."

Egan Cates pulled himself up, his face white and strained. The miner had lost blood, and the lack of water was not helping him.

Will turned to Val. "You and Dobie load. Make every move count now. I believe they're planning to do us in."

When they came it was from scarcely thirty yards off. They seemed to spring directly out of the rocks. They fired a volley and charged.

All the guns were loaded, and the Apaches were met by a crashing volley, the men firing as fast as they could work the levers on their rifles. Val knew the attack would have to be beaten back or they would not survive, and he emptied his rifle as swiftly as possible.

Three Apaches made the circle of rocks. A barrel-chested one vaulted the rocks from behind and rushed at Will's back, a knife in his hand.

Val, unable to think what to do, threw his rifle at the Indian's legs, and the man stumbled and went to his knees. Both boys leaped on him, Dobie striking hard with a rock.

The Apache threw them off and lunged to his feet. They grabbed his legs and he swung down with a knife at Val's back. Will, hearing the scuffle behind him, wheeled and fired his Winchester at point-blank range.

The heavy slug caught the Apache squarely in the chest and he fell back. Will fired again, then turned and clubbed his rifle at one who was fighting desperately with the wounded Cates, who had only one useful hand. The butt caught the Apache behind the neck and he went down, his skull crushed right at the top of the spine.

The two Apaches were tossed over the rocks. The remaining one of the three was backed against the rocks with Bridger Downs's .44 jammed into his belly.

"Hold him, Bridger," Reilly said. "We mustn't let him go to warn the others. Our boys haven't had time to get around to the other end of the pass. If he gets away and tells the others about all the rifles and ammunition we've got, they'll know it's a trap."

The drummer was quick. "We'd better send up the signal for the attack. As for him"—he gestured toward the Indian and drew his knife—"we'd better let him abscond right here."

The Apache lunged suddenly, springing to the top of the rocks, then leaping over. Reilly fired a shot in the air, and let him go.

"Let's hope it works," the drummer said. He glanced at Bridger. "I had to trust you knew what abscond meant, and I was sure the Indian would not."

Bridger Downs spat, and gave the drummer a hard look. "I know what abscond means, my friend, and if I was you I'd forget what it means."

The drummer smiled. "Of course. This is all among friends, isn't it?"

There was a sudden rattle of horses' hoofs, and they saw the dust of the fleeing Apaches. The trick had worked.

"Come on." Will Reilly got to his feet. "We'd better go while the going is good."

"Just for luck," Cates suggested, "throw a fire together. The signal smoke will sort of help them along."

Sponseller came down from the rocks. He had a bullet burn along his ribs, but was otherwise unhurt. He helped get the horses ready, and when they were all mounted up they moved out, three of the horses carrying double.

It was a good fifty miles to Ralston's, and Val never forgot that ride, nor the walking he did on the way.

After that it was Silver City, where Val went riding with Billy, the son of the woman who kept the boarding house. Dobie was with them, too. They raced their horses through the streets and out into the hills beyond the town.

"You people stayin' around?" Billy asked.

"Nope," Dobie said. "Ma's going over to Las Vegas. Her sister—my aunt—lives there. Ever since pa died we been traipsin'."

"You better hope your ma doesn't marry again," Billy said. "Mine did, and he's drunk most of the time. He beats me when he can lay holt of me . . . which ain't often."

"We're going to El Paso," Val said. "Maybe to New Orleans."

They circled around the town and came in from the other side, talking about Indians. "I never seen any real wild Injuns," Billy said. "There was some in Kansas folks said had been wild a while back, but the ones in Colorado were mostly just hanging around."

After supper they stood outside the Antrim House and Ash Upson talked to the boys. "A pleasure," he said, "a real pleasure to talk to Will Reilly. It isn't often we find anyone with his knowledge of literature. He's an admirer of Scott, as I am."

The other boys did not know who Scott was, but Val recalled Will's mention of him. After a while Will came out. "We're leaving tomorrow, Val."

Then came a week in El Paso, three days in San Antonio, and a ride on a steamboat from Indianola, Texas, to New Orleans. It was a fortunate time for Will Reilly. The cards ran his way, and he played them carefully, arriving in New Orleans three thousand dollars richer than when he left Tucson.

After that there was Mobile, Savannah, Charleston, Philadelphia, and New York. . . .

And then a year in Europe. Val was growing taller and stronger, and he learned to speak French, picked up some German and Italian. As they traveled, Will Reilly gambled in every city in which they stayed. Yet sometimes weeks would pass during which he would not touch a deck of cards, nor enter a gambling hall, though even during such times he never really released himself from the hold of gambling.

His wagers were polite ones, developed during conversations, and often evolving from some casual discussion of history or genealogies; on these, too, he was well informed. Often the fact that he was an American gave his antagonists greater confidence, as did his manner, which was almost apologetic, though insistent at such times. Somehow—and Val often wondered how it happened—it was always Will who was challenged. But Will Reilly was not a man to allow himself to grow slack in his physical condition. He boxed, he fenced, he went to shooting galleries, he rode horseback, he wrestled.

But Will Reilly was changing. They were in Innsbruck now, and one night after midnight he returned from the gaming rooms in a black mood. He threw a handful of money on the table in their room. The gesture was one of irritation, even of disgust.

He looked at Val. "You should be asleep. You're too young to keep such hours."

"I wasn't tired."

Will glanced at the book. "*Faust?* Where did you get hold of that?"

"It was a lady. The one you were talking to this afternoon. Louise, I think you called her."

"You talked to her?"

"Yes, sir. She was asking about you. If I was your son."

Will Reilly was silent for a moment, then he muttered to himself, "So she didn't believe me? But why should she? I'm a gambler." His tone was filled with self-contempt, and Val watched him curiously. He had never seen Will like this before.

Will gestured at the book. "Read that—and then read Byron's *Manfred*. That's the only Faust who acted as if he had any guts. The rest of them were a pack of sniveling weaklings who learned nothing that was of any help to them."

Val never knew why he said what he did, but he knew his friend was in trouble. "Have you learned anything of any use to you?" the boy asked.

Will gave him a quick, hard glance. Then he chuckled. "Why, now, there's a likely question if I've ever heard one. Yes, I've learned a lot, but there are some situations where all a man knows is of no use to him. Val, I've been an ungodly fool. I've stepped in where I had no business, and the best I can get out of it is the worst."

"What are you going to do?"

"Play my hand out . . . as far as it will take me. I've taken chips in the game, and I'll not back out now."

"And if you fail, sir?"

Reilly gave Val one of those flashing Irish smiles that lit up his face. "Why, then, Val, I'll need a lot of luck and a fast horse."

Well, Val thought, it would not be the first time they had left town in a hurry. And he wondered if Will had actually given any thought to the fast horses.

Val was not yet ten years old, but he had been reared in a hard, dangerous school. The next morning when he saw Will mount up and ride off toward the forest alone, he went over to the stable where horses were for sale or for hire. He had talked to the hostlers before, and the owners, too. There were two gray horses that he particularly liked, and he stood looking at them now.

"Would you sell those horses," he asked, "if I could get my uncle to buy?"

"The horses are for sale." The hostler was an Italian, and friendly. "Everything is for sale if the price is right."

He waited until another hostler, a German, walked away and then said, "Your uncle should be careful. He is making a dangerous enemy."

"You are our friend?"

The Italian shrugged. "I like him . . . your uncle. He is a man."

"Then sell me the horses and say nothing about it."

The hostler stared at him. "You are serious? You're only a child."

"Sir, I have traveled with my uncle for a long time. I know how it is with him. He lets me do things."

"Yes, I have seen that." The man rubbed his jaw. "You have the money? It is quite a lot."

"Yes, sir. I can get it."

They haggled briefly, but it was largely a matter of form. Val knew he would have to pay a little too much, but he remembered what Will Reilly often said: "The cost of something is measured by your need of it."

"And the horses? Where will you keep them?" the Italian asked.

"Take them tomorrow, when nobody is watching, to the red barn. I shall want them saddled and ready."

That called for some more haggling but to a boy who had spent his life among men, and who had more than once watched Will make preparations for a hurried leave-taking, it offered no problems.

The old stone barn was deserted, a place where, as Val knew, the Italian hostler often met a girl friend. Sometimes Val had walked to the barn with him and they had sat talking and looking

_ across the valley until the girl came, at which time Val would leave them alone.

So, sitting in the pleasant shade of the barn, or in the sunlight, if the hour was early, Val had indicated his impression that the mountains before them could not be crossed into Italy, nor into Switzerland. This the Italian was quick to deny.

"There are smugglers who cross them all the time," he said. "They have secret paths over the mountains. In fact," he added, "I know some of the smugglers, and have used some of the trails."

Now he said after a while, "Why do you think my uncle is in danger?"

Luigi shrugged. "It is plain to see. Your uncle is a handsome man, a strong man. The woman he is in love with, and who, I think, is in love with him, comes of a very important family in Russia, and it is said she is to marry a man here who is of a very old family. This is arranged by her cousin, Prince Pavel, and all is well. Then comes your uncle.

"The lady is out riding. They meet, and your uncle comments on the view. The lady replies . . . and it had begun.

"I was riding with her to be sure all goes well with her, and when we have passed the lady asks me about him. They meet again. By accident? I do not think so. This time they talk of mountains, of the Urals, the Rockies, and these Alps. Your uncle talks well, very well.

"Again they meet, and again. Someone with nothing better to do speaks of it, and her cousin, Prince Pavel, is furious. It is his wish for his cousin to marry the German, who is very rich and of noble family. The lady is warned . . . I know it is so, although I did not see it—only their faces afterward.

"They meet again, and then your uncle is warned."

Will Reilly warned? They did not know him as Val did. He was a proud, fierce man under that cool face he showed to the world.

They warned Will Reilly, who had killed three men in gun duels, and another with a knife in a dark room where they fought to the death? Who had fought the Sioux and the Apaches?

Suddenly Val was afraid. He was afraid for Will, and he was afraid for those others who did not know Will Reilly as well as he did.

# FIVE

Val had walked out very early in the morning to see if the gray horses were in the barn, and when he returned he strolled along to the café where he was to meet Will.

He loved the quaint old town which had been a trading post, which had been founded in the twelfth century, or before. He loved standing on the bank of the swift-flowing Inn River, and watching the water. He loved the mountains that loomed so close to the city, and the picturesque buildings of a bygone time. Sometimes he thought he never wanted to leave Innsbruck, but he knew the wishing was useless, for they never remained long in one place.

In Innsbruck Will had done no gambling. Here he thought only of Louise, and Val liked her himself. He had met Louise twice, and they had talked for a long time on both occasions. The first time was at the Munding, and she had bought him a pastry. That was when she had merely met Will Reilly when riding, and had not really known him at all. She had been very curious, but Val was used to that; women were always curious about Will Reilly.

Val never said that Will was a gambler. He was a mining man, a story in which there was some truth, for Will did have a mining claim in Nevada, and he owned shares in several mining ventures.

45

Val walked along the Maria-Theresien-Strasse to where it became the narrow Herzog-Friedrich-Strasse, and went on until he
came to a little café where Will told him Goethe used to come to
sip wine. He went inside and found a table near a window where
he could watch the street.

A man came walking briskly along the street, but when he was
opposite the café he stopped and loitered idly.

Val was curious. For more than five years Will Reilly had been
training him always to observe anything that seemed unusual or
out of place, and this man had been hurrying as if he was afraid of
being late, and then had stopped and merely loafed. The hour
was early, the café had just opened, and there was no one else
about.

Then another man strolled up the street and, without paying
any attention to the one who waited outside, he entered the café
and seated himself at a table facing that of Val, with the doorway
between them.

A couple of minutes later two men came up the street and
stopped outside to talk.

Val had eaten breakfast at that café for several consecutive
mornings, and had never seen any of these men there before.
Suddenly, he was frightened, and he remembered what Luigi,
the Italian hostler, had told him.

He started to get up, but the man facing him lifted a hand.
"Stay where you are, boy. You will not be hurt."

"I am going because I do not wish you to be hurt," Val said.

The man seemed amused. "Us? Hurt?" he said, and added, "I
am sorry you have to see this, boy, but your uncle must be taught
a lesson, and it will do you no harm. You may learn from it."

"My uncle has learned a great many lessons."

"But evidently not the essential one. Ah, here he comes."

Will Reilly strolled up the street with that casual elegance that
was so much a part of him. As he opened the door Val started to
cry out, but a rough hand was placed across his mouth, stifling his
shout.

Will stepped through the door and the two men on the street
pivoted sharply about and stepped in after him, seizing both his
arms from behind.

Will did not struggle, but merely glanced at the man at the

table, who was obviously directing the operation. "Where is the Prince? I am sure he would want to witness this."

They were somewhat taken aback by his calmness, but Val was not. He had seen Will Reilly face such situations before, although not for the same reason.

No one else had appeared in the café, nor was there anyone on the street. They were taken outside to a carriage that appeared from nowhere driven by the man who had arrived first. Inside the carriage were four men, one of whom held a pistol. Will and Val were put in the carriage and the two men who had held Will got up behind the carriage and the leader mounted the box beside the driver.

Val sat very stiff beside Will, trying not to show his fear. Yet in spite of his fear he found himself a little contemptuous of these men. Obviously hired for the job, they were so inept that they had not even searched Will Reilly, and they were utterly unaware of the kind of man they dealt with.

How could they know? He seemed merely a handsome, well-set-up young man, well-dressed and poised. How could they know what lay behind him?

Their destination was only a short distance beyond the limits of the town. Val glanced out of the coach window and across the fields. Just over there, not half a mile away, was the deserted barn with their two horses. The coach came to a sudden halt beside a small grove, where two saddle horses were tied.

Val saw Will give them a quick glance, and knew what he was seeing. One of the horses was the one Louise rode. Was she to be here?

They walked through the trees to a small clearing, perhaps half an acre in extent. Across the clearing, in riding clothes, stood Louise and a tall young man. She wore a gray riding habit, and looked lovely, but her eyes were wide and frightened.

The young man wore a beautiful fur-trimmed coat, which he now removed and dropped over a rock.

Louise spoke, "Pavel . . . *please!*"

"No, my cousin, we are going to teach this American some manners. I hope you will also profit by the lesson."

"Pavel—"

"Remove his coat, if you please," he said to the men holding Will. They stripped off his coat, and he made no resistance. The soft material of his white shirt was ruffled by the breeze. He was smiling.

Val, unnoticed by the others, had edged nearer.

"Now, peasant, you are going to get a whipping. The kind of whipping we reserve for such as you."

"This is rather absurd, don't you think?" Will asked. "If you wish to call the whole thing off, Prince Pavel, I will accept your apology."

"*My* apology!" Pavel's features went taut with anger.

"I must have heard about you, Prince Pavel. I have heard you do not pay your gambling debts, and that you will marry your cousin to this wealthy man so he will pay them for you."

"Stand back," Pavel said to the others, "and give me the whip."

It was a long whip, not unlike the western black-snake or bull whip.

Val was amazed, not so much that they should plan to whip his uncle, but that they were so sure they could.

"Let me do it, sir." The man who stepped forward was a husky brute, and Val saw Will glance at him, marking him for future attention. "I have some skill at such things."

"Of course not," Pavel replied shortly. "I reserve the pleasure for myself." He coiled the whip, drawing the lash almost lovingly through his fingers.

During his early years Will Reilly had made a trip over the Santa Fe Trail, working as a teamster. He had used just such a whip, and he had seen and participated in the brutal whip battles fought by teamsters, who could flick a fly from the shoulder of a bull without touching the skin.

He knew the tactics well, and when Pavel swung the whip and shot the lash at him, Will stepped an easy pace forward, blocked the whip with his forearm, and the lash coiled about it. Instantly his hand dropped, grasped the whip, and gave a tremendous jerk.

Prince Pavel was jerked off balance, the whip flying from his hand as he went to his knees on the turf.

One of the men lunged toward Reilly, but Val promptly tripped him. Will reversed the whip and snapped it viciously at Pavel. The tip of the whip snapped at the young Russian, ripping his shirt and starting blood from his shoulder.

Pavel screamed and, moving lightly as a dancer moves, Will Reilly stepped about quickly. The husky man who had begged for the chance at the whip was next, and the lash whipped his shoulders, snapped at his belly, laid open his cheek.

The action had been so swift that the others had been caught off guard. They were not fighting men, as such, just strong bullies hired for a job. Will moved, now a deadly dancer, his whip a darting snake that drew blood wherever it landed. It struck Pavel's cheek, ripping the flesh, and the Prince screamed again, clapping his hands to his face. The lash popped again, and this time the end dug into his forehead.

Suddenly the man who had been the leader of the group, the one who had sat opposite Val in the restaurant, dug a hand into his coat pocket and came up with a pistol.

Will stepped back closer to Val. "Now!" he said, and from under his coat Val took the pistol he had carried for Will, and tossed it to him. Deftly, he caught it with his left hand even as he moved.

The man had leveled his gun to fire, and Will Reilly fired, almost casually. The man rose on his tiptoes, his gun went off into the turf, and he fell forward on his face in the grass.

At the sound of the shot, its report echoing against the mountainsides, there came a silence. It was no longer a few men giving a whipping to a man for a price. It was death.

Prince Pavel was on his knees, blood streaking his face and neck, his shirt soaked with it. He was staring at Will, stunned horror in his eyes. "Don't . . . don't kill me!"

The other men were backing away, looking for a chance to run. "You'll pay for this!" one of them shouted. "You will never leave the country alive!"

Will Reilly dropped the whip, and walked over to where his coat lay. He put it on, shifting the gun from hand to hand as he did so.

Only then did he look at Louise, who stood shocked and white, unable to believe her eyes.

"I am sorry, Louise, that this happened in your presence," Will Reilly said. "I am not a man to accept a whipping for any reason— least of all, for loving you."

"You have killed him."

"He would have killed me. He was armed, and he was intending to shoot. I had no choice."

He glanced at Pavel. "Had he challenged me, I would have

fought him. Or we might have met together and talked of this. Instead, he chose this method."

"I fight only with *gentlemen!*" Pavel was on his feet, shaken, but with a show of confidence returning.

"Judging by the company you keep," Reilly said coolly, "you need have no fears."

He turned to Louise. "Will you come with me now? I shall return to my own country."

She seemed to hesitate, and stared at him.

"No!" Pavel shouted. "You can not!" He grasped her arm. "He is a murderer! He will be hunted down and thrown into prison, then executed! You would ruin us all!"

Will Reilly stood quietly, while Val shifted from one foot to the other, anxious to be away. Some of the men were already away through the trees, and it was no more than thirty minutes of fast walking to the edge of the city. And these men would be running.

"Louise?"

"No . . . I can not."

One long moment he looked at her. "Good-bye, Louise." He had thrown in his hand, and Val knew it.

"Come, Val." He turned, thrusting the gun into his waistband. He stumbled once, and glancing up, Val saw Will's face was drawn and pale.

Val caught his hand. "We must hurry, Uncle Will. Those men will have almost reached Innsbruck, and people there may have heard the shot."

With Val leading the way, they turned abruptly from the road and went down a path that led across the fields, partly concealed by a line of trees.

"Wait a minute." Will stopped. "We've got to get horses—"

"They're waiting in the barn over there," Val pointed. "I had Luigi put them there. I paid for them," he added, "out of your anchor money."

That anchor money had been a joke between them. It was a little money Will Reilly always kept for a road stake in the event he had to move swiftly. He had once jokingly referred to it as his up-anchor money, but the phrase had somehow been trimmed over the years.

They walked swiftly. Will Reilly was no fool. He was a traveler with no local standing, and no influence, while Prince Pavel came from a powerful family with connections in many European countries. If Will Reilly was arrested now there would be small prospect of escape.

"We're going to be in trouble," he said to Val. "I haven't been gambling lately, and I've spent a good bit. I wish we dared go back and get that anchor money."

"We don't need to," Val replied, "I've got it here."

They dipped down through a stream bed, crossed a stone wall, and went up the grassy slope to the barn. Luigi got up from where he had been sitting. "The horses are saddled," he said, "but you must hurry."

There were three horses, and Luigi said, "You would never get over the mountains without me, and if I take you over the mountains you might take me to America."

"That we will," Reilly said, and swung into the saddle.

They followed footpaths and cart roads to the village of Axams, then across country toward the Sellrainer.

It was clear and cool. The wind from off the Alps was fresh, the horses lively, eager to go. The meadows were matted with wild flowers. The mountain slopes were dark forests of pine. Once a small blue butterfly lit for an instant on the mane of Val's horse and then was gone.

There was no sound but the beat of hoofs. How long before their route would be discovered? How long before pursuit could be organized? A man was dead, and another man of power and influence had been beaten with a whip. They would come, Val was sure of that.

Will led the way Luigi had pointed, and Luigi fell back beside Val. "Tell me. What happened?"

When Val had told him, his only comment was, "It is what I said, he is a man, that one!"

"Where are you taking us?"

He pointed at the vast wall of the Stubaier Alps. "Over that. On the other side is Italy; or if you wish we can go west, and there is Switzerland."

"But they will follow us."

He shrugged. "They will try all the roads first. It will give us time. Not many know the way we are going, although the mountaineers would guess. They will not know at first that we are mounted, and they will try to close the best-known roads. By the

time they know what we have done, we shall, with luck, be lost
back in the Alps."

When they reached the Sellrainer there was a good cart road
that followed the stream as far as the village of Gries, where a
footpath continued on up the gorge of the Melach. It was wild
and picturesque. Somewhere near was the hunting lodge of the
Emperor Maximilian I, but they had no time to think of such
things. Soon they would leave the horses at the farm of a man
known to Luigi, and from there on it was walk all the way.

"We can get what we need from my friend," Luigi said. "He
has warm clothes, boots, packsacks . . . everything."

"I will want a good rifle," Will said.

Luigi shrugged. "That, I think, is impossible. We will have
enough to carry without it."

They were climbing steadily. Around them the high fields were
green, and there were many butterflies, mostly of the small blue
variety, and many birds. Twice he saw what Luigi told him were
golden eagles, and once the feared *lammergeier*, or bearded
vulture.

The farm of Luigi's friend was a pleasant place when they came
to it, a barn for the cows, sheepfold, and a rather larger than
usual house with white walls and an overhanging roof. They rode
into the yard and a short, stocky man appeared in the doorway,
studied them carefully for a moment, and then came down the
grassy slope to meet them.

"Friends of mine," Luigi said, "they are going over the
mountain."

The man scarcely glanced at them. "Come in, then." He turned
his back to them, went back inside, and they followed him.

Seated at a table cleaning a rifle was a young man with a buxom
woman, and two equally buxom flaxen-haired girls. A fire was
going, for the evening was chill at the altitude. "You will spend
the night," the man said. He glanced at Val. "The boy is too
young. It is a hard climb."

"He is a strong boy," Will said. "He is accustomed to mountains."

The man took his pipe from his mouth. "I have told you," he
said simply. He turned to his wife and spoke to her in Italian.

"He is Tirolean," Luigi explained, "but his wife is Italian . . .
from Merano. They have many friends," he added, "in Italy as
well as in Switzerland. He knows everybody."

Luigi left the room with the Tirolean, returning after a short time. "He wants too much," he said, "but he will accept the horses."

"I'll bet he will," Will said. "And everything else he can get."

"We can make a deal on the horses because I have threatened to take them back to Gries, where I know a man who will buy them." He accepted a cup of coffee, and added, "There is no fooling him. Men do not come this far into the mountains at such an hour without a special reason."

"Did you tell him what happened?"

"He does not wish to know. You come, he sells, he knows nothing . . . he does not suspect anything, you see? If the police ask he will tell them nothing important. He is a master at it."

They were silent then. Will Reilly sipped his coffee and stared into the fire, remembering. Val dozed, woke once, and dozed again.

After a long time Luigi spoke again. "You know what lies ahead, do you not? The trail is narrow, part of it is all right, part is very steep, very rough. And there can be storms—and if you have not seen a sudden storm in the Alps, you have seen nothing."

Will shrugged. "Is there an alternative?"

"No."

"Then . . ."

# SIX

It was dark and cold when Val woke up. Will Reilly was sitting on the edge of his bed, dressing. "Better get dressed, Val. We've got to be moving."

"Where is Luigi?"

"I don't know. His bed is empty."

Val put his feet to the floor and dressed in silence. He might have expected this, for Will was moving true to form. Always the unexpected . . . always the quick start, and then travel faster than anyone could expect.

When he was dressed he went into the kitchen. Will was making coffee. "A warm drink will do us good. Get your gear together, Val. You'll be glad of those heavy boots before the day is over."

"Will we be in the snow?"

"Not until dark, I'm thinking."

"What happened to Luigi?"

"He's around, I believe, but if he isn't, we will move out on our own. I'm ashamed, Val. I was tired, and that and the fresh mountain air made me sleep sounder."

They heard someone stirring in the other room, then the door opened and the Tirolean came out, stuffing his shirt into his pants. "You make free," he said.

"We hoped we would not disturb you," Will said, smiling. "After all, why should you and your family get up just because we must? And we thought an early start would be advisable."

The man looked sour, but whether it was the early hour or something gone awry with their plans, Val could not guess.

He dragged their packs to the door, then went to the table. Will had made chocolate for him. There was bread, jam, and some cold meat on the table.

"You cannot see. It is early to walk on the mountain," the Tirolean said.

"Oh, we'll manage!" Will had not seated himself, Val noticed, and knowing the ways of his friend he held himself ready to move quickly. Anything unusual made Will Reilly wary, and Luigi had no reason to be gone—or none they could think of.

Suddenly Will put down his cup. "All right, Val. Get your pack on."

"You leave without Luigi?" the Tirolean protested.

Will shrugged. "He's probably waiting for us. If not, he'll catch up."

Never turning his back on the man, Will helped Val with his pack, then held the door open for him and stepped into the doorway after him.

"Thank you," he said, smiling pleasantly. "You have no idea how we appreciate this." And he drew the door to behind him.

Will moved out at a good pace and Val was hard put to keep up. It was a cart track, then a herdsman's track, and almost at once it began to climb steeply. Each of them had a staff, which helped.

Below them a few lights showed in the village, and then they rounded a bend. Will slowed his pace. By now they were about half a mile from the village.

"What happened?" Val asked.

Will paused a moment, looking back, giving Val a chance to catch his breath without mentioning it. "Val, most people are sadly, weakly human. Don't ever forget that. All but a few mean to be honest, but sometimes their ambition, their greed, or their need for more money will lead them into error. Probably there is a simple explanation for Luigi being gone. Probably the Tirolean was annoyed because we were up before him, in his own house, and made so free as to prepare our breakfast.

"On the other hand, they may have had second thoughts. Prince Pavel would probably pay a good sum to know what became of me, and after all, the police will be after me. They may have persuaded themselves they should report me."

"I don't think Luigi would do it."

"Maybe not. I don't like to think so, either. Let's give him the benefit of the doubt, and keep moving while we are doing it."

They walked in silence for better than a mile, and then paused for a brief rest.

The stars were out, although far up in the sky over the mountains it was growing light. Presently they could distinguish one tree from another, and they could see where they were putting their feet. The green valley of the Otz lay far below them now, shadowed still, although they walked in sunlight. Val was a good walker, and at one time or another he had done a lot of walking. He had always loved the mountains, and much of his walking had been done at much higher elevations than this. He had gone over passes twelve or thirteen thousand feet up in Colorado; and if what he had heard was correct, few of these passes were anywhere near that.

The men who lived in this region were all mountain men who hunted on these high slopes, and would be making better time if they tried to follow, but as Will told him, "We've a good start, Val, and they know I am armed. Most of them are family men who would have little sympathy with such men as Pavel Pavelovitch."

Will kept their pace easy, and made frequent stops. Shortly after noon they made a longer one, ate a little bread and cheese, and drank from a cold stream that ran off the mountain nearby.

By mid-afternoon, Val was having a hard time of it. His legs were tired, and the climb had become steeper, or so it seemed to him. Once, when they had stopped, they sat watching a golden eagle swing against the vault of the sky.

"It's almost worth it, Val. We'd never have taken this hike otherwise."

"Will, I've been thinking. Won't they send word over the Brenner Pass? A rider or a coach could make the trip to Merano, and officers could be waiting for us when we cross into Italy."

Reilly smiled. "Yes, you are right. That's why we aren't going into Italy. At least, we'll see. There are two ways, and the shortest and probably the best route does take us into Italy, but for just a few miles."

The wind off the mountain was cold. Val plodded on, no longer thinking of anything but the moment when they would stop. Will seemed to be looking for something, and suddenly it was there . . . a narrow ravine that fell away steeply for about a hundred yards, and then ended in a precipice. He turned and descended the ravine.

"Careful now, Val," he said. "One slip, and it will be the end of you."

They came abruptly to another crack in the plateau that ran diagonally into the ravine they followed. Will Reilly took Val by the hand and climbed down into this smaller ravine. Under an overhang was a small stone hut.

Lifting the latch, Will went in, and Val followed. The place was snug and tight. There was a fireplace and a stack of wood sufficient to last for days, for the hut was built against the cliff, and the overhang was deep enough for a storage place for fuel.

"How did you know about this place?" Val asked.

For a moment that Irish smile came over Will Reilly's face. "I listen, Val, as I have taught you to do, and sometimes I cultivate strange company. You might wonder why, but I've learned always to keep one hand on the door latch, mentally, at least.

"There are smugglers' caves and hide-outs all over the mountains. You see, we're near the meeting place of three borders here, Austria, Italy, and Switzerland, and smuggling can be profitable."

He built a fire. He was quick and sure, as always, and his fire flared up with the first match.

"I've brought some tea. We'll have tea and then we'll bathe our feet and wash out our socks. That's the first thing on a long walk, boy. Keep your feet happy, and a change of socks will help."

They started off again before daybreak, and it was piercing cold. They struggled against the wind, but after a while it began to let up and snow began to fall. After an hour of that they could scarcely see. In any event, their tracks were covered. During lulls in the storm they could catch glimpses of a vast sweep of peaks, some looming amazingly near, some far off.

\*       \*       \*

Many times in the years that followed Val tried to reconstruct that escape from Austria. They branched off at the head of the Venter.and went west of the mountain, into Italy. They went through small villages—villages they did not know the names of—and passed a fourteenth-century castle; then over a steep pass, and they were in Switzerland. It was footpaths and dim trails most of the way.

After that there was Zurich . . . Paris . . . London—and New York. . . .

Will Reilly was never quite the same again, and he had never quite forgotten Louise.

He was colder, harder, and he laughed less often. He kept Val with him, and they were just as close; they talked of books, they went riding and shooting together. Will Reilly gambled, and he led a gambler's life, and over the next few years he paid attention to a dozen women with the casual ease that was typical of him, but he was serious about none of them.

When Val was fourteen they parted for the first time, when Val hired on at a cattle ranch in Texas. It was hard, grueling work, but he loved it, working from sunup to sundown, with only occasional rides into town. Will was operating a gambling house in New Orleans, but after six months he sold out and rode west to Texas.

Val was now a tall boy, broad in the shoulders and strong in the hands. Fantastically quick with a gun, he had never drawn one in a gun battle; expert with cards, he cared nothing for gambling.

"It's good to see you, Val," Will said when he saw him. He looked at him thoughtfully. "You're growing up, boy."

With Will there, it took little urging for Val to quit his job, and with a pack horse they started riding west to San Antonio. As they rode, Will kept watching their back trail. He was silent for a long time, but after a while he said, "They're hunting me, Val."

"Who is?"

"That's the hell of it. I don't know."

That night in the Variety, Will told him more. "Somebody took a shot at me in New Orleans. They missed. Two days later they tried it again, and they missed again. . . . I didn't."

"You got him?"

"I killed a man I had never seen before, and you know that I never forget a face. I would swear I never ran across him anywhere, let alone gambled with him."

"Mistaken identity."

"No . . . it was me he wanted. He lived long enough to say that they hadn't told him I could shoot."

"They?"

"That's what he said."

"So it's over?"

"No. Two weeks later they tried again, while I was in a card game. They burned me that time, and they got away."

"They?"

"There were two of them." Will Reilly rubbed a hand over his face. "So I quit. I sold out and drifted west. How can a man gamble when somebody he doesn't know is shooting at him? If you have an enemy you know it, and you know him; and if it is a matter of shooting, you shoot. This is different. Anyone who walks in the door may be the one, and they can't all miss."

Val had never seen Will Reilly worried before, but to sit in a gambling game knowing that any one of the players, or any bystander, may be there to kill you . . . well, how do you concentrate on' your cards?

From San Antonio they drifted to the German settlements around Fredericksburg. They camped three nights on the Pedernales to see if there was any pursuit. When none appeared, they rode to Fort Griffin. There, in a poker game, Will Reilly won sixty dollars, and Val won twenty at handwrestling. Although still only a boy, he had an unusually powerful grip, and had the arms, shoulders, and chest of a grown man.

They rode the grub line west, and then they hired two wagons and four skinners and went up the Canadian to hunt buffalo. As both of them were dead shots, they did well. They followed the buffalo with a few other hunters, banding together for protection against the Indians. A tall young man named Garrett was one of them, and he was a good shot with a rifle.

Val, who had a natural aptitude for weapons, and who had done a lot of shooting, killed nine buffalo at his first stand, eleven at his second. When the herd became nervous he stopped shooting for a few minutes to let them get over their uneasiness.

He had made his stand near a buffalo wallow where the buffalo were scattered over the grassy plain below. He waited, enjoying the warm sun after the cool of the night, and watching the huge, shaggy beasts grazing.

Will Reilly was half a mile away at the other corner of a triangle of which the apex was their wagons. Suddenly a rider appeared, a tall man with long flowing hair to his shoulders, riding a magnificent black horse.

"How are you, boy?" He glanced over the terrain. "You have a nice stand here. Why aren't you shooting?"

"I'm letting them get settled down. They were in half a mind to stampede."

The man studied him thoughtfully. "Nice rifle you have there. May I see it?"

"No, sir. I never let anybody look at my guns."

The man smiled. "Are you Will Reilly's boy? I heard he was out here."

Val got to his feet slowly, and the tall man noted how the boy wore his gun, and the stance he took.

"Will Reilly might be around. Who should I say is looking for him?"

"You tell him Bill Hickok wants to talk to him."

Val studied the man. Hickok was a friend of Will's, he knew. In fact, Will had loaned him a horse one time when he had been badly in need of one.

"Mr. Hickok," Val said, "Will said you were a good friend of his, so I take that as truth, but if you've become one of those hunting him, you'd better know you'll have two of us to face."

Hickok looked at Val for a moment, then he nodded. "As a matter of fact, I came to warn him. Will Reilly was a friend to me when a friend was needed, and I hoped to return the favor. There are three men over on the Arkansas, and they are hunting him."

"We'll ride over and talk to Will," Val said.

Will Reilly left his buffalo stand and came to meet them and he listened while Hickok told him the news. "One of them is Henry Sonnenberg," Hickok said. "He said he'd know you when he sees you."

"And the others?"

"Thurston Peck and Chip Hardesty. But don't underrate

Sonnenberg. He's been building a reputation out in the Nevada gold camps. He killed some stranger out at Ruby Creek stage station, and another one in Pioche."

After a short silence Will Reilly said, "Bill, I've got a favor to ask. If you can, without stirring up trouble for yourself, find out who is back of this. They're being paid, and I want to know who is doing the paying."

"You don't know?"

"I haven't the foggiest idea. That's what makes it so bad."

They rode back to camp, put coffee on the fire, and started stirring up some grub. The skinners were still out.

After they had eaten, and Hickok and Will were lighting cigars, Wild Bill looked over the match at Will. "Do you know a man named Avery Simpson?"

"Should I?"

"He was in Wichita for a few days, then traveled to Hays. I understand he has ten thousand dollars to be paid to the person who kills you . . . no matter how."

Will Reilly just stared at him. Val got up to bring more fuel for the fire. When he had put the buffalo chips on the flames, he said, "Maybe we ought to look him up and ask why?"

"Yes," Will said. "The hell of it is knowing that anybody may try to shoot or knife or poison you, and not even knowing why."

"Want me to talk to him, Will?" Hickok asked.

Reilly smiled, without humor. "I'll admit, Bill, that this business is getting under my skin, but not that much. I can still fork my own broncs."

"Of course." Hickok leaned back on his elbow. "Don't forget Sonnenberg while you're looking for this man Simpson. From what I hear, Sonnenberg is a sure-thing operator. If I was you I'd shoot on sight."

Bill Hickok stayed the night with them and rode on in the morning. The next morning they rode out, too. Only this time they rode east, and then north.

Val and Will rode into Hays on a frosty morning, and went to the hotel to make inquiries. Avery Simpson had checked out, leaving as a forwarding address the Peck House, in Empire, Colorado.

"All right," Will said quietly, "we'll go to Empire and find out what Avery Simpson has to say for himself."

Val walked to the window. There was a terrible sense of foreboding in him. Why did Avery Simpson want to have Will Reilly killed?

And did he want to kill Val too?

# SEVEN

The Pecks had arrived in Empire with considerable means, and over the years they had enlarged their house, imported furniture from the East, and lived in a degree of comfort known to few in the mining regions. For nine or ten years they entertained travelers, known or unknown to them, until bad times came to the country and the Pecks turned to entertaining for a small charge.

The Peck home, always the center for everything in that part of Colorado, had now become a hotel, and it was there that Will Reilly and Val arrived late one evening.

A fire was blazing on the hearth, for the night was cool. It was a pleasant room, and after the chill of the long ride on the stage it felt comfortable.

Val looked around the room thoughtfully. He saw a young girl, perhaps younger than himself, and there was a man, obviously an easterner, who sat in a big leather chair reading a newspaper and smoking a cigar.

The girl was small, with large eyes, and was very pretty. Val went over to her. "Do you live here?" he asked.

"No." She looked at him with interest. "Do you?"

"We travel," Val said. "In this country—and we spent a year in Europe."

63

"I've never been there, but I will be going, one of these days."

"I'm Val Darrant," he said. "What's your name?"

"Maude Kiskadden." Her chin lifted proudly. "I am an actress."

"An *actress?*"

"Yes, I am. So is my mother."

Will Reilly had come up to them. "How do you do?" he said, offering his hand. "I am Val's uncle. Did you say your father's name was Kiskadden?"

"Yes."

"I knew a Kiskadden up in Montana. In Virginia City."

"That was my father."

Will Reilly looked at her curiously. "Your mother was named Virginia? Who used to be married to Joe Slade?"

"No, sir. My mother is named Annie. She's an actress."

"Sorry. I guess Kiskadden must have married again." He glanced around the room, then his eyes came back to her. "Are there many people stopping here?"

"Only four. There's my mother and me, and there is a mining man from Denver, and some easterner."

"I had expected more. . . . This easterner now—can you describe him?"

"He is a tall blond man, sort of heavy. He smiles a lot, but I don't like him," Maude Kiskadden said.

Val watched Will Reilly go up the stairs, his face serious. Two hours later, at the supper table, they saw Avery Simpson for the first time.

He came into the dining room after Will and Val were already seated. The Kiskaddens were there too, and Simpson nodded to them, then seated himself at a table at one side of the room and lighted a cigar before opening his paper.

Will Reilly got up. "Excuse me a minute, Val. I will be right back."

He crossed the room to Simpson's table. "Mr. Avery Simpson, I believe?" Will drew back a chair and sat down.

Simpson took the cigar from his mouth and looked at Reilly. "Do I know you?"

"Apparently you do not, or you would be a wiser man."

"What does that mean?" Simpson asked.

"I understand you have been offering ten thousand dollars to have me killed. I am Will Reilly."

The cigar almost dropped from Simpson's lips, and he fumbled for it. His face had gone white. "I don't know what you are talking about," he said.

"You know perfectly well, Mr. Simpson, but if you are carrying a gun, you may call me a liar."

"I did not say that. I did not call you a liar."

"Then what I have said is the truth? You have been offering ten thousand dollars for my scalp?"

Avery Simpson was frightened, but he hesitated. There were at least seven witnesses in the room, and all of them were listening. The man across the table was cool, even casual, but suddenly, desperately, Simpson wished himself far away.

"Well, I—"

"If I am not a liar, Mr. Simpson, you have offered ten thousand dollars for my death. Am I a liar, Mr. Simpson?"

"No. No, no."

"Then you have offered that sum?"

"Yes."

Never in his wildest imaginings had Avery Simpson expected to be confronted with such a situation. From all he had heard, this man across the table had killed other men, and was quite capable of killing him. He waited, his mouth dry, cold sweat beading his forehead.

"Mr. Simpson, as of this moment I want you to revoke your offer. I want an item published in the press in Denver, El Paso, Tucson, and in other papers in a list I shall submit to you, revoking your offers. You need not mention what offer, just that any offers you have made are revoked and no money is to be paid to anyone for any offer previously made. When you have written those letters in my presence, and mailed them, you may leave town. You may go back to where you came from, and if you appear in the West at any future time, for whatever reason, I shall shoot you on sight."

Avery Simpson pushed back his chair. "I will. I will write the letters now."

"That is correct. However, you will not need to leave the table. I will see that paper is brought, and you may write the letters here and now. At this table."

Simpson licked his dry lips and was about to protest, but thought better of it.

"You know, of course, that I could shoot you right now and no western jury would ever convict me. You have tried to buy my death." Will Reilly smiled pleasantly.

Avery Simpson watched as Peck brought paper and pen to the table. Slowly, carefully, he wrote as Reilly dictated, and when he was finished with the last letter, Will Reilly said, "There is one more thing. As you did not know me, and have no reason for wishing me dead, I take it that you have been acting for someone else? Am I right?"

Simpson nodded.

"I want the name of that person. And I want it now."

Some of Simpson's courage was returning. During the process of writing the dictated letters he had been slowly growing more angry. Now, suddenly, the anger burst out. "I'll be damned if I will!"

Almost casually, Will Reilly backhanded him across the mouth. In that room only Val and Simpson knew the jolting force of that blow, Val because he had seen it used before, on other occasions. A slow trickle of blood started from Simpson's mouth.

"The name, Mr. Simpson."

Avery Simpson looked wildly about the room, but those present either seemed to be ignoring what was happening, or they looked at him with cold, unfriendly eyes. The men who hired their killing done were not respected men in Colorado.

"Prince Pavel Pavelovitch."

It was Will Reilly who was surprised. "Him? After all this time?"

"You horsewhipped him. He still carries the scars, and the story follows him wherever he goes. Or so I have been told."

"What else were you told?"

"That the Princess Louise will no longer have anything to do with him."

"She is married?"

"I do not believe so."

Will Reilly was silent, then after a pause he said, "You will leave in the morning, Mr. Simpson, and keep going until you reach wherever you came from."

Deliberately, he stood up and walked back to his table. After a moment, Avery Simpson got up and left the room. Val watched him go, wondering what the man must be thinking.

Will Reilly seemed uninterested in his food. Slowly he took a cigar from his case and bit off the end, and then sat for several minutes holding the cigar in his fingers and staring into space.

"She isn't married," Val said.

"We don't know . . . but I could find out. She's a well-known person."

"You would be going where he is."

Will gestured impatiently, as one brushes away a fly. "It doesn't matter." He put the cigar in his teeth, and lit it. "I am thinking of her." He looked at Val. "I am a gambler, Val, and a gambler is not simply a nobody, he is worse."

"Many of the people she knows gamble."

"Of course. But there is a difference between a man who gambles and a gambler. I have never quite been able to persuade myself of the difference but others have . . . long since."

"She loved you."

He looked at Val. "Did she? I wonder."

"You don't have to gamble. You could invest some money. Right now," Val lowered his voice—"you have money, and you own mining stock. You could—"

Will Reilly got up suddenly, almost overturning his chair. "We will, Val. We will go in the morning. I will speak to them at the stable about having our horses ready."

Filled with his plans, he opened the front door and stepped out.

They must have been afraid of him, for they used shotguns—at any rate two of them did. The other used a Spencer .56 that fires a slug as big as a man's thumb.

He stepped out the door and it swung to behind him and he had no warning. Even so, in his reflex he cleared his gun from its holster.

The blasting roar of the shotguns shook the room. Val left his chair running, and burst out the door.

There were three of them leaving, and one looked back over his shoulder. It was Henry Sonnenberg.

# EIGHT

W ill Reilly had drilled Val in the procedure so many times that he acted now without even thinking. He glanced once at Will; he had seen dead men before, and he knew that Will could never have known what hit him.

He went back inside and up the stairs to their room. He was not thinking, he was as yet only feeling the terrible shock, but he did what Will had taught him to do. He went to Will's trunk and got out their stake money. It was a considerable sum.

Unbuttoning his shirt, he stuffed the gold coins into the money belt with those already there. Then he got out the three letters that had been delivered by hand from Louise to Will, back in Innsbruck, and he put them in his pocket. Only then did he go back downstairs.

He was shaking now, and he was suddenly afraid. Already the sense of loss was beginning. Will was gone, and Will Reilly had been his world. He had been father, uncle, brother, friend, all these in one; he had been his partner against the world, and it was considering that which made Val Darrant realize that he was suddenly without anyone—he was all alone.

Valentine Darrant was nearly fifteen, and he had been traveling most of his life. Not only that, but he had often made all the arrangements himself for both of them. Will might be in a game where it was unsafe to win; a signal to Val, and Val would make the arrangements. And so he made them now.

People were still gathered on the hotel steps, talking, when he went to the livery stable. He saddled their horses and led them out back of the corral, where he tied them in a concealed place. Then he went back to the hotel.

"Mr. Peck," he said when he found him, "I want a decent burial for my uncle." He produced two gold pieces. "Will you see to it? They will pay attention to you."

"Of course, son, but you don't need to think of that now. You're welcome to stay right here at the hotel until everything is settled. Everything will have to be impounded until we find his next of kin."

"He was an orphan," Val said. "He had no kinfolk, except me."

"Well, we will have to see about that. In the meantime, don't you worry. We will attend to everything."

They had taken Will to a dark shed that housed the materials for coffins, a place where bodies were kept until buried. The burial would be the following morning.

Val went to the shed and talked to the man at the door, a pleasant, middle-aged man who had two boys of his own. "May I see him?" Val asked.

The man studied him a moment. "I reckon so, boy. You an' him seemed mighty close."

"We hadn't anybody else."

"How come they killed him? Gambling fight?"

So Val told it to him there by the door, very briefly but clearly, about Will and Louise, and the horsewhipping Will had given Prince Pavel.

"Served him right," the man said. "I'd like to have seen that. You go ahead on in there, boy, an' take your time."

So Val went in.

A lantern was standing on a table and it shone on Will, who was lying there as if he were asleep.

Val stood beside him, knowing what he had to do, but dreading it. This, too, had been a part of it, and from the time Val was six years old, Will had drilled it into him.

"Remember, Val, these home guards are mostly good folks . . . but there's larceny in some of them. You know where I carry my money—in that secret pocket inside my vest. No matter what happens, you get it. And get the money hidden in the hotel, and then you get out.

"You've been around enough—stay in the best hotels if you can. Tell them you're expecting to meet your uncle, or any story they can believe, Val. Don't let anybody know you've got more than a few dollars, but money can be your friend, and your best protection."

Val hesitated a moment now, and then put his hand on Will's body, felt for the vest buttons. They were caked with dried blood, but he unbuttoned them. Sure enough, it was there, a small packet of greenbacks, and something else . . . a locket, it felt like, and a small square of paper.

Quickly he put them into his pocket, buttoned up the vest, and rearranged the blanket.

"Thanks, Will," he said softly. There was a lump in his throat and he could feel the tears coming, and fought to keep them back. "Thanks for everything. I . . . I guess you know how it was . . . you an' me. I love you, Will, and I never had anybody else, and may never have again.

"I'm going to get out, Will. I'm going to take off the way you said I should, but I'll see that you're buried, with a marker and all. Then I'll come back, you can count on it. And that isn't all. One of these days I'll find them, Henry Sonnenberg and the others, and when I do, I'll make them remember you, Will."

He went outside, and the man at the door put his hand on his shoulder. "That's a good boy. I know how you feel."

"He was all I had. We were all either one of us had."

"Sure, now." The man's voice was husky. "Boy, if you're of a mind to, you can come out to our place. We ain't got much, but you're welcome."

"Thanks. Will Reilly told me what to do if this ever happened."

Val walked away in the darkness and back to the hotel. There were people standing in the parlor talking about what had happened, but they stopped talking when he came up.

"Mr. Peck, can I speak to you?" Val said.

When they had gone into another room, Val took the small packet of money from his pocket. "Uncle Will always told me you were honest, and this here is mine. I don't know what is going to happen, but I wish you would be my banker. Take this, keep it for me, or invest it . . . whatever you think best."

Peck hesitated, studying the boy. "Where did you get this, son?"

"It's mine. He wanted me to have everything he had, but he always left this money with me in case we were separated. You know, sometimes folks did not take kindly to his winning."

"I guess not." Peck took the money. "All right, boy. I'll take care of it. I haven't had much luck with money these past years, but it has been the times. I'll care for it like you were my own son."

"He wanted a round stone," Val said, "like a rolling stone. All he wanted on it were the dates, and the words, *Here's where Will Reilly stopped last*."

Val went up to the room, and closed the door behind him. He looked at Will's clothes . . . all those handsome, beautiful clothes.

He worked quickly, making a small pack of his own belongings, including the six-shooter Will had bought for him. He took down Will's Winchester, checked the load, and placed it ready on the bed, changed into range garb, and went to the window.

After a quick look around he slipped out, went down the slanting roof and dropped his stuff to the ground, then lowered himself to arm's length and dropped. Gathering up his gear he went through the alley and across a dark vacant lot to the back of the corral where the horses waited. There he stopped long enough to belt on the six-shooter.

Somewhere, not too far away, was Henry Sonnenberg. Val considered that. He was good with a gun. Will had seen to that. He had been shooting alongside Will for almost ten years, but he did not think he was ready for Henry. Nor for the others . . . but there was time. Will had always advised patience.

He mounted his horse, and with Will's horse on a lead rope, he took the trail out of town. He rode at an easy lope for a short time, and then walked his horse. Just short of daybreak he stopped and rested the horses; after that he mounted Will's horse and rode on.

He kept to the back country, riding west and south. He avoided people, sometimes by turning off the trail, returning to it only when the people had gone by. He knew where he was headed.

It was a small remote log cabin, high in the mountains north of

Durango. On two occasions, when drifting through the country, Will and he had spent the night there, and one other time they had stayed a week. At that time they had done some work on the cabin and had explored the country around.

The cabin stood at the edge of a grove of aspens. A spring was nearby, and there were a few acres of meadow for grazing. There were fish in a nearby stream, and plenty of game.

Riding the wild country gives a man time to think, and Will Reilly had encouraged thinking. "You have to be objective, Val," he had said. "That is the first thing a gambler learns. Each problem must be taken by itself, and you have to leave emotion out of it. Be stern with yourself. Don't pamper yourself."

Well, he no longer had Will to guide him, but he had what Will had taught him, and that teaching had been of a kind to give him strength within himself. Will rarely had positive answers, but he always offered the means to arrive at answers.

Val Darrant considered what lay before him. Henry Sonnenberg must not go unpunished. The law would hardly try very hard to find the killer of a dead gambler, and the law in the West was, in most places, still merely local law. If Henry Sonnenberg was to pay for his crime, it was Val's job to see that he did.

Three men had been involved, and Val knew their first effort would be to find Avery Simpson and collect their blood money. With Will Reilly dead, Simpson's misson was accomplished, but some rendezvous must have been arranged for the payoff.

But what was to prevent Simpson returning east by the fastest means possible, and keeping all the money for himself?

Many men had a streak of larceny in their makeup, and it was unlikely that Avery Simpson was free of it. He might simply return to his usual habitat. But he was a shrewd man, and would be cautious, so he would start in the direction of the rendezvous, wherever it had been.

Hickok had seen him in Wichita, but he had left for Hays . . . it was likely that contact had been made there, and that might be the rendezvous point. In any event, he had nothing else to go on.

That night, after he made camp, Val practiced his draw, then fixed himself something to eat, and practiced again. He had a natural speed of hand and eye, developed over the years by handling cards and guns, and by juggling several small balls, a practice started by Will.

Each night he practiced drawing, but he did no firing, for he was not anxious to attract attention to himself, and had no idea who might be in that part of the country.

In Durango he got a newspaper and found the item Will had made Simpson write. Val himself mailed those letters the first morning after the killing. He smiled at the thought of Henry Sonnenberg meeting Simpson after seeing that item.

Val folded the paper and placed it on the table beside his plate. Then he reached in his pocket for money, and found he had none there. But there was gold in his money belt—in both money belts, for he was carrying several thousand dollars.

He hesitated a moment, then took up the paper and opened it. Using it as a shield, he slipped a hand inside his shirt and took out three gold coins. As he started to place them in his pocket one slipped from his fingers and rolled on the floor.

Several heads turned. Embarrassed, Val got up to retrieve the coin, which had stopped rolling near a heavy boot, stained with red earth. As Val reached for it, the boot moved and came down hard on the coin.

Val stepped back and straightened up, his heart pounding. He had seen Will Reilly face such situations, but he had never faced one himself.

There were three men at the bar, and the foot of the man on the end was on the coin.

"You've got your foot on my money," Val said. "Would you move it, please?"

The man made no move, but he glanced at the others, chuckling. "Listen to that talk. Real gent, ain't he? Now look here, boy. That coin dropped out of my pocket. It ain't yours, it's mine."

A dozen men were watching, their eyes on Val. He was only a boy, but he was wearing a gun, and any man who carries a gun must be prepared to use it.

"There's a twenty-dollar gold piece on the floor, and it belongs to me," Val tried to keep his voice from shaking. "Take your foot off it."

"It ain't yourn," the man said, "but if you can get it, you can have it."

Deliberately, he moved his foot and Val stepped forward to pick up the coin. Instantly, he saw his mistake. As he bent over he saw the man's boot swing for a kick, only inches from his face.

His reaction was instantaneous, from long training. He struck
the boot aside even as it swung toward him, and the slap threw
the man at the bar off balance and he started to fall, catching
himself by his right hand on the bar just in time.

Val stepped back quickly, gun in hand. "Pick it up mister," he
said quietly, "and put it on my table."

Slowly the man pulled himself up. The other two had spread
out a little. "Put that gun up, kid. We were only funnin'."

"Pick up the money and put it on my table." Val's voice was
suddenly cold and steady. He did not want to kill, but he didn't
believe he would have to. These were bad men, but dangerous
only when the odds were with them. "I'm not funnin'," he added.

The big man stooped for the coin, and then he lunged in a long
dive. Val did a boxer's near side-step and brought the barrel of
the Smith & Wesson down on the back of the man's head. He
went to the floor, out cold.

Without removing his eyes from the others, Val picked up the
coin and backed off. Then he went to the bar and paid for his
meal. He took up his change and pocketed it.

"You won't get away with this, kid," one of the other men said.
"He'll kill you."

Val knew what a good bluff could do. He holstered his gun and
faced them. "How about you? You want to try?"

The gesture worked, for the man very carefully put both hands
on the bar, away from his gun. "It ain't my fight," he said
hoarsely. "I'm just with him."

Val backed to the door, aware of the quiet-faced man at a table
near his own, who had sat watching him. Had he seen that man
before? Who was he?

Val stepped out and let the doors swing to. His horses were
right down the street. He turned and walked swiftly toward
them.

When he glanced back the man with the quiet face was standing outside the saloon, lighting a cigar. Val mounted, and swung
his horse.

He reached the cabin on the mountain near dusk, and drawing
his horses into the shadow of the aspens, he watched it for some
time. There was no smoke from the chimney, no sign of life.
When half an hour had passed and it was nearly dark, he rode
forward.

There was no horse in the corral, no fresh manure on the ground. He tied his horses and went to the cabin, taking the thong off his six-shooter. He was almost at the door when he noticed it was slightly ajar, and there were dark spots on the split logs that formed the steps. He touched one of them, and it seemed to be damp.

Whoever was in there must have heard him at the corral, and he spoke quietly. "I am friendly. You want to strike a light?"

There was silence.

All was darkness within. For several minutes Val waited, then moved closer. He heard breathing, and stepped up to the door. The breathing was uneven, the breathing of someone injured, he was sure.

With his left hand he pushed the door wide, but nothing happened.

Then deliberately, he stepped in and to the right against the wall. There was no reaction.

"Who's there?" he asked. "Who is it? I am a friend."

There was still no response, and taking a chance, he struck a match.

Beyond the table which occupied the center of the room a man lay sprawled on the floor. A gun lay not far from his hand. The bunk from which he had fallen was bloody.

The match burned down, and Val struck another and lit the coal-oil lantern on the table. Then he went around the table and stared down at the man. The back of his buckskin jacket was bloody, and torn by a bullet. Carefully, Val turned the man over. It was Tensleep.

There was a cut on his scalp that looked to be several days old, and the blood from the bullet wound had dried.

Val straightened up and looked around the room. Tensleep, several years before, had been riding with Henry Sonnenberg, and despite what Val had heard about Sonnenberg, Thurston Peck, and Hardesty, Tensleep might have been one of them.

Never before had Val been faced with anything of this kind, although more than once he and Will had taken care of wounded people. But it had always been Will, decisive and sure, who had taken command and had known what to do.

The first thing was to take care of Tensleep. He straightened the bed, then slid one arm under Tensleep's hips and put the other around his body under the arms, and he picked him up.

Val was strong, but the wounded man was limp, and like a dead weight. Maybe moving him was the wrong thing, but Val got him on the bed, and unbuttoned the bloody shirt. The sight of the wound turned him sick at his stomach.

Turning from it, he put sticks together in the fireplace, started a fire, and put water on to boil.

Then he went outside, stripped the saddles from the horses, and turned them into the corral. He found a stack of hay, scarcely enough for two days, and pitched some to the horses. After that, he carried his gear into the cabin and dumped it on the floor.

The water was boiling, and he carried some of it to the table and with a clean handkerchief he bathed the dried blood away and cleansed the wound as best he could. He made a pad of another of his handkerchiefs and bound it in place over the wound. He did the same at the point of exit, and then washed the blood from the wound on the scalp.

He shaved some jerked beef into a tin and, adding water, made a thin broth. He didn't know whether he was doing the right thing, but Tensleep had been without food at least a day or two, so he tried him with a little of the broth. The wounded man swallowed it, and then accepted more.

At midnight Val prepared his own bed and went to sleep.

# NINE

He awoke suddenly, starting from a sound sleep into sharp attention. He stared up at the cabin roof for a moment. Where was he? The cabin in the mountains . . . Tensleep . . .

He swung his feet to the floor. Tensleep was awake, and was watching him. "I ain't sure who you are, *amigo*, but it looks to me like you come along at the right time. I'm hit hard, ain't I?"

"Yes."

"You think I'll make it?"

"I'm not a doctor, but Will used to say that he'd seen men with guts pull through injuries where by all accounts they should have died. He used to say two-thirds of it was in the mind."

"Will? Ah, now I got you! You're that kid of Will's . . . from ten years back. Sure, an' I'd heard you were still with him. What d' you know about that?"

"Will's dead. They got him."

Tensleep lay quiet, staring at the ceiling. "I'd have staked my life they couldn't do it, not even the three of them."

"He was coming out of a doorway, and they gave him no warning. They used shotguns."

Val pulled on his clothes and got a fire started. He didn't know what to do except to make some more of the broth. There were

77

herbs that might help, and Will had taught him a little about them, but he remembered no herbs that grew around where they were now. With what he had, he would have to try to build some strength back into the man.

"What happened to you?" he asked.

"It was them, Hank and the others. They wanted me with them, but I wouldn't go against Will. First place, I knew he was faster and a better shot, but mostly it was because I always liked his style. He was my kind of man—the kind I'd like to have been. . . . I never was anything but a wild kind of hombre with no more sense than the law allows. . . ."

His voice trailed off, and in another minute Val saw that he was asleep. While the water was getting hot he went outside and led the horses from the corral and picketed them on the grass. Tensleep's horse had evidently been taken away, for there was neither horse nor saddle, and they must have taken his weapons too.

Val gathered fuel, and considered the situation. If he was going to catch Simpson or Sonnenberg he had to be riding, but Tensleep would never make it here alone. There was not one chance in ten for Tensleep to make it anyway, but without Val's help there was not even that chance.

The cabin stood on a gentle slope with a thick grove of aspen behind it, the trees climbing the mountainside in a solid mass. Still higher up were stands of Engelmann spruce and balsam fir. Below and to the east were slopes covered with yellow pine. Here under the aspen columbine was growing, with its lovely lavender, purple, or sometimes almost white flowers, and mingled with them some tiny yellow flowers he did not recognize. Near the cabin a stream came down the slope in a steep fall, supplying water for whoever lived in the cabin and for their horses.

As night came on, Tensleep grew feverish, and sometimes he was wandering in his mind. "Save me, kid," he cried out, "for God's sake save me long enough to find Hank!

"Watch out for him! He's mean, poison mean! He'll hate you, kid, like he hated Will! He was afraid of Will—I told him he was afraid. That's why they used shotguns out of the dark. That's why he hated Will, because he was scared of him."

After that a pause, and then he spoke more calmly. "He shot me under the table, kid, sneaked a gun out and shot me. Never gave me a chance. He gut-shot me an' left me to die—told me he was takin' my horse and outfit."

"You get well," Val said, "and I'll give you Will's horse and outfit. I brought it along."

Tensleep slept then for almost an hour, and woke up begging a drink.

"Val," he said hoarsely, "I seen men gut-shot afore this. Mostly they die in less than a half-hour, at least the ones I've seen. Some of them take a while, but if they live as long as I have, they usually have a chance. You know, boy, that bullet might have gone clean through me and never clipped a thing. Seen it happen. But I'll have a bad time tonight, I'm figurin'.

"Val, there's a plant grows down on the slope below here. I seen it a time or two over east of the stream. It has a purple flower—called cinquefoil. You find it, pick some of the leaves, and make me some tea. It's good for fever, boy. It'll help me."

Val got up. "I'd better go then. There isn't much light left."

"East of the stream, nigh that big gray boulder with the moss on it. There's a lightning-struck tree close alongside, and sumac on beyond it, higher up."

Val went out quickly, taking his rifle. The sun had set, but it was still light enough to see. He checked landmarks, choosing those useful after dark when everything looked different, and he crossed the stream and hurried down the slope, making the best time he could. He found the plants where Tensleep had said they would be, and gathered a hatful of leaves.

Tensleep was sleeping restlessly, his face already hot from fever. He threw his head from side to side and muttered unintelligibly.

Val steeped some of the leaves in hot water, and then held the wounded outlaw up so that he could sip some of the tea. Again and again he repeated the proceeding, though he was afraid he might be doing the wrong thing. If the man really was cut up inside, he certainly was; but in such a case Tensleep would die, anyway. The nearest doctor was at least sixty miles away, and Tensleep might be wanted in Durango.

At last Val slept, and when morning came he saw that Tensleep was resting easily. He fed the horses and busied himself outside, but still the outlaw slept.

Val cleaned his guns, washed out the handkerchiefs he had

used on the wounds, and cut some wood and laid it ready for a fresh fire. Then he went outside again and practiced with his six-shooter.

He was fast . . . maybe as fast as Will, who had always said Val had a gift for it. And he could shoot straight. He felt no desire to shoot anyone, yet he knew that if he could find Sonnenberg he would kill him, for there was no evidence to convict him of the murder of Will Reilly. He would do the same for Hardesty and Peck . . . if there was no other way.

He came back to the cabin to find Tensleep awake. The outlaw had been watching him through the open door. "Pretty handy with that thing, ain't you, kid? Well, you'll need to be."

"I don't intend to stay in the West. After I've had a go at Sonnenberg, I'm going back east. I'll stay there, I think."

"Maybe. But this here country has a pull on a man. You get to looking at the mountains, and at the stretches of wide-open, empty land . . . and it gets to you.

"I never had no chance to live no place else. When I was growin' up the thing I wanted most was to be a mountain man, but by the time I'd got some years on me, it was punchin' cows. I was a fair hand . . . and one of the best bronc riders around. An' then one night some of the boys were broke and we wanted to throw a wing-ding so we rounded up ten or twelve head of cows and sold them . . . and the law got wind of it, and they was after us for rustlin'."

Tensleep had gained a little strength, and he wanted to talk. So Val listened.

"I never figured to be an outlaw. I'd known too many as a boy . . . on the dodge all the time, and never anything in sight but prison or a rope. But one careless evenin' an' there I was . . . runnin' from the law.

"I never was a hired gunman, though. Fact is, the first time I killed a man it was over that. He was always hirin' out for rough work like burnin' out nesters, or killin', and he wanted me to he'p him. I told him what I thought of that and he grabbed iron. I never had any thought of bein' fast at that time, an' wore a gun because ever'body did—out on the range from time to time a body needed it."

"You killed him?"

"I got off two shots before he cleared leather, and I been outlawin' it ever since."

He was suddenly tired, and he lay back on the bed while Val rolled a smoke for him and put it between his lips. When he had the cigarette drawing he said, "You do that, kid—you get shut of this country and go east."

In the days that followed, Val was restless. Sonnenberg and Simpson would be meeting, and parting. After that there would be small chance of finding them. But he stayed on. And Tensleep gained strength every day.

Val remembered hearing an Army doctor talking to Will about western men. "They're made of rawhide and iron, and they don't die easy. It's what meat and beans and a lot of hard work and fresh air will do for you."

The day that Tensleep got up Val told him he was leaving. "All right, Val," Tensleep said. "You light out. I can manage all right now."

"Like I promised, I am giving you Will's horse and saddle, his six-shooter, and my rifle. I am going to hang onto Will's rifle myself."

Tensleep turned away abruptly. "Kid, you'll do all right," he said. "If ever I get the chance to make it up to you, I will."

Val Darrant hesitated for a moment over what he was about to say—that door to the past was closed so long ago.

"Tensleep, you knew my mother. You knew Myra Cord."

Tensleep turned to look at him. "That's a closed book, Val. You forget her."

"What was she like?"

"You've forgotten?" Tensleep's tone was rough. "She was no good, Val. She turned you out, she would have had you left to freeze. She was heartless and mean."

"Where is she now?"

Tensleep sat down and rolled another cigarette. "Look, kid, nobody knows anything about that. Me, and maybe Hank recalls it. So leave it lay. Go build yourself a good life and forget her. Will Reilly was born on the wrong side of the tracks and became a gentleman, Myra was born on the right side and became a—a shady lady and a thief. Yes, an' folks suspected her of murder, a time or two."

"Did you know my father?"

"Better than Will Reilly did. I packed for him one time, into the mountains not far from here. He was a well-off man, Val, and that's how you came to be."

"Me?"

"Myra set her cap for him. She was a tramp, workin' down on the line like the rest of 'em, but she had eyes for a good thing. She latched onto Darrant, and when she knew you were going to come along, she tried to get him to make a will in her favor.

"Darrant was no fool. He didn't believe she was going to have a child, and he could read women better than most, so he told her to forget it and she got mad and threatened him.

"Well, he laughed at her, and then she got all soft and weepy and said how she never meant it. Me, I couldn't keep my nose out of it. I'd spent time in the mountains with him and liked him, so when she bought that rat poison, I told him about it.

"He just looked at me, and said, 'There are rats in that old hotel. I've heard them.'

" 'Uh-huh. And they been there ten years, and nobody made any fuss about 'em, so how come all of a sudden she buys enough rat poison to kill half the rats in Colorado?'

"The next day he was gone out of there . . . just like that.

"Oh, you should have seen her! She was fit to be tied! Somehow she'd learned that he was well fixed, and she hated to lose."

"Did you ever see him again?"

"No. He went back east, I think, or maybe to Canada."

"And Myra?"

Tensleep shrugged evasively. "You stay away from her, boy. Forget her. That there's a downright bad woman."

"What about Van?"

"He's with her, wherever she is, unless she's got tired of him and kicked him out—or poisoned him."

The next morning Val rode out of the mountains. He followed the trail to Hays, and lost it there. Then he rode south into Texas.

The gold in the twin money belts rode heavily on his hips, but he used it sparingly. One night, camped in a sheltered draw near some mesquite, he fed his fire. A feeling of loneliness possessed him. He was missing Will's companionship, and the talks they'd had about people and books and cards. He was realizing that he wanted to leave all this behind and go somewhere very different . . . he wanted to go east.

For some time he had been conscious of a growing sound in the distance, and now there was the rattle of trace chains, and the creak of a heavy wagon. A voice called out, "Halloo, the fire!"

Val stepped back into the shadows. "Come in if you're friendly. If you're not, just come a-shootin'!"

He heard a chuckle from the darkness. "Now, there's an invite if ever I heard one! Come on, Betsy, looks like we're to home!"

# TEN

The wagon rolled up to the edge of the firelight and a tall old man got down, peering toward the fire. "It's all right, stranger," he said. "We ain't meanin' no harm. Seems like Betsy an' me, we got lost out here."

He walked into the light, carrying a rifle in his right hand, muzzle down.

Val studied him. He seemed like any drifting landhunter. Val's eyes went to the wagon. Whoever Betsy was, she was not in sight. The muzzles of four rifles were.

He was still deep in the shadow and he was sure they could not see him, but he was in no position to fire. If he did shoot, they would sweep his position with rifle fire in the next instant.

"If you're friendly, why the rifles?" Val kept his tone pleasant. "And don't count on them being any help. They might get me afterward, but I'd nail your hide before they did."

"Looks like a Mexican standoff, don't it, son?"

The old man walked up to the fire. He was shabbily dressed, but he looked as if he made a try at cleanliness, at least. "You all alone, boy?" he said.

"No, I'm not alone. I've got a six-shooter and a Winchester," Val said. "They're all the company I need."

The old man chuckled. "See? I tol' you he was our kind of folks. 'Light an' set, Betsy."

The wagon curtains parted and a girl swung down lightly and easily, then she turned and faced the fire. Her hair was black, and her eyes were the same. Her skin was clear and creamy. She was beautiful.

"I am Betsy," she said simply.

"Why don't you have the rest of your outfit get down, too?" Val said. "I'd feel a lot easier in my mind if you just gathered around."

Two young men, not much older than Val himself, got down from the wagon, and Val stepped into the open. He held out his hand. "I am Val Darrant," he said, "and I am hunting a place to light."

"Same here." The taller of the boys said, "I am Tardy Bucklin. This here's Cody, an' Pa you've met." Then he turned to the girl. "And this here is Western Bucklin, our sister. We call her Betsy."

"There's coffee," Val said, "but I haven't enough grub for you all."

"Never you mind," Cody said, "I'll get a bait from the wagon."

The old man turned toward the wagon and called out, "All right, Dube, you can come out now."

Another tall boy got down from the wagon and walked toward them, grinning.

Val was annoyed with himself. He had been a fool to gamble, and they had acted wisely, keeping their ace in the hole hidden until sure of him. "Is that all of you?" he asked. "Or do you still have another rifleman somewhere?"

The old man smiled, his eyes twinkling. "Matter of fact, Boston's out yonder checkin' your sign to see if more than one of you came in."

Then Val saw the dog, a big rough-haired one, part airedale and part mastiff, or Great Dane perhaps. He was not unfriendly, but watchful.

Boston walked into the firelight then, and this was another beautiful girl, younger than Betsy.

"You'll have to watch your step, young feller," Pa Bucklin said. "These here girls ain't seen a likely young man since they left home. You'll be lucky if you get away without them catchin' onto you."

*"Pa!"* Western said indignantly. "What will he think of us?"

"Just a-warnin' of him, same's I would if I seen a rattler. An' he'll need it, won't he, boys?"

"Gals do beat all when it comes to takin' after a man," Cody said dryly. "Not," he added "that they ain't good gals. I wouldn't have you get any wrong ideas about 'em."

One of the boys took his rifle and moved out into the darkness, and the girls began putting on some food. "You set up, son," Bucklin said. "These girls cook up mighty able vittles, and no matter how much you et, they'll git you to have more."

Val did sit up, and the food was all Pa Bucklin had said.

While they ate, the old man explained. "We're like the rest of 'em, son. We're huntin' a fresh start in the western lands. We got nothin' but a little grub, some good horses, a cow, and a lot of hands used to work, but we aim to make good."

For the first time in many days, Val relaxed. They were pleasant, easy-going people. They had come from the mountains in Virginia, and they were headed west to try ranching. Pa Bucklin had been a horse trader, and occasionally had driven stock to the eastern cities for sale. Cody and Dube had been west before; they had hunted buffalo, and had taken part in two of the early cattle drives.

"They tell me there's good land in Colorado," Pa Bucklin said. "Me and the boys figured to git ourselves some while the gittin's good."

"Holding it is harder than getting it," Val said.

Tardy Bucklin smiled at him. "We get it, we hold it," he said, "don't you worry your mind about that. We got to get cattle, too, and horses. We figured to round up some wild horses to start off with. Cody says it can be done."

"Fact is," the old man said, "we got ourselves a claim staked out. We got ourselves a place. Cody an' Dube, they scouted the country when they were buffalo huntin', and they found us a spring with a good flow of water. We're a-headin' for it now."

"Mind if I ride along?" said Val. "Might lend a hand in case of Indians."

"Welcome," Pa Bucklin said, and that began it.

For three slow days they traveled down-country, three wonderful days. The Bucklins were good-humored and hard-working. Val did his part of the work, and tried to do a little more, and in the meanwhile he was thinking.

"This water hole now," he said. "Is it just sitting there?"

"It's Comanche country," Dube said, "and not many will hanker for it, but we built ourselves a soddy and Uncle Joe stayed on to sort of see after it."

They rode up to the springs on the late afternoon of an overcast day. Dust devils were stirring among the short grass, and worrying the trees around the spring—a small but sturdy grove of cottonwoods and willows. Cody and Dube started ahead to scout the layout. Val swung alongside them.

"Uncle Joe, now," Dube said. "He should be expectin' of us, I reckon."

There was no sign of smoke, no sound of axe. They spread out a little and, rifles in hand, rode closer. Then they saw the body, a dark patch on the slope of the hill, away from the trees.

Cody swung wide, circled warily, and approached the body. Then he rode back to them quickly, his face white with anger. "It's Uncle Joe. He was shot, drug, an' left to die."

They closed in swiftly on the soddy. It was a low but solidly built sod house with a pole corral next to it. As they approached the door they could see a sign on the door.

THIS LAND CLAIMED BY DIAMOND BAR
STAY OFF!!

"Well," Dube spat. "He might have talked us out of it, but he began the shootin'."

"Maybe your uncle shot first," Val suggested mildly.

"Uncle Joe? Not him. He was half blind. He couldn't see well enough to shoot at anything that wasn't close up to him, and he didn't hold with shootin', unless set upon."

"His rifle is gone," Cody said.

"We'll know the rifle," Dube said. "One time or another we'll come upon it."

The sod house was empty, but it had been rifled, the food thrown in the dirt for the wild animals and the ants to eat.

"You tell Pa, Dube. Val an' me, we'll sort of set tight."

When Dube had gone, Cody said, "Pa will be upset. Uncle Joe

was the only kin of my mother, an' Pa and him thought a lot of one another. I reckon we'll have some huntin' to do."

"You may be outnumbered."

Cody turned cold eyes on Val. "No Bucklin is ever outnumbered, young feller."

The wagon rolled in, and the girls began to make the little house comfortable. They slept in the soddy, the men slept outside.

The next day they began work on enlarging the house. They also dug rifle pits on the hills close around, and a man stayed on watch all the time. At night there was another on watch—the dog, a powerful beast, friendly as a puppy among the family, but deep-voiced and ready to be fierce to anyone who approached from the outside.

"We got to round us up some horses," Bucklin said the first day, "and hunt us some meat."

"You ought to run cattle," Val suggested. "You can't sell many horses, except to the Army, and the Indians will steal them."

"A body does what he can," Bucklin said grimly. "We got nothing but our milk cow."

Val threw his saddle into place, cinched up, and stood staring at the rolling hills. These were good people, poor but solid, and they were workers. Maybe he was a fool, but Will had always taught him that character was the most important element in judging horses, dogs, or men. And women, too, he supposed.

"Mr. Bucklin," he said, "I am of a mind to talk business."

Pa looked at him, surprised at the sudden change of tone. Cody looked at him, too.

"Are the boys all here?" Val said. "Let's sit down together."

They came in, those tall, quiet young men, Dube, Cody, and Tardy, and the two girls.

"You don't know me any better than I know you," Val said, "but I like the way you work together and the way you handle yourselves. I can feel you're honest people, and I think you're going to make a success of ranching." He hesitated, then took the plunge. "I want to buy in. I want a partnership. I won't be here much of the time—I've got to go east, and I've got some looking around to do. In fact, I've got to find a couple of men . . . three, in fact. That's why I can't work with you much of the time."

"What you figurin' on?"

"You need cattle. I will put up the money for six hundred head if you can get them for ten dollars a head."

"We can buy cows for four to five dollars in Texas," Cody said. "You got that kind of money?"

"Yes," Val said. "I inherited it from my uncle, and I can get more."

They looked at one another, and Val could see they were doubtful. He opened his shirt and took out one of the money belts. Opening the pockets he took out two thousand dollars in gold and greenbacks. "There you are. When you're ready, we can ride south and east and buy cattle."

Cody heaved a great sigh. "Well, Pa, there she is. More'n we ever hoped for. I say we go partners with him."

Bucklin rubbed his jaw. "You want half?"

"One-third . . . you do the work, I put up the money for the cattle. You take that, buy what you can. I'll come in with more later."

"Don't see's we could do better, nohow," Bucklin said. "We're with you, son."

After that several days passed, during which they scouted the range in every direction, riding in pairs for self-protection, with always one man on watch at home. The grass was good, and despite the claims of the Diamond Bar, they saw no cattle wearing any brand at all.

They did see a small herd of buffalo, numbering not over sixty head. One, grazing off to one side, they shot for meat. There were numerous antelope, and once, far off, they glimpsed a wolf.

Water holes were scarce. The one by which they had settled had a strong flow, but it was the only water hole in several miles. Its value was immediately apparent. Whoever controlled that water would control about forty square miles of range. A longhorn steer would walk three days to get to water, though cattle weren't going to fatten up much unless water was easier of access.

About a hundred yards from the soddy, they dug out a low place, shaping the sides and lining three sides with stones, to form a crude tank. Into this they directed the runoff from the spring.

"Pa," Cody said, "I don't like it much, about Uncle Joe. He was a kindly man."

"Maybe we ought to fetch it to them," Dube suggested.

"No," Pa Bucklin said, "we'll wait. We settled in this country of our ownselves. We aim to stay here, so we ain't goin' to push no fight. They started it, an' they'll come a-huntin' us soon or late. Meanwhile, we got to think about cattle, mostly about breedin' stock."

He glanced at Val. "You know anything about beef cattle, boy?"

"A little. I've worked on the range a mite, and I've sat and listened to the cattle buyers talk deals by the hour. I've waited a lot in hotel lobbies and I'd hear them talking the fine points. When Will and I punched cows a little, we worked with a very canny cattleman who used to tell us what was wrong with this one or that one. Yes, I know a little."

"None of us knows too much, when it comes to that. No more than a sight of others who are choosing land in this western country. Son, you, Cody, and me, we'll ride up to town."

"How about us?" Boston asked. "Western and me, we'd like to see the lights."

"Ain't many lights where we're a-goin'," Cody said. "You all saw that town. It's a one-street town of weather-beaten shacks, mostly saloons."

"You stay," Pa said. "There might be trouble. There might also be trouble here too, but you two can handle rifles good as any man."

Before the light came the next morning they were riding the short-grass plains toward town, startling the rabbits, which ran off a ways and then sat up, ears pricked. They rode with their Winchesters in the saddle boots, and spurs jingling.

They came into Cross-Timbers, and the first thing they saw was a Diamond Bar wagon and two Diamond Bar ponies standing three-legged at the hitch rail in front of the Cap-Rock Saloon.

The street was lined with eight buildings and a corral—there were four saloons, two general stores, a blacksmith shop, and an eating place.

They tied their horses and went into the saloon, letting the batwing doors swing behind them. Pa and Cody, they walked up to the bar, but Val did what Will Reilly had always done, and stayed inside the door, looking into the darkest corner to get his eyes accustomed after the glare. He did not drink, anyway, so he sat down at an empty table near the door.

There were four cowhands and a teamster in the saloon, as well as a couple of men in broadcloth suits at the bar. With them was a man who looked as if he might be the blacksmith.

Pa ordered a drink and then looked over at these men. "Beggin' your pardon gents," he said, "but I am in the market to buy cattle."

For a long moment no one spoke, although all turned to look at him. Then one of the cowhands at the table spoke up. "You picked the wrong country, friend. There's no range around here, not for miles. This here is Diamond Bar country."

"Seems a mighty spread-out place for one outfit." Pa spoke mildly. "Anyway, we've settled in on a nice water hole over west of here. We like it there."

"That water hole was posted by the Diamond Bar."

"I noticed that," Cody said quietly, "and they murdered an almost blind old man to mark their sign."

For a moment there was dead silence, and then the cowhand said, "That old man was armed."

"That old man was not armed," Cody said flatly. "He was my ma's oldest brother, and he couldn't see across this here saloon."

The cowhand's face tightened. "You callin' me a liar?"

"If you were there, and shot that man, I am callin' you a liar and a murderer," Cody said coolly. "If you just heard the story told, I am tellin' you whoever told you that story was a liar and a murderer."

One of the others spoke up. "You'd better say that easy, cowboy. The man who told us that was Chip Hardesty."

Val interrupted. "Cody, sorry to butt in like this, but Chip Hardesty belongs to me."

They all looked at him, and the teamster snorted.

"Kid, you keep your mouth shut. Hardesty is a mean man, and the fastest one around."

"You can tell him for me that he is a murdering skunk. He killed that old man. He also killed another man, he and two others, with shotguns, without warning as he came out of a door in the dark." Val sat facing the men at the table, and he fixed his eyes on the teamster. "And you, mister, you take a long time thinking before you tell me to shut my mouth again."

"Don't you talk to me." The teamster was shaking with anger. "You ain't dry behind the ears yet."

"This gun is," Val said, "and it speaks plain language. You just put a hand on that gun you've got and I'll write my initials in your belly."

The teamster's fury was suddenly penetrated by a cold arrow of caution. The boy was young, but the gun could be just as deadly, and the distance between them was less than fifteen feet. In any event, it wasn't his fight unless he was foolish enough to make it so. Let Hardesty do it. That was what he was getting paid for.

"You settle it with Hardesty," he said. "Like you said, he belongs to you. And I'll tell him," he added, with deep satisfaction. "He'll be huntin' you before sundown."

Val looked at him. "Mister, you get on your feet right now. You ride right to where Hardesty is, and you tell him to come on in. I'll be waiting . . . right here."

The teamster got to his feet, very carefully.

"You go with them," Val said to the cowboys, "just in case they don't believe him. And you tell the boss of the Diamond Bar he can stay in this country just as long as he's willing to stay off our backs. We want no trouble, and we aren't going to cause him any."

"Except for them that killed Uncle Joe," Pa Bucklin said. "You tell your boss to hang them before night falls or we will hang him within thirty days."

"You're crazy!" the teamster cried. "Plain crazy!"

"You tell him that," Bucklin said. Then he turned to the others. "Let's go eat. Be an hour or more before he can get here."

# ELEVEN

It was a quiet meal. Nobody felt much like talking, Val Darrant least of all. He had said what he wanted to say, but now he would have to back it up. He had never met any man in a show-down gun battle, least of all a veteran killer like Hardesty, but Hardesty was one of those who had killed Will Reilly.

Pa and Cody were quiet, too. Only toward the end did Cody speak up. "They may bring an army, Pa."

"Then we'll have to take care of an army," Pa said shortly. "Let's stay under cover until we see what they look like."

"I'll go out," Val said, "I've got this to do."

They were silent for a few minutes, and then Cody said quietly, "Val, you're a good friend or I wouldn't say this, but you bein' a boy and all, I—"

"Thanks, but I told him what I could do. I've got to put up or shut up. This is my proposition."

"You ever been in a gun fight before?"

"I've fought a couple of times," Val said, "but never man to man, like this."

"Then you make the first shot count. Don't give no worry to being fast. If he shoots first, you got to face it, but take your time and put that first one where it can be the last one."

93

"Thanks."

There was nothing elaborate about the saloon. It had a bar fifteen feet long at one side. There were four square tables, each surrounded by four chairs, the kind called captain's chairs. The bar had obviously been shipped in, as had the chairs; the tables had been made in the town.

The stock of liquor was not large, but was adequate for men who liked strong drink and cared little about age or flavor. Several dog-eared decks of cards were on tables, and idly riffling one, Val noticed that somebody had been marking them with a thumbnail—clumsily, too.

One of the men at the bar, dressed like a western man who had been east more than a few times, came over, drink in hand. "Mind if I sit down?" He smiled. "I promise to get out of the way before the shooting starts."

There was something familiar about the man, and Val, who had been taught to remember, recognized him as the quiet-faced man who had been present when he had the showdown over the twenty-dollar gold piece.

"You travel a lot," Val commented, and the man smiled at him. "Sit down," he added.

"You mentioned buying cattle. Do you plan to start ranching?"

"We have the ranch," Val said; "now we need cattle."

"I might be interested in investing a little, if you come out of this all right."

"Thanks, but we have all we need."

"My friend over there," the man said, "is a cattle buyer. He occasionally sells, too. And sometimes we grubstake a good outfit."

Val made no comment, but he was curious. Will Reilly had taught him never to accept men at face value, and he did not. He knew that there are all kinds of men appearing in all kinds of guises.

"I am Steve Kettering," the man went on. "My friend over there is Paul Branch."

Val introduced Pa and Cody, and waited. This man was building up to something, and it might be interesting to know what it was. "What's the matter with your friend?" he asked. "Isn't he the sociable type?"

Kettering turned. "Paul, come on over and meet these gentlemen."

Branch came over and sat down. "I am sorry, gentlemen," he said, "I'm not in the best of moods. I came into town for a poker game and Kettering promised me one. If I am a bit restless, please forgive me."

"What do you play for?"

They looked at him. "I mean," Val said, "do you gentlemen play for money, or for cigar coupons?"

Branch reached down in his jeans and pulled out a thick roll of bills. "I play for that," he said, "and there's more where that comes from."

It looked to Val like what was known as a Kansas City bankroll, a couple of tens wrapped around a thick wad of ones, or even around brown paper.

This man Kettering had seen him before, seen him drop a gold coin on the floor, and now he heard him trying to buy cattle, and needing no backing. Which Val knew would be evidence enough that he had money.

"Would you boys be interested in a little game?" Branch asked. "I mean, you have some time to kill, and I thought—"

How many times had Val watched the routine? Reilly was an honest gambler, and roped nobody into a game, but he had often pointed out such developments to Val, who was amused at how clear the pattern was.

"We've got business," Pa Bucklin said. "If you've cattle to sell, we'll talk. We got no time for cards."

"I might have a little time," Val said. "I might just have enough. A man standing in my shoes can afford to take a chance. But these cards look pretty used up—"

"I am sure the bartender has a fresh deck around," Branch said. "Shall I call him?"

Val smiled. "Now there's a gamble, right there. I'll lay you three to one he does have a fresh deck. Is it a bet?"

Kettering's eyes had grown suddenly wary. He looked at Val thoughtfully, but Branch shrugged it off. "That's no bet. Most bartenders have a deck of cards for sale."

The bartender brought a deck of cards and Branch broke the seal, and shuffled the cards. "Shall we cut for deal?" he said, and promptly cut the cards. Val saw the finger tap the stack gently as Branch reached to make his cut and knew he had a slick ace, its face treated with shellac to slide easily.

Branch turned up the ace of hearts. "You can't beat that. Shall I deal?"

"But I might do just as well. Mind if I shuffle them first?"

He did . . . and promptly cut an ace.

Branch's face stiffened, but Kettering only bit the end from a fresh cigar and lit it.

"Let's just put these aces aside." Val had picked up the cards again, and was shuffling them idly as he talked. "And try again. Maybe you can beat me this time."

"It's getting to be a warm day," Kettering got to his feet. "You boys play if you like. I'm too restless." He walked to the bar and ordered a drink.

Branch started to reply, his irritation showing, but Cody interrupted. "You ain't goin' to have time. I think I hear horses a-comin'."

"One hand," Val said. "Just you and me, Branch, and we play what's dealt . . . no draw."

Branch hesitated only a minute. The deck was marked to indicate face cards and he had two aces in a sleeve holdout, so there was little to worry about.

Val dealt the hands, and Branch saw the five cards Val dealt to himself had not a face card among them. Branch picked up his hand. Two eights, two queens and an ace.

Val was studying his cards, Pa Bucklin had walked to the bar again where he could watch the street, and Cody's eyes were on the door. Branch made the shift without trouble, replacing the eights with the aces.

Branch put five gold eagles in the center of the table.

"You're a piker, Branch," Val said, "I'm just a greenhorn kid, but I'll go five hundred." And he put the money on the table.

"Forget it, Paul," Kettering's voice held an edge. "Throw in your hand and I'll buy you a drink."

Branch considered his cards. He now had a full house, aces and queens, and the chances that this boy could better it were small. He glanced at his cards and at the five hundred dollars in the middle of the table. There was a good chance this kid would be shot full of holes in the next few minutes, and somebody would steal the money from his pockets. . . .

"I'll see you," he said. The horses were stopping now in front of the saloon. Branch placed five hundred on the table, and spread his cards . . . three aces and two queens. He started to reach for the pot, but Val spread his own hand . . . four tens and a trey.

Paul Branch felt himself suddenly go empty. Val reached over and swept the money to him with his left hand.

"Paul"—Kettering's voice broke through the fury that was mounting within him—"I'll still buy that drink. Come here!"

Branch started to rise. Through a red haze of anger he remembered how Kettering had suddenly pulled out, how Kettering had tried to get him away. Kettering had seen something, sensed something, but he himself had been rooked—and good—by a mere boy.

It was in his mind to kill. He was opening his hand to reach for his gun when the doors smashed open behind him.

"I'm Chip Hardesty!" The tone was hard with challenge. "Where's that kid?"

Val Darrant stood up. His mouth was dry and his heart was pounding. "Will Reilly was my uncle," he said quietly, holding his voice down for fear it might become shrill. "You murdered him. You never gave him a chance."

"I don't fight kids!" Hardesty sneered.

"But you murdered a blind old man," Val said, "and don't worry about this kid. You were afraid to tackle Will Reilly when he had an even chance, and Will often said I was faster than he was."

Hardesty laughed, but the laugh broke off. *Faster than Will Reilly?* It couldn't be. He never knew when his hand started to move. He could not remember thinking that he was going to draw, only that his hand almost of its own volition was dropping, grasping the butt, lifting . . .

He never heard the sound of the gun, although it must have been loud in the room. He felt himself taking a step backward, and then he was sitting on the floor, and he was rolling over, and the last thing he saw were the gray slivers in the planks of the floor, and then a gray mist that crept over them.

Paul Branch was looking at the sprawled body of the gunman, feeling the icy chill at what he had almost done. He had been about to draw on this kid, and if he had done so he would now be dead.

Pa Bucklin stepped into the door. The teamster and two cowhands were outside. "You'd better come in and pick up your man.

Take him back to your boss and tell him we Bucklins and Mr. Val Darrant are staying on at the Springs."

Paul Branch said to Kettering, "If you are still in the mood to buy it, I'll have that drink."

Kettering ordered, and then spoke to Val. "You said Will Reilly was your uncle? Did he teach you about cards?"

Val put his palm down to holster level. "From the time I was that high," he said, and he walked out.

He did not want to look at Hardesty. He did not want to think about what he had done. He wanted to be out in the air, and away from people. He no longer wanted to kill Thurston Pike or Henry Sonnenberg.

He did not want to be a gambler or a gunfighter. He did not want to die as Hardesty had, or Will Reilly, or as Tensleep almost had. For a long time he had wanted to go east . . . now was the time.

He was going to keep five hundred dollars and he was going to leave the rest of it with the Bucklins to buy cattle and operate the ranch.

If he ever needed to come back, he could come back there, to the ranch. . . .

# TWELVE

B ut he did not go . . . not quite yet. He rode with them to
round up their cattle buy on the plains west of the Neuces,
and started the long drive overland to the ranch, mostly young stuff
with a few older steers to steady the herd. They wanted breeding
stock, for they were not thinking of next year, but of the years to
come.

After the first two days the cattle strung out, and for two weeks
they moved the herd, first through dry country, and then across
swollen streams and land that was soggy from the sudden rains.

At last Val pulled off to one side and said to Pa Bucklin, "I am
leaving it to you. You will hear from me, and one day I will come
back. In the meantime, build the herd, and when there is money
for me, bank it in my name."

They shook hands, and Pa said, "The womenfolk are going to
miss you mighty. My girls set store by you, boy."

"I will come back."

Cody rounded the herd and rode up to him. "If you ever need
help, you send out a call and we'll come a-runnin'. We reckon
you're kin of ourn now."

"I never had a family. Only Uncle Will, who wasn't rightly my
uncle."

"You've got one now. From grass roots to cloud."

The day was threatening rain when he turned his horse away from the herd and pointed north for Kansas and the railroad. He held to low ground because of lightning, but he kept a steady course. When night came there was nothing around him but dampness, the clouds, and the dark. He camped several times before he saw the lights of Dodge, and when he came up to the town he was wearing sodden clothing, several days of whiskers, and a bedraggled look.

He rode past a cheap saloon and did not see the man who suddenly gave him a second look, then spoke over his shoulder into the saloon.

He drew up opposite a restaurant and leaned over to stare in the rain-wet window, trying to see how inviting it looked inside. He swung down and was about to tie his horse when two men in boots and spurs came up the boardwalk.

"Shed right back yonder in the alley," one said, "where you can put your horse out of the rain."

"Thanks," Val said, and followed the man into the alley. They were scarcely within its darkness when he heard the man behind him take a quick step. Val started to turn, but not in time. The gun barrel caught him a sweeping blow over the ear and he went down.

He heard a voice saying, "He's wearing a money belt an' packing about three thousand dollars."

He felt hands fumbling at his shirt, but he could neither move nor speak. A voice was muttering, "Hell, there ain't that much here!"

He felt rough hands seize him, and then he lost consciousness. He remembered nothing after that. When he opened his eyes it was daytime, and he was sprawled on his back.

He heard a whistle, and he realized he was on a train, lying on the floor of an empty freight car. His head was throbbing.

He tried to sit up, and finally made it. The car door was open and he saw that it was still raining—the rain, slanting across the opening, was like a steel mesh. He felt at his waist—the money belts were gone.

His gun was gone, too. He searched his pockets, but he found nothing, not so much as a two-bit piece.

The car was empty except for himself, and he had no idea how long he had been lying there. Through the night and most of the day, no doubt, for, judging by the light, it was already getting on toward evening. Several times he saw the lights of houses, so they must be in eastern Kansas or Missouri. He lay back, rested his head on his arm, and went to sleep.

A boot in the ribs awakened him, and a voice spoke. "Come on! Get up!"

The train was standing still on the outskirts of a village. The voice came again. "Get out of here, now! An' don't let me catch you on one of our trains again!"

He ducked a blow, stood up, and dropped to the ground, but his legs were weak and he fell, rolling. Slowly, he pulled himself up. The train was starting, with jerks and a rumble.

He stood watching it vanish into the town. His head was throbbing, and when he put his fingers to his skull he found lacerations.

His mind fumbled over the sound of that voice. It belonged to somebody he had known or heard once before, and obviously it was somebody who knew he was carrying money—for he had known exactly where to look, and even how much had been there.

Val shivered with cold and wetness. Hunching his shoulders against the rain, he looked around. He stood at the bottom of the embankment. Ahead of him in a shallow valley, was a small stream, which the railroad crossed on a trestle. Clumps of willows grew along the stream, with here and there a cottonwood.

He saw a thin trail of smoke rising from a point downstream. Beyond the hollow he could see a house painted white, a red barn with a weather vane, and a windmill. Sitting down on a rock, he took off his spurs and dropped them into his pocket, then he started toward the trail of smoke.

A path led to an open place among the willows where three men were sitting around a fire. Two were older men, the other in his early twenties, Val judged.

They looked at him. "Man, you look as if you really got it rough," the younger man said. "They throw you off that rattler?"

"They sure did." Val touched his scalp. "But they didn't do this. I got pistol-whipped in Dodge City."

They looked at his outfit, and his boots. "You been punchin' cows?"

It was simpler to put it that way, so he agreed. He dropped

down on a log across the fire from them. "Somebody rolled me and dumped me into a boxcar. Where are we, anyway?"

"Missouri." The younger man leaned over and filled a tin cup. "Have some coffee. Do you good."

Neither one of the older men, both of whom looked capable and tough, had spoken.

"Which way you headed?" Val asked.

"East. I got an uncle in Pennsylvania. I'm going there."

One of the older men leaned back under the makeshift shelter and said, "New Orleans for me. I can make it good, down south."

"Ain't much to do," the other one said, "and they don't pay nothing, Fred."

"I'll make out. I always have."

The coffee was hot and strong, and it was just what Val needed. He felt the warmth of it go through him. "I got to find work," he said. "They took all I had."

"You got anything to sell?"

Val thought of his spurs. They were large-roweled, California-type spurs, not too common in this area. "I've got some spurs." He showed them. "That's about all."

"You might get a dollar for them—maybe two if you hit the right fellow. Say, there's a boy about your age up at that farm" —he pointed—"who might fancy those spurs. I seen him trying to rope a post up there. Fancies himself a cowhand."

"You got to be careful," Fred offered. "You can get six months for putting the bum—" At Val's blank expression Fred explained. "I mean, for begging. You ask for grub or money, and they'll put you on a work gang."

"And it don't make any difference that you're huntin' work," the other man said. "I'm a millwright, and a good one, if I do say it. There just ain't any work to be had." The fire as well as the coffee had warmed Val, and he grew sleepy. All of the others dozed, but when a train whistle blew the three ran for the train and left him sitting there.

He stared into the ashes of the fire. The rain had stopped, and he should be getting on. He was fiercely hungry, his head still ached, and he was unbelievably tired. He got to his feet, kicked dirt over the fire, and took the path that led toward the farm where the boy lived who might buy the spurs.

The road was muddy, but he kept to the grassy border. Cows

stared at him across the fence, and at the ranch a dog barked. He walked more slowly as he neared the farm, not wanting to enter. He had never sold any of his personal possessions, and did not feel sure how to go about it. He dared not ask for food—not if he could get six months in jail for it. And he knew that some jails hired their prisoners out as laborers and collected a fee from whoever hired them.

He hesitated, then turned in at the gate. A big yellow dog barked fiercely, but he talked softly and held out his hand to it. The dog backed away, growling.

A woman in a blue apron came to the door and looked at him suspiciously. "Yes? What do you want?"

"I was wondering if you had some work I could do? I can split wood, dig . . . I guess I can do anything."

"No." Her voice was sharp. "We don't need any help, and you're the fourth man who has been here this morning."

A tall boy had come into the doorway behind her, and the contempt vanished from his eyes as he glimpsed Val's cowboy boots. They had been made by the best maker of cowboy boots, and were hand-tooled, with fancy stitching.

"Are you a cowboy?" he asked.

"I was," Val said. "I was robbed in Dodge City. Somebody put me on a train and here I am."

"Tom, you stay in the house!" the woman ordered. "You don't know who this man is."

"He ain't no older than me. Look at his beard—it's only fuzz!"

Val was irritated by the comment, but he kept his peace. "Are you a cowpuncher?" he asked, knowing well enough that the boy was not.

"Well, not really." The boy had come outside. He was about Val's age but somehow seemed much younger. "I plan to be. Only my folks, they don't cotton to the idea."

He walked out and leaned on the top rail of the fence. Val sat on the rail beside him. "It's hard work," he said, "and some of those old mossy-horn steers get mighty ornery."

They talked for a time while Val's stomach gnawed with hunger. Finally he said, "I got to go. I want to find somebody who'll buy my spurs."

"Spurs? Let's see them!"

Val took the spurs from his pocket. The Californios liked their

spurs fancy, and these were an elaborate job, each with two tiny
bells. He could see from the way the boy's eyes shone that he
wanted them.

"You can see," Val said, "these are no ordinary spurs. Fact is,
they were a gift to me. From Wild Bill Hickok."

"You knew *him?*"

"He was a friend of my uncle's. He warned my uncle that some
men were looking for him. To shoot him," he added.

The boy handled the spurs. "I'd like to have them," he said,
"but I've only got two dollars."

"Well," Val said, "if you could rustle me a meal, or some meat
and bread or something, I'd sell them to you for two dollars."

"You just wait right here."

In a few minutes he was back with a paper sack and the two
dollars. Val took the money and the sack. "You'd better go now,"
the boy said. "Pa's coming home and he's dead set against tramps."

"All right . . . and thanks."

He started for the gate, then hesitated. "Look, if you ever get
into west Texas, you hunt up the Bucklin outfit. They're this side
of the cap-rock—you ask at Fort Griffin. You tell them Val Darrant
sent you."

He walked out of the gate, and when well down the road he sat
down under a tree. There was a big hunk of meat and cheese in the
sack, and several slices of homemade bread, as well as an apple.
Val took his time, eating a piece of the bread, most of the meat,
and the apple. Then he walked on.

Two days later he was in St. Louis. He rode the last few miles
on the seat of a wagon beside a farmer who was carrying a mixed
lot of hides, vegetables, and fruit. "Work's mighty scarce, boy,"
the farmer told him, "and you will do yourself no good in St.
Louis. Ever since the depression hit, there's been three men for
every job."

Idle men stood about the streets of the city, and Val paused on
a corner, considering. He had nothing to sell. Nor was he in any
position to look up any of Will Reilly's friends, for he lacked the
one thing Will had always insisted he keep. He must have a
"front," he must have the clothing, the neatly trimmed hair, the
polished boots, even if he did not have a cent in his pockets.

Standing on the corner watching the traffic, he tried to gauge
his talents and abilities. He had great card skill, but he did not

want to be a gambler. He had skill with guns, but he did not want to use it. He had received from Will an education in literary and historical matters. But to do anything with any of these abilities he needed money.

All day he walked the streets, and wherever men were working he asked for a job. In every place it was the same. "We don't have enough work to keep our own men busy."

When night came, he wandered back to the river front and sat down on the dock. For the first time he realized that Will Reilly, while showing him much of life, had also shielded him from much. To be with Will Reilly had given him a position, and as Will was treated with respect everywhere, Val had also received respect. Suddenly now it was gone, and he stood alone, and unknown.

There were friends of Will's in St. Louis. They had stayed at the Southern Hotel, and Will had been accorded the best treatment that hostelry had to offer, but he could not walk into that lobby looking as he did now. He might write to the ranch for money, but the postal service was uncertain, and it might be weeks before anybody from the ranch went into town, or to Fort Griffin.

Before, even during periods of separation, Will had always been not too far away, and Val had always known there was somebody, somewhere, who cared. Now there was nobody.

That night he slept on a bale of cotton under the overhang of a warehouse. He put a newspaper under his coat for protection against the cold, huddled in a ball, and shivered the whole night through. Several times he awoke, turned over, and fought to get back to sleep again. Always there were places where the cold reached him.

At last he got up and walked down to the edge of the wharf. The river was running through the piles, sucking around them. Further up a river boat was tied, lights showing, but the lights were obscured by the falling rain.

It was still dark; he was hungry, and his eyes heavy with weariness. After a while he walked back to his cotton bale, tucked the newspaper more firmly into place, and went back to sleep.

He awoke in the cold gray of dawn. The rain had stopped, but the clouds hung low. The river rolled by, and he sat staring at it, wondering which way to turn.

An old man, puffing on a meerschaum pipe, was plodding along the dock, carrying a lunch box. He glanced at Val over his steel-rimmed spectacles. "Mornin', son," he said. "You're up mighty early."

Val grinned at him. Hungry, stiff, and cold, he still felt a streak of whimsy. "Mister," he said seriously, "you have just walked into my bedroom unannounced. I did not wish to be disturbed."

The old man chuckled. "Well, now that you're disturbed you might's well come along and have some coffee."

Val dropped off the bale. "That's the best invitation I've had for a whole day. In fact, it's the best invitation I've had in several days."

They walked along to an old steamer that lay alongside the dock, and the old man led the way over the gangplank, and along the deck to the cabin. He unlocked the padlock and they went inside.

"Sit down, boy. I'll rustle around and make some coffee." He set the lunch box on the table. "Ain't seen you around before, have I?"

"No, sir. I'm hunting work."

"What's your line?"

"Well, I've never worked much. I've punched cows a little, and I've hunted buffalo. But I'm strong—I can do anything."

"That's like saying you can do nothing. Folks who do the hirin' want carpenters and such-like. You got to have a trade, son. Ain't there anything special you can do?"

"Nothing that I want to do."

"What's that mean?"

"I can deal cards, and shoot a gun."

The old man eyed him over his glasses. "Hmm. You a gambler, son?"

"No, sir. My uncle was, and he taught me. He said it was self-defense, like boxing. Only he didn't want me to be a gambler."

"Smart man. What do you aim to do, son? I mean, a man ought to be going somewhere. You're young, boy, but you'd best be thinking of where you're going to be at my age. When I was a boy I drifted, too. Always aimed to settle down and make something of myself, but somehow that was always going to be next year—so here I am."

He had bacon frying, and the coffee water was boiling. "I bring my lunch, most times. I can stand my own cooking just so long, then I have to go out and buy something somebody else has fixed."

"You're not married?"

"Was . . . one time. Fine woman. Had a son, too."

"What happened to him?"

"Went west . . . never seen hide nor hair of him since. He was a good boy." The old man paused. "Can't complain. I done the same thing as a boy. Went west with a keel boat and spent my years trapping fur."

He glanced at Val. "You ever see the Tetons, son? Or the Big Horns? Or the Wind River Mountains? That's country, son! That's *real* country!"

"I've seen them."

The old man put slices of the bacon on a plate, and then poured coffee. Got some bread from a bread box, "It ain't much, son, but you fall to."

Val took off his coat and sat down at the table. "You don't need a deck hand, do you? I'll work cheap."

The old man chuckled, with dry humor. "Son, I'm lucky to feed myself. Ain't had a job of towing to do in five months now, and only a little work then. There was a mite of salvage I was countin' on, but there wasn't much in the cargo . . . only flour. And water-soaked flour won't do anybody any good." Val put down his coffee cup. "Where was it sunk?"

"Bend of the river—maybe thirty mile downstream. She hit a snag and tore the bottom out. It ain't in deep water. A body can land on the Texas."

"You want to try for it? I could help. I'm a good swimmer and diver."

"No use. That flour's ruined."

"Not necessarily. I saw some sacks of flour out west that had been in the water, and only the flour on the outside was ruined. It soaked up water and turned hard as plaster."

"This flour was in barrels."

"All the better. You want to try for it?"

"That water's almighty cold this time of year." The old man hesitated, but Val could see that he was turning it over in his mind.

"We'd better keep it under our hats," he said finally. "That cargo is worth something, and there's some might want to take it from us."

"Do you have a gun?" Val asked.

"An old shotgun, that's all."

They talked it over, and Val went out on deck with the old man to examine the gear. It was in good shape, and the steam winch was usable. The steamer had operated on the Missouri River and on some of its branches. It had been used to push flatboats up the river and log rafts down the river, and to tow disabled steamers. It was a real workhorse of the river.

"The water's muddy," the old man said. "You'll have to locate a hatch, and if one ain't open, you'll have to open it."

"I'll make out."

Val had never done anything of this sort, but he was right in saying he was a strong swimmer and a good diver, and he had read stories of salvage; and in San Francisco he had heard talk in the hotel lobbies about such things. There is no better place than a hotel lobby in a boom town for picking up information . . . at least, he reflected, he would be sure of some good meals.

The old man studied him with shrewd attention. "You're an educated boy."

"No, not with schooling. I never went to school. But I've read a lot, and I've discussed what I've read."

The old man shrugged. "It could be the best way maybe. You think quickly, and you seem to have a good mind. Why don't you study law?"

"I hadn't thought of it."

"Well, think of it. Even if you don't want to practice the law you can use it in many ways. And just knowing it can be important."

They talked a good part of the day, returning again and again to their project. They looked over the gear once more.

One thing disturbed Val. "We should both be armed," he said. "There are too many drifters in town. Most of them are probably good men out of work, but there will be some bad ones among them. Such men can smell money, and if we get the flour up . . . How many barrels are there?"

"On the manifest, five hundred. Some will be damaged—maybe all of them."

"It will take us a while, and somebody is sure to be curious, so we had better be prepared."

"I have no money," the old man said. "The shotgun is all I have, and not many shells for it."

Val thought of something suddenly. He and Will had stayed at the Southern. Perhaps the manager there might loan him money. They had been very attentive to Will Reilly, and there was just a chance.

He borrowed old man Peterson's razor and shaved. He had now been shaving for two years, although even now he rarely needed to shave more than once every few days. And the old man had a black dress coat that did not fit him too badly.

Night had come before he started up the street toward the hotel. He felt ill at ease, knowing that he did not look right; nevertheless, this was a chance he had to take.

The Southern's lobby was spacious, and it was busy. At the desk the clerk glanced at him, then ignored him, but Val said, "May I speak to the manager please?"

The clerk studied him with cool eyes. "The manager? What do you want to see him about?"

"Just tell him I am Will Reilly's nephew."

There was a change in the clerk's manner. "Oh? Just a minute."

He was back in a moment to show Val through a door into an inner office, where the manager sat at a roll-top desk.

"I am Valentine Darrant, Will Reilly's nephew."

"Yes, I remember you. How is Mr. Reilly?"

"He's dead. He was killed."

"Oh?" There was ever so slight a change in the manager's manner. "So what can I do for you?"

"I arrived in town a few days ago, and I am broke. I have a job but I need a little cash. I was wondering if you—"

The manager got to his feet. "I am sorry, Darrant. We do not lend money. Mr. Reilly was a valued client of our hotel, but as you have said, he is no longer with us. Now, if you will excuse me—?"

A moment later Val was standing in the street. Well, he had no right to expect a loan. It had been a foolish idea. Still, how different it had been when Uncle Will was here!

He started to turn away when he heard a voice. "Val?"

He turned. It was Bill Hickok. "This is a long way from the buffalo ranges, sir," Val said.

"It surely is." Hickok came closer. "I wasn't sure it was you, at first." Then he added, "I heard about Will. That was too bad, Val."

"Thanks, sir."

"Are you staying here?" Hickok gestured toward the hotel.

"No, sir. As a matter of fact, I'm broke. I don't have anything at all." He told Hickok all about it: the ranch, the blow on the head, the arrival in St. Louis, the old river boat. "So I need a gun," he added.

"Boy, I'd like to help you. As a matter of fact, I haven't been doing too well. I have no stomach for acting, boy. All that make-believe goes against the grain. So I am going back west to guide a couple of hunting parties."

He reached into his pocket. "Val, I don't have much, but here's a twenty-dollar gold piece, and if you'll come upstairs with me, I've got a spare gun you can have."

They went into the hotel. The manager came forward and spoke to Val. "I don't think you have a room here, young man. I would rather—"

"I do have a room here," Hickok said sharply, "and this boy is a friend of mine—a very good friend. Treat him as such," he said, "or hold yourself accountable to me."

"Yes, sir. I am sorry sir. I only thought—"

"On the contrary, you did not think." Hickok brushed by him.

Upstairs he opened his valise and came up with a new Smith & Wesson Russian. "This was given to me, Val, and I think it may be the best of all the guns of the frontier, but I like the feel of the guns I've always carried." He dug out a handful of cartridges. "Here, take these. You'd better get more, though, if you're expecting trouble."

Hickok stood before the mirror, combing his hair, which fell to his shoulders. "It was Sonnenberg, Hardesty, and Thurston Pike who got him, wasn't it?"

"They ambushed him with shotguns when he was coming out of a door. He never had a chance."

"They never could have gotten him any other way. I knew Will Reilly, a good man with a gun. Well, they'll get theirs. That kind always does."

"Chip Hardesty is dead."

"Hardesty? I hadn't heard that."

"It was down in Texas, sir. Just west of Fort Griffin. He was a hired gunhand with a cattle outfit."

Hickok's eyes met Val's in the mirror. "And you said your ranch was down that way?"

"I killed him, sir. He brought it to me."

"Good boy. Anybody who would dry-gulch Will had it coming." He straightened his tie. "Will told me you were one of the best shots he had ever seen, and the fastest."

"He liked me, sir. I think he exaggerated."

"Not to me. Will never exaggerated on a thing like that in his life." Hickok dipped a washcloth in cold water and held it to his eyes. "Makes them feel better," he commented. "Too many nights sitting over a card table, I guess. I am better off when I'm on the hunt."

Val got up. "I've got to go, sir." He paused. "Thank you very much. I'll pay you back one of these days."

"And I may need it. Luck to you, boy. If you come out around Cheyenne or the Black Hills country, look me up."

When Val was out in the street, the weight of the gun in his waistband felt good. Along the river front it was cold and foggy. His footsteps echoed as he walked along the wharf toward the "Idle Hour."

Tomorrow they would be on their way, and in a few weeks, more or less, he would have money. He could go east.

# THIRTEEN

The night was overcast, the wharf was damp, the black waters of the river glistened where the few lights reached it. There was a somber stillness over everything.

At the last minute they had taken on another man, a broken-nosed Irishman with a glint of tough humor in his eyes, and an easy way of moving and talking. Both Val and Old Man Peterson had passed the time of day with him along the river front. He was broke, like themselves, and he was ready to take a chance, so they hired him on as a deck hand.

Paddy Lahey had been a tracklayer, a rough carpenter, a tie-cutter, and a miner. Somewhere, back in the years before he left the old country, he had been a fair-to-middling prize fighter.

"It's up to you," Val told him. "You'll come in for a fifth of what we make. Peterson gets two-fifths because the boat belongs to him. I am getting two-fifths because of my knowing the flour could be saved, and because if there's trouble I will take the brunt of it."

"You're young for that," Lahey commented, studying him doubt-fully. "Better let me handle the trouble. I'm an old roughneck, and used to the ways of fighting and brawling."

"You'll be needed, I'm thinking," Peterson said, "but I've confidence in Val."

"Have you done any fist-fighting?" Lahey asked.

"Not to speak of. Will Reilly taught me a little, and we boxed some."

"Then we'll spar some. You're a well-setup lad, and it could be you've got the makings. Will Reilly, was it? It's a good Irish name he has."

They cast off their lines and eased the small steamer into the current. She would sleep six, but she was short on cargo space. If they were lucky enough to get the flour up, they would have to make more than one trip to get it all to the docks in St. Louis.

They slid silently past the boats moored along the river, edged into the current, and headed south.

Just around a bend of the river they saw the steamboat they hoped to salvage lying in shallow water. After hitting the snag, the pilot had made a run for the shore to try to save his boat and his cargo, and he had almost made it.

"What we got to watch for," Captain Peterson said, "is river rats. They try to get all they can lay hands on, and you can be sure they've been down there, looking around. They're a pack of cut throats."

"That they are," Paddy agreed. "You can't trust 'em an inch."

They watched the shore, but they saw no one before they neared the wreck. The shores there were heavily wooded right down to the water, with cottonwood, box elder, elm, and willow.

After they had tied up to the wreck itself, Val stripped to dive. This would be the first time he had ever swum for any reason other than for pleasure. His activities would be shielded from the shore by the bulk of their own small steamer.

The Texas, with its pilot house, was visible above the water. A quick examination of the pilot house told Val that it had been looted of everything valuable. Even the wheel had been ripped out and taken away, as well as the brass lamps and other fixtures.

The Texas, where the officers as well as the boat's crew had their quarters, came next. This too, had been thoroughly looted.

Peterson got out a fishing pole and after lighting his pipe, dropped his line over the side. Beside him on a hatch he had his shotgun. "Let 'em figure I'm just fishing," he said. "It mayn't fool 'em for long, or at all, but it might."

Val belted on a crudely made canvas belt with large pockets attached, into which he had placed stones to weight him down. He climbed over the side to the hurricane deck, and from there he climbed down a stanchion to the saloon deck. Here, ranged around the saloon, were the first-class cabins—staterooms that on Mississippi River boats were named for the states of the Union.

The water was murky, but there was still light enough to see, and if there had been a search down there Val realized that it had been a hurried one. On the fourth dive he found a long wooden case in one of the cabins. It was an elegant, highly polished box. Tying it to the end of a line, Val signaled for it to be hoisted.

Later, on deck, they examined it. On it was the name Steven Bricker, which Val had seen before.

"Let's bust it open," Lahey suggested.

"No, let's not. The man that owns this box is at the Southern Hotel. I saw his name on the register there when I was waiting to see the manager. He might pay us for it. Anyway, I think I know what it is."

It was a gun case, Val felt sure. He had seen such cases before, and they usually held guns treasured by sportsmen, weapons often inlaid with gold, and sometimes covered with ornamentation.

The following morning he dived deep, going at once to the main deck. This was littered with boxes and crates, and on the foredeck he found some heavy lines, evidently used in mooring the boat. These could easily be sold along the river front, or used by Captain Peterson himself, and they were hoisted aloft.

Lahey made two quick dives after that. He could not stay down as long as Val, but he went directly to the hatch on the main deck and knocked out a couple of wedges and removed a batten. By mid-morning when they stopped for coffee they had the forward hatch opened and had exposed the barrels. Peterson had steam up and had turned on the power so they could use it in hoisting the barrels.

"There's a cargo net down there," Lahey said. "We've only got to roll the barrels into it. They weigh nothing much under water."

Huddled under a blanket, Val sipped coffee. He had never been in the water so much before, and had not gone so deep more than once or twice. But he was excited by the search, and there were still several cabins to be examined.

It was hard work, but by nightfall they had fifty barrels of flour aboard their own steamer. They were covered with tarpaulins, some of which had been salvaged from the wreck. So far they had seen no sign of anybody about.

They examined one barrel of flour, and found that the flour next to the outside of the barrel had settled into a hard crust for about three inches, while that in the center of the barrel was still as good as ever. This flour they kept for their own use.

Reluctantly, they cast off, leaving Paddy Lahey aboard to watch their cargo. They steamed back up the river, and when they reached the water front at St. Louis Val went ashore and headed for the Southern Hotel with Steven Bricker's gun case under his arm.

This time there was no interference. He was given Bricker's room number, and went up.

The man who answered the door was short and stocky, with graying hair and beard. He had sharp blue eyes, that went from Val's face to the case. "Well," he said, "you'd better come in." He added, "I never expected to see that again."

"I was in the hotel the other night and saw your name on the register, so when we found this . . . well, I imagine they are favorite weapons of yours, and that can be important to a man."

"They are important," Bricker said. "They were the last gifts to me from my father. What do I owe you?"

"Nothing, sir. I am merely returning your property."

Bricker looked at him shrewdly. "If you'll permit me to say so, you look as if you could use the money."

"I could," Val admitted frankly, "but I'll not take money for returning your property."

"How did you come by it? I thought the 'Gypsy Belle' was a total loss."

Val explained. He told about how he had learned about the flour, and what they had done so far. Captain Peterson, he added, had even now gone to the insurers to make a deal for recovery of the flour.

Bricker listened, lighting a fresh cigar. "Had you ever thought they might just take over and continue the salvage themselves, allowing you nothing?"

"We did think of that. I hope they will be decent about it, sir."

Bricker got up and took his coat from the wardrobe. "Let's just walk over and see how Captain Peterson is doing. He might be able to use some help."

Captain Peterson, cap in hand, was just being shown through the gate at the office of the insurers. His face was red with anger. "Boy, they've threatened us with arrest. They've said—"

Steven Bricker stepped past him and opened the door of the inner office. "Danforth, I think we had better discuss this matter of salvage," he said. "Come in, Darrant. You, too, Peterson."

"Now, see here! What's your part in this, Bricker?"

"These gentlemen are friends of mine, Danforth. And, I might add, they will be represented by my attorneys."

Danforth sat down and took up a cigar. "You can't mean that, Bricker. I've known of Peterson for years. He's nothing but a water-front bum, scavenging along the river for whatever he can pick up."

"And now he has picked up a beauty," Bricker replied, "and you're going to pay him for it. I happen to know that after the initial survey you abandoned that wreck. As it happens, if you remember, I was a passenger on the 'Gypsy Belle.' I had personal effects of considerable value aboard.

"You can buy out the interests of Peterson and Darrant," he went on, "or they will proceed to salvage it themselves. I happen to know that you have offered to settle with some of the shippers at a very modest price."

"That is none of your business, Bricker."

"I shall make it my business." Bricker got up. "You have been notified. I shall instruct my attorneys to proceed at once."

When they were outside, Bricker turned to the others. "Are you gentlemen willing to fight? I mean, can you fight?"

"We can, sir," Val answered.

"Then you get back down to that steamboat and tie up to her. Unless I'm wrong, they will make an effort to drive you off. I will get help to you as soon as possible. When my men come, they will be carrying a blue flag."

Val Darrant had grown up in a hard school, in which one often moved fast, or not at all. There was no time for contemplation, and he knew it. Peterson would arrive at the right decision but he would take too long, and Lahey was content to abide by whatever they decided.

"Captain," Val said, "you and Paddy unload the cargo. I'm going to take a boat and go back to the wreck."

He wasted no time. There was a skiff on the "Idle Hour" which he quickly launched, and then without delay he shoved off. He had a small packet of food, a keg of water, and the Smith & Wesson pistol. There was a good current in the river, and he was a strong hand with the oars.

He had not gone many miles when suddenly he heard the chug-chug of a steam engine and the thrash of paddles. Glancing back, he saw a small steamer, not much larger than the "Idle Hour," steaming toward him. At once he was sure this was a boat sent by Danforth to take possession of the wreck.

For a moment he was swept by dismay, but almost immediately he had an idea. Taking up a line from the bow of the boat, he fashioned a hasty slip knot. He had learned roping long ago while herding cattle, and although no great shakes as a roper, he knew the roping of a bollard would not be too difficult a trick. She was a side-wheeler running at no more than half-speed, but he was going to get no more than one cast and it had to be good. Still, the bollard would be as large as a calf's head, and certainly wouldn't be bobbing as much.

He coiled his line, giving himself as much slack as he could after making the other end fast, and as the steamer swept past he made his throw. It shot straight and true, and instantly he dropped into place and grabbed his oars and managed to get in a couple of good strokes to ease the jerk as the slack came to an end.

Despite that, it gave him quite a jolt, but the line held fast and the next thing he knew he was proceeding downriver at a good clip. He sat back and relaxed. It was night, no one was on deck aft, and probably the only man awake was in the pilot house.

They made good time, but he knew that when they rounded the bend they must slow down because of the risk of running upon the wreck. That would be his chance.

He was waiting for the moment, and when they swept into the cove and cut the speed to slow, he waited until the steamer swung around broadside to the wreck. Instantly he slashed the line and caught up his oars. He made two sweeping strokes before he was seen; there was a shout from the steamer's deck, but he kept on.

Suddenly there was another shout, this time a command to

halt. He pulled hard on his right oar, easing on the left, swung out of line, continued on.

A shot rang out and struck the water to his right, and then with one more strong pull he turned quickly, caught hold of the Texas and pulled himself hand over hand around it to the sheltering side. Then he tied up his skiff and climbed aboard, taking his food and water.

By now it was almost light. He climbed into the pilot house. There seemed to have been no one aboard since they had left. There were ladders on both sides of the pilot house to the hurricane deck, where the Texas was. The hurricane deck was under water, but if necessary he could retreat to that more sheltered area.

These were tough men, sent to do a job, and no doubt had been well chosen for it. They would shoot to frighten him, and when he did not frighten they would shoot to kill.

Some of the hatch covers they had taken out when opening the hatch had floated against the Texas and lay there among the other driftwood. They were about six feet long and three inches thick, so he carried several of them up and used them to thicken the pilot-house bulkhead, an added protection against bullets.

Then he made coffee on the little pilot-house stove, ate a piece of cheese and some crackers and sat back to keep watch, and to wait. And he knew he had very little time to wait.

There were at least a dozen men on that steamboat, and he could see them gathering near the rail—evidently a boat was to be lowered.

A heavily built man came near the rail. The steamer was not more than thirty yards off, and his voice was loud and clear. "You, aboard there! We're from the owners! We're comin' aboard to take possession. You can get off of your own free will, or you can be thrown off!"

"Nothing doing!" Val shouted. "I am in possession, and I intend to stay here. I am armed, and if necessary I will shoot."

There was a moment of hesitation, then the big man shouted back, "All right, boy, you're askin' for it!"

A boat was brought around to the side and men started to descend a rope to get into the boat. The Smith & Wesson Russian was a powerful gun. He aimed the .44 at the water line of the rowboat and fired. Then he fired again.

A man on the rope ladder scrambled back aboard, and there was a shout from the boat. "Hey! He's put a hole in us!"

Another man yelled, "She's leakin'!"

"Bail her out!" the big man ordered. "An' row over there! You can make it before she sinks."

Val Darrant loaded the empty chambers of his gun. He had no doubt that by plugging the holes and bailing they could make it. He was no kind of a show-off, but sometimes a demonstration of what could be done was enough to prevent having to do it.

On the ledge by the pilot house window was a bottle. He took it in his hand and stepped to the door.

"Just so you gentlemen will understand that I can do what I say," he called, and tossed the bottle into the air. Lifting the gun, he fired, breaking the bottle; fired twice more, smashing the largest of the two falling fragments, and then smashing it again. The three shots sounded like one solid roll of thunder in the small cove.

When the sound died, he said, "I hope I won't have to demonstrate on any of you."

The rest of the men, despite the protests of the big man giving the orders, climbed back aboard, and Val could hear loud argument. Meanwhile he waited, desperately anxious, for the arrival of his friends. The trouble was, these men might seize the "Idle Hour" and force Val to give up his position to save his friends.

The steamer had drifted closer now. "All right, you can shoot. So we just set here and wait. When night comes you ain't goin' to see very good. We'll come then."

Despite his doubts, Val kept his voice confident. "Fine! You can just wait out there until the United States marshals arrive. They'll be glad to see you, with all of those John Doe warrants they'll be carrying. And I imagine they will know some of you boys very well! You just stick around. I've got a thousand rounds of ammunition and grub enough for two weeks."

He had nothing of the sort, nor did he have any idea that United States marshals would be coming, but it gave them something to think about.

As Will Reilly had often said, "Let them use their imagination, Val. Nine times out of ten they will think you are holding more than you are. So just wait them out."

He was not tired, the morning was dawning bright and beautiful, birds sang in the trees along the river bank, and his gun was loaded again.

It was a bird that warned him. A mud hen was swimming near the stern of the steamboat carrying the attackers. It had flown up briefly at the shots, then settled back. Now, suddenly, with a startled squawk, the mud hen took off.

Val sat up quickly. Instantly he knew what they were doing. They were coming now, swimming underneath the water. There might be one or two, there might be a dozen, but they were coming, and he was one against them all.

# FOURTEEN

H e could feel the softness of the air, see the sunlight and cloud shadows on the trees and water. He could see the men along the rail yonder, and four of them now had rifles.

The men swimming to attack him were probably coming from around both the bow and the stern to take him from both sides. He did not want to kill anyone, both because killing was no solution to one's problems and because he had an idea the courts might be more inclined to hang him than not. And he had no witnesses . . . or none that he knew of.

"Call them back," he said, shouting to the big man who watched from the pilot house. "Call them back or I'll have to shoot."

"You fire that gun," the big man shouted, "and we'll riddle you with bullets!"

There is a time for all things. He had offered not to kill, the men were closing in, and he was alone. The attackers were thugs paid to do their work, but the director of it all was that big man yonder.

"Call them back," he said again, knowing they were almost at the wreck. Incongruously, he noticed that the mud hen was back again, swimming complacently, and would still be there when all of them were gone.

There was no answer, so he lifted the Smith & Wesson and shot the big man through the shoulder.

He saw the man knocked backward, heard his cry of shock and astonishment, and Val yelled at him. "Call them back. It's you I'm going to get if you don't."

The man dropped from sight, but unless they had reinforced their walls as he had done, that pilot house was no more protection than cardboard. Yet even as the man dropped from sight, the four riflemen opened up on him. He heard the ugly smash of the bullets into the bulkheads, the whine of ricochets. From the door, flat on his belly, he fired and saw one of the riflemen spin around and drop his rifle.

He fired again, and one of the others stumbled. All of them were running now. Hastily, he fed a couple of shells into his gun, and heard a splash in the water down below. At least one of the men was now inside the Texas, and right below him.

When he had tied up his skiff alongside the wreck, he had carried his oars up to the pilot house so they might not steal the boat. Now he caught up one of the oars. He thrust his pistol into his waistband and stepped quickly out on the shore side of the pilot house. A man was just scrambling up the ladder and catching the oar in both hands, above shoulder height, Val smashed the butt end of the oar into the man's chest, knocking him back into the water.

Even as he splashed, Val heard running boots on the other side and wheeled around, drawing as he turned.

The man held a knife, an Arkansas toothpick, and he held it low down for thrusting.

Val held the gun on him. "You can drop that thing and dive off, or I'll kill you," he said. "I've already shot the big fellow."

"Him? You wouldn't dare, that's—"

"I shot him. You boys better look at your hole card. Who's going to pay you now?"

The momentary flicker of doubt in the man's face told Val that he had struck a nerve. He tried again. "Look at it—nobody else is going to do it. Do you suppose the company will admit it had anything to do with what you're doing here? If that big fellow doesn't live, you can't collect a quarter. Not a lousy two-bits."

Nobody was trying to shoot from the steamer now, for their

own men were aboard and they awaited the outcome. "See?" Val said. "They've stopped shooting. They know the show is over."

The man hesitated, in doubt. Val knew his every urge was to come on, to finish the job if he could, but the gun muzzle was pointed at his belly, and no doubt Val's argument undermined his resolution.

At that moment he heard a whistle, and around the bend came the "Idle Hour," Paddy Lahey standing in the bow with a shotgun in his hands. Moments later another boat rounded into the cove, this one with four armed men standing in the bow.

"There you are," Val said. "Now you just swim back to your boat—or swim to shore, for all I care."

"You ain't heard the last of this," the knife man declared. "We'll find you in St. Louis."

The second boat, flying a blue flag, drew alongside the wreck. The man in the bow looked up at Val. "Are you all right?"

"No complaints," Val said, "but you got here just at the right time."

Seven days and nine trips later they had emptied the wreck of its cargo of flour as well as nearly a ton of lead, and odds and ends of salvage from the staterooms. The latter would be returned, wherever possible, to the original owners.

The flour, which was currently selling for twelve dollars a hundred pounds, brought them a good return, although several barrels had been completely destroyed and others had been a total loss from water damage. When they settled up, Val found himself with something more than four thousand dollars.

Steven Bricker was in his room when Val called on him to settle up for the four men he had hired.

Bricker accepted the money, but waved away any suggestion of payment for legal fees. "Danforth was bluffing," he said. "He thought you didn't know what you were doing and he'd scare you off. It has been done before."

He studied Val. "You've a lot of nerve for a youngster," he said, "but they raise them that way out west." He bit off the end of a cigar. "I can use a lad like you. My business is building railroads, and I can give you a chance for a lot of hard work, wild country, and education."

Val shook his head. "I think I'll go east for a while. I want to study law."

"Good idea. You do that. When you decide to go to work, you write to me." Bricker scribbled an address on a piece of paper. "I will make a place for you. We can use your kind."

He got up and held out his hand. "Good luck, boy. We will meet again, I am sure."

Outside in the street it was raining again, but Val had proper clothes now, and wore a good raincoat. Earlier, he had said good-bye to Captain Peterson and Paddy Lahey. Now he walked down the street to the railroad station. He had checked his bags there earlier.

He was going east. He was going to New York.

The next few years went by so swiftly that he was only vaguely aware of the time passing. They were years spent in hard work, in study, in learning. For a year he stayed in New York, reading law in an attorney's office, and reading almost everything else he could find. He went to the opera whenever he could.

He grew taller and heavier. He became friendly with several prize fighters and spent hours in the gymnasiums boxing with them, or out on the roads when they did their road work. He wrestled, punched the bag, and skipped rope. At twenty he weighed a hundred and ninety pounds, and was six feet two inches tall.

After New York he spent a year in Minnesota, and later in Montana. He was first an assistant and secretary to Steven Bricker, who was building branch-line railroads, opening mines, dealing in mining and railroad stocks, as an associate of James J. Hill.

From time to time he had letters from Pa Bucklin, always written by one or the other of the girls. They had drilled four wells, they had bought more stock. They were now running three thousand head of cattle and planned to make their first real sale. There had been small sales from time to time, the money defraying expenses or being used to purchase more breeding stock.

It was in the autumn of his twentieth year when he was in New York that he left the gymnasium where he had been working out and walked up the street to the corner. He stopped on the Bowery, watching the faces of the people as they passed. Suddenly a hand touched his sleeve. "Sir? If you could manage it, sir, I haven't eaten today."

It was a moment before Val turned, for he knew that voice, would have known it anywhere. When he did turn, the man had already started away. "Just a minute, please," Val said.

The man turned, and Val was right—it was Van . . . Myra's man, who had left him with Will Reilly, fifteen years back.

Van's hair was grayer, his face thinner, his cheeks more hollow, he seemed not much changed. His clothes still looked neat, although he had perhaps slept in them.

"Yes?"

"Would you dine with me, sir? I should take it as a pleasure."

Van's eyes searched his face, his expression almost pleading. "You are serious, sir? If you are, I accept, most sincerely."

Val's heart was pounding strangely. He had always liked this lonely, weak man, this man who had been kind to him. He had told him stories, he had been gentle when no one else seemed to care.

"If you don't mind, we'll walk up the street. There is a good restaurant where I occasionally eat."

They walked along together, neither speaking, until they reached the restaurant, which was one with notable food.

"You are sure—? I do not look as presentable as I might," Van said.

"Come along."

Only when they were seated did Van look at him. A faint frown showed on his face. "Do I know you? I can't place you, but there is something familiar about you."

Val ignored the question until they had ordered, and then he said, "Tell me about yourself. You seem to be a gentleman."

Van shrugged. "I would have claimed so once, but no more. I am nothing."

"What became of Myra?"

Van stiffened, and stared at him. "What do you know about Myra?" He scowled. "You have known me then . . . but where?"

"What about Myra? Where is she?"

"If I had done what I should have done she'd be burning in hell. A dozen times I planned to kill her—"

"You weren't much inclined toward killing, Van."

"Damn it all! *Who are you?*"

"You haven't answered my question. Where is Myra?"

"Right where she planned to be, one way or another. Myra

Cord is a rich woman, rich and dangerous. If you plan any dealings with her, forget it. She would eat you alive."

"She must have altered her profession."

"I don't know whether she did or not. Myra is a vicious woman, who used prostitution as you might use a stepladder. Where she is now she doesn't need it, although I haven't a doubt she'd use it if it was to her advantage. She's come a long way, but she hasn't changed." Van continued to stare at him. "What's your interest in her, anyway?"

The food was served, the waiter left, and Val said, "She was my mother."

Van dropped his fork. His face turned white.

Slowly the color came back. He pulled at his tie, loosening it. "You're Val? Valentine Darrant?" he said.

"Yes."

"I'll be damned!" The words came slowly.

"I don't think you will be, Van. You kept me alive, you know. You saved my life, and did me the greatest favor a man ever did for another."

"What was that?"

"You left me with Will Reilly. He kept me, Van. He raised me. He taught me a way of life for which I owe him, and you, more than I can say."

"So? Maybe that was why we never saw him again. I was always expecting to have to meet him, and I was afraid—not of what he would do, but of the way he would have looked at me. I liked the man, damn it. I respected him. And then I had to abandon a kid on him."

"You think he avoided you and Myra?"

"He must have. You know the West. It's a small community, after all. The men of the mining camps were known in them all. They followed every boom. The same in the cattle towns. And Will Reilly was a known man. I had run into him fifty times before, but never after I left you with him."

They talked the meal through, and much of the night.

"What about you?" Van asked at last. "Where are you going? What are you going to do?"

"I'm going West. Not for long, I think, but I want to see some people out there and look at a ranch. And I made an investment a long time back, and I want to see what became of it."

He went on: "I passed my bar exam, Van. I can practice law if I want to. In fact, I have had some experience along that line. And I told you I worked with Bricker."

"It's a wonder you didn't run into Myra. She's done business with him. Knows him well, in fact."

"Myra Cord? If she had done business with him, I would know of it."

Van smiled wryly. "You don't think she would keep the old name, do you? She's too shrewd for that. She dropped that name a long while ago. She's Mrs. Everett Fossett now."

Val stared at him. Myra Cord . . . his mother . . . *Mrs. Everett Fossett?*

"You must be joking."

"No," Van said grimly, "I am dead serious. She married Old Man Fossett, married him for his name and his money. He was a respected man, you know, and a well-liked man, but he was no match for her. She tricked him and married him, and then murdered him in her own way. Oh, I know! It wasn't anything the law could call murder, but it was that, just as much as if she had used poison."

"She's worth millions."

"Yes, and not an honest dollar in the lot. She wasn't a pauper when she married Fossett. She had robbed every man she knew, I expect, and she had spent very little of it. Fossett was only another stepping stone."

"Have you seen her lately?"

"Not over two weeks ago, right here in New York. She didn't see me. I took care that she didn't, because I am one page she forgot to turn under; or rather, I got up nerve enough to run before she could do me in. She didn't see me, but I saw her." He was silent for several minutes. "She's a beautiful woman, Val, even yet. She's not much over forty, and even in the early days, mean as she was, she had good looks."

"I have seen her. I just never dreamed . . . I mean, I had heard talk of her, but the idea that she was Myra Cord never entered my mind."

"Now that it has, don't go near her, Val—she'd kill you. Don't look at me like that. She wanted you killed when you were a helpless child, didn't she? And you'd open up a whole bag of tricks she wants forgotten. She's an important woman now, socially and financially. And she's completely ruthless. Once she sets her mind on something, there's nothing in God's world can stop her."

"I wonder."

"Don't wonder—don't even think about it."

Val pushed back from the table. "Van, what can I do for you?"

"Maybe a ten-dollar gold piece. Any more would be a waste."

"Van, why don't you go home? I mean back to your own people? Your own world."

"You're crazy." He chewed on his mustache. "Oh, I'll not deny I'd like to. They know I'm alive, but almost nothing else. But I couldn't. I've no money, no clothes, no way to make a living."

"Would five hundred dollars help? I mean, five hundred dollars and clothes? I'll stake you, Van. I think it's a good gamble."

"Damn it, Val, I couldn't. I just couldn't. And what would I say to them? My parents are alive. I have two sisters. I—"

"Just go back and don't say anything. They will make up better stories than you ever could. You've been traveling, seeing the West . . . you've come home to settle down. I'll give you the money. I've done well, Van. I can afford it."

Actually he could not—not that much. But he was young, and the way looked bright ahead.

"All right," Van said at last, "I'll take it. If you will let me pay it back."

"Whenever you can . . . but go home. Go back to your own people."

# FIFTEEN

T he butler paused before the portly man in the dark suit. "Mrs. Fossett will see you now, Mr. Pinkerton."

He got up and followed the butler over the deep carpets, through the tall oak doors, and into the library. He rarely entered this room, and was always astonished when he did. As the guiding hand of the largest and most successful detective agency in the United States, if not in the world, he had met all manner of men, and women. This was the only one who made him uneasy, and a little frightened.

Yes, that was the word. There was something about her cold, matter-of-fact mind that disturbed him. He had the sensation that she was always at least one jump ahead of him, and that whatever he said she already knew.

She sat behind the long desk, only a few papers before her, including, he noticed, several newspapers that he recognized as coming from various cities.

"You said you had news for me?"

"Yes." He paused. "I have found him."

"Well . . . that's something, at least. Where is he? On the Bowery?"

"No, ma'am. He has gone home. He is with his family."

129

Myra Fossett felt a cold thrill of anger go through her. Was it, as Van himself had once said, that she never liked to have anyone to escape her?

"You have made a mistake. He is a proud man, whatever else he may be. I am sure he would not go home without money."

"He has money. A little, at least. He paid his bills. He bought new clothes—an excellent wardrobe, by the way—and he went home in some style."

"There must be some mistake. How could he get the money? Nobody would lend him money any longer, and he was always a rotten gambler."

"That we do not know, except that—"

"What?"

"Well, he was seen to meet a man—a young man—and they dined together. They talked for several hours. It was after that that he bought clothes and returned home."

She pondered, considering all the possibilities. Van knew too much; and a sober, serious Van who had gone home to his family might prove more dangerous than a casual drifter and drunk whom nobody would believe. Moreover, he had run away from her, and that she could not forgive.

"What sort of young man?"

"A gentleman, ma'am. Handsome, athletic, well-dressed, well-groomed. He was young . . . perhaps twenty-five. . . ."

"What was he doing on the Bowery? Is he a bum?"

"No. Nothing like that," he said. "We made inquiries . . . nobody would tell us anything, if they knew. He comes to the Bowery to train. To box and to wrestle. Incidentally, he is very good, they say."

"A professional?"

"No. I do not believe so. He is a gentleman."

Myra Fossett gave him a glacial look. "Sometime you must define the term for me, Mr. Pinkerton. I am not sure I know what a gentleman is, or how one becomes one. I doubt if I have ever met one."

"Present company excepted?"

"No," she replied shortly. "A man in your business, Mr. Pinkerton, is certainly no gentleman. In any event, I am not paying you for your moral standards. Rather," she added, "for your lack of them."

He got to his feet. "I resent that, madam—"

"Resent it and be damned," she said. "Now sit down and listen, or get out of here and send me your bill."

He hesitated, his face flushed. He knew suddenly that he hated this woman, hated everything about her, but she paid him well, and she seemed to have an unlimited amount of work to be done. He stifled his anger and sat down.

"You do not have a name for this young man? They must call him something around that gymnasium."

"Well, we do have a first name, but that is all. One of my men heard him called Val."

*Val* . . .

Myra Fossett sat very still. Pinkerton, who had watched the emotions of many people, had the sensation that the name had struck her a body blow.

After a moment she said, "Mr. Pinkerton, if Van Clevern has returned to his people I am no longer interested in his actions. As of this moment, you may recall your investigators.

"However, I am interested in this young man. This Val, as you say he was called—I shall want a full report on him, his associates, his actions."

"It is going to be very difficult—"

"If that means you will want more money, the answer is no. If you believe the task will be beyond your scope, Mr. Pinkerton, I believe I can find somebody who will find it less difficult. Surely, the investigation of one unsuspecting young man cannot be such a problem."

"We have no idea who he is, or where he lives."

"But he goes to the gymnasium to box, doesn't he? Have him followed. Ask questions of those with whom he boxes. . . . I do not need to tell you your business, I hope."

"If I had some idea—"

"Of why I wanted the information?" Myra Fossett smiled. "Mr. Pinkerton, I have known for some time that you are eaten with curiosity as to the reason for my investigations. You might just tell yourself that in business matters I find the human element is always important. I like to know the manner of man with whom I deal, and what his associations are. You are valuable to me for that reason. Do your work and keep your mouth shut, and you will have a valuable client; make trouble for me, and I will ruin you. . . . I believe we understand each other, Mr. Pinkerton."

He got to his feet, his features set and hard. "We do, Mrs. Fossett. I shall have a report for you within the week."

When he had gone, Myra Fossett sat staring straight before her into the darkening room. She had told the truth and she had lied, at one and the same time. Information she wanted, but only in part for business reasons, and in part only for the malicious satisfaction of knowing the secret lives of her associates. Knowledge was indeed power, but it was for her more than a weapon, for it fed her contempt for the men with whom she associated and for the sheep who were their wives.

The information she required about Van was for an altogether different reason. For twenty years he had been a part of her life, and there was little in those twenty years that he did not know or suspect. When he had suddenly broken with her and run away, she had been furious, both with him and with herself for not recognizing the signs. The trouble was that he had threatened to leave so many times that she no longer believed him.

He had become necessary to her, for exactly what reasons she did not venture to ask herself. He was, even yet, a fine-looking man, acceptable in any company; and although a drinker, he had never yet allowed it to show in company to any degree more than dozens of others whom they met at one time or another. She had no intention of letting him leave when he wished, but she had already recognized the fact that a time was coming when he would be more of a handicap than an asset. To be realistic, that time had arrived.

Had he guessed her intentions? He might have suspected. Certainly, he knew enough about others who had gotten in her way. She remembered a day long ago when he had been just drunk enough to speak out, and he had told her in that curiously speculative way he had of talking when drunk, "Myra, you are a moral cripple. I mean it. Just as some people are born with physical defects, you were born with a moral defect. You have no conception of right and wrong. Things are good or bad as they serve your purpose or do not serve it."

Val? It was impossible, of course. Val was dead. He had died out there in the night and the cold after Van had abandoned him . . .

She had never believed Van would have the guts for it. She had been surprised when he returned without the boy, but when he had suggested they leave at once, she thought that he might really have done it. And Van had never referred to Val again, never mentioned him even once, so he must have left him to die.

But suppose he had not? Where could he have taken the boy? Where might he have left him? All she had now was that twenty years later Van met somebody who might be twenty-five years old and called him Val . . . or perhaps something that sounded like that. This person, whoever he was, might have given Van money; might have talked him into going home.

If so, what did it mean to her? It could mean everything, or nothing. Van close to her, under her thumb, frightened of her, was one thing. Van free of her, back with his own family . . . would he want to forget all that lay behind? Or would he have an attack of conscience?

Myra Fossett, who now had wealth and power and was close to the position she craved, could not afford Van's conscience. He simply knew too much. A Van Clevern who seemed to be headed down into the gutter was no danger, but a Van Clevern back with his family, that self-righteous family of which she had heard so much, was a very real danger. One minute or two of talking on his part could destroy everything she had so carefully built.

He even knew about Everett Fossett, or suspected. And Everett had friends and perhaps relatives of whom she knew nothing who might start an investigation.

She considered the question coolly and made her decision about Van Clevern. Of course, she admitted, that decision had really been made a long time ago, but then he had been useful to her.

It would have to be an accident. There would be no chance for poison in this case.

She considered the others. It had worked well with them. Seven men and two women, and each one had been a step toward the success she wanted. It had been poison with all but one, and that one was knocked on the head when he started to wake up, and was left out in the mule corral. Van still believed he was covering something that could be called an accident, that she had hit harder than she wished.

Val . . . Could it be that she had a son still alive?

She had never wanted the child, had planned it merely as a trap for Darrant, and he had gotten away from her before she could spring the trap. And then she was saddled with a child.

But now she was curious . . . did he look like her? Or like . . . what was his name?

Andy . . . that was it. For Andrew, she supposed, or possibly André, considering the fact that he was partly French.

Val . . . suppose he really was alive? What then? What difference could it make?

Van had always had a weakness for the child, and Van might talk too much . . . no, he wouldn't. Not to Val. Yet Van might tell him where she was, who she was, and Val might come to her for money.

Scarcely a week had gone by when Pinkerton's report was on her desk.

The young man's name was Valentine Darrant . . . *so her son was alive* . . . he had read law with the firm of Lawton, Bryce & Kelly . . . *a good firm* . . . had been admitted to the bar. Seemed to have come from the West. Had worked for Steven Bricker . . . *that tall young man she had passed in the doorway* . . . a young man of very definite ability who seemed to know many people of doubtful reputation . . . *maybe he did take after her* . . . spent much time in shooting galleries, never played cards, rarely gambled except an occasional friendly wager on some fact of sports or history. Went often to the theater and the opera, well-educated, but nothing known as to his academic background.

It was little enough, and left a number of questions unanswered. Where had he been during the intervening years? Who had reared him? Who had given him his education? How long had Van known him?

Myra glanced at the report again. The last line told her that Val had left town. He had bought a ticket for St. Louis.

Well, enough of that. Now there was the problem of what to do about Van Clevern.

Nevertheless, she found herself beset by a nagging curiosity: What was her son like? Was he like her? Or like Darrant?

For Darrant she had a grudging respect. He had had sense enough to get away while the getting was good, and not many had done that, not before she had bled them dry.

Some people said a child took after his grandparents. She had no idea what Darrant's family had been like, but for her own she had only contempt. They had been good, God-fearing people by contemporary standards, and her father had done well in a limited way. Well, no matter.


Van Clevern had indeed returned home. He had taken a little while to get himself looking presentable. He had stopped drinking, had eaten regular meals, had caught up on his sleep. And as Val had said, his family were glad to see him, and they asked few questions. If they did ask he had a story to tell them. He had been involved in mining deals out west. He had made money, lost it, and now was planning to find a local connection and stay home. . . . Only at times did he think of Myra, and uneasily wondered what she would do.

He shook off his doubts, doubts brought on by an all too clear memory of her fury at being thwarted, of her ruthless, relentless nature. But then, he told himself, she would be glad to be rid of him.

Slowly, his manner changed. He became more confident, and began to pick up old associations. It was discovered that he had acquired a lot of information about mining and railroad stocks, and possessed a good deal of on-the-spot information. Three weeks after his return he was hired as a consultant by an investment house in which his father was a partner.

By the time two months had gone by he had proved himself worthwhile to the firm. He met people easily, and his knowledge— much of it acquired from Myra—was proving of value.

Another month passed, and Van Clevern had obtained several new accounts for the firm, so it was with a distinct shock and sorrow that they heard of his death.

He had been riding in the park on a Sunday morning, and had evidently been thrown from his horse. His skull was badly shattered and he had been dead for at least an hour when they found him.

Val Darrant, stopping at Knight's ranch, in New Mexico, read a brief notice of the death in a newspaper somebody had left at the ranch. It was a Chicago paper, several weeks old, and the item was a small one, on an inside page; it gave only the barest details.

Val put the paper down and sat back in his chair, a curious emptiness within him. Of all those whom he had known, next to Will Reilly himself, he had loved Van Clevern the most.

A weak man, but one who had been kind, who had taken time to talk to a small boy when nobody else so much as noticed him, and who had saved him from death.

And now he was dead. An accident, they said.

As to that, Val was not so sure. Van had been an excellent horseman, often riding the half-broken mustangs of the western country. It seemed unlikely he would be thrown by any rented-out horse in an eastern state. It could be, but it was unlikely.

# SIXTEEN

V al Darrant had no liking for open country, and a good stretch of it lay before him. Beyond it the Burro Mountains bulked strong against the sky. He drew rein at the mouth of an arroyo and studied the terrain before him.

He had a feeling that he had glimpsed a faint cloud of dust only minutes before, but now, with a full view of the plain, he saw nothing. He touched his Winchester to be sure it was not jammed too deeply into the scabbard, and then touched his heels to the buckskin.

The gelding was a good horse with black mane and tail and just a suggestion of black spots on the left shoulder, as if there might have been some appaloosa strain somewhere in the buckskin's past. It was a strong horse with a good gait, mountain- and desert-bred.

The country ahead looked innocent enough, but he stayed where he was, knowing that to trust innocence too much could lead to trouble.

He had ridden the stage from the little village of Los Angeles to Yuma and thence to Tucson.

He had believed he'd had enough of the West, but now he was singing a different song. He now knew this was the country for

137

him. No matter how far he might travel, he would always come back here. He was riding now for Silver City, then across country to Tascosa and to the ranch below the cap-rock.

Suddenly, he heard the soft beat of horse's hoofs behind him.

He turned his mount and waited. It was one rider, on a shod horse. This ride from Tucson had been enough to get his eyes and ears tuned to the western lands again. He waited. . . .

The horse was gray, with a black mane and tail, the rider a slender young man wearing a battered black hat, his hair down to his shoulders.

"If you're riding east," Val said, "I'd be glad of the company."

He was a good-looking young man, almost too good-looking, except for two prominent teeth. They did not disfigure him, but did mark his appearance. He weighed not more than a compact one-fifty, and he was probably about five-eight. His hair was blond, his eyes gray.

"Ridin' east myself," he said. "You alone?"

"Yes."

Val looked at him. "Say, now I know you. You're Billy Antrim."

The rider rolled a smoke and glanced at him quizzically. "It's been a while since I been called that, but come to think of it, you do look familiar."

"Your mother ran the boarding house in Silver City. I came into town traveling with Will Reilly. Remember? You, Dobie, and I took a ride into the hills a couple of times. We swapped yarns, too."

"Sure, I recall. Where you been all the time?"

"Drifting," Val said. "Will's dead. He was killed up in Colorado a few years ago."

"Heard about it. The way I heard it he was shot from the dark. Never had a chance."

"That's right. It was Henry Sonnenberg, Hardesty, and Thurston Pike."

"I heard that, too. Sonnenberg was in Fort Sumner a couple of years ago. Hardesty's dead."

"I know."

Billy looked at him quickly. "Say! You were the one who got him! Over at some ranch in Texas."

"In town. He wasn't much."

They rode for several miles, both watching the country, and

suddenly Val said, "You mentioned that nobody ever called you Billy Antrim any more. Knight's Ranch is up ahead, and maybe I should know what to call you."

Billy looked at him. "My name's Bonney," he said. "They call me the Kid."

It was a name on everybody's lips. Even the eastern newspapers knew about Billy the Kid and the Lincoln County War.

"Are you all right at Knight's? If you aren't, I'll ride in and buy whatever you need."

"They're good people. They know I am wanted, but I never trouble them and they don't trouble me. Anyway," Billy added, "so far as I know, only Pat Garrett is hunting me. The rest of them either don't care, or they don't want to borrow trouble."

Shadows were growing long, reaching out from the Burro Mountains ahead. The ranch lay in the mouth of the canyon of the same name, and had become a regular stop on the stage line. Richard S. Knight had built the fortlike adobe in 1874, and sold out a few years later to John Parks, who now operated the ranch.

Val led the way into the ranch yard and Parks came out to meet them with two of his seven children. He glanced at Val.

"Valentine Darrant, sir. I think you know Mr. Bonney."

"Yes, I do. How are you, Billy?"

"Middlin', Mr. Parks, just middlin'. But I'm shaping up to feel better when I've eaten some of your good grub."

"Too much of your own cooking, Billy?"

The Kid laughed. "I'm not much of a hand at cookin', Mr. Parks, not even when I have it to cook. I ain't been close to food in three days."

"Go on inside. Ma will put something on for you."

Val swung down. "I'll look after your horse, Billy. Go ahead."

He led the two horses to the water trough and let them drink, then to the corral, where he stripped the gear from them. Parks was pitching hay to his own stock.

"You know Billy pretty well?" he asked.

"We met a long time back. When his mother was boarding people over at Silver City. We played some together as boys."

"A lot has happened since then."

"I've heard some of it." Val rested his hands on his buckskin's back. "I like him. So far as I've heard, he's done nothing his enemies weren't doing, only he ended up by being outlawed and they didn't."

"He's stopped by here several times, and he's always been a gentleman. Shall we go in?"

After supper Val went outside and sat down on the steps. He felt a growing irritation with himself. He had a right to practice law, but he had done little of it, and then merely as an employee. He owned a part of a ranch which he would soon visit, but he had no taste for ranching. He had a good deal of experience with railroads and investments, but not enough to qualify him for the kind of a job he wanted, nor was he very interested in business.

Here he felt at home. He liked the West, and he liked the drifting, but it was no use. Beyond every trail there were only more trails, and no man could ride them all. He had known a few girls in passing, but had never been in love. Within himself he felt a vast longing, a yearning for something more . . . he did not know what.

He did not believe that anything was to be solved by killing, yet the memory that Thurston Pike and Henry Sonnenberg were still at large, and undoubtedly still involved in killing, nagged at his mind.

Was he hoping that something would intervene? That somebody would do his job for him? When he remembered Sonnenberg he felt a kind of chill. He was a great brute of a man . . . he seemed invulnerable. Was he, Val Darrant, afraid of Sonnenberg?

Yet Sonnenberg's hand had only held the gun and squeezed the trigger. Equally to blame were Avery Simpson, who had traveled the West offering a price for a man's life, and Prince Pavel, who had hired the killing done.

Will Reilly would have known what to do, and Will Reilly would have done it.

Was that why he could settle down to nothing else? Was that what subconsciously worried him? Was it the feeling that he had left the murderers of his best friend, Will Reilly, unpunished?

And what about his mother? What about the woman who now called herself Myra Fossett? Should he go to her and identify himself? To what purpose? He wanted nothing from her, and she had never shown any interest in him except to be rid of him.

Billy came out and sat on the stoop beside him. "Nothing like a desert night," he said. "I always liked riding at night."

"Where's Sonnenberg now?"

Billy turned his head and looked at him. "Don't mess with him, Val. Not even if you're good with a gun. He's poison mean, and he's fast—real fast. I wouldn't want to tackle him myself."

"He was one of them."

"Forget it. Look where followin' up an idea like that got me. After Tunstall was shot, well, I figured to get everyone of that crowd that done it. Well, we got several of them, and now the war's over an' everybody else is out of it but me."

"You didn't tell me where Sonnenberg was."

"Reason is, I don't know. Somebody said he was up Montana way." Billy paused. "I know where Pike is, though."

"Where?"

"If you're goin' back to that ranch of yours you'll be pointing right at him. Last I heard he was in Tascosa. He's got him a woman there."

"You going that way?"

"No," Billy said after a minute, "I think I'll set for a spell. This here's good grub, they're nice folks, and I just think I'll rest up a few days. It ain't often I get a chance to rest these days."

"I'm pulling out, come daylight." Val stood up. "So long, Billy, and good luck."

He went inside, and to bed. Before he got into bed, however, he checked his gun. It was the Smith & Wesson .44 Russian that Hickok had given him. He liked the balance of it, liked the feel. Val Darrant rode away from Knight's Ranch before daylight, curving around the mountains, over a spur, and down across the rolling country beyond. This was still Apache country, and he had had his fill of them as a boy in the bitter fight when they had attacked the stage on which he'd ridden with Will, so he kept off the skyline and was wary of the route he chose. He avoided possible ambushes, studied the ground for tracks, watched the flight of birds. All of these could be indications of the presence of people.

At night he chose a hidden spot, built a small fire, and prepared his coffee and whatever he chose to eat. Then he put out his fire and rode on for several miles, masking his trail as much as possible.

The country he was passing through after the first day or so was the area touched by the Lincoln County War, and many of the hard characters connected with that fight were still in the area. He stopped in Lincoln itself and tied up at the hitching rail in front of a small eating place.

Inside there was a short bar and half a dozen tables. He sat down and a plate of beef stew was placed before him. In many such places there was no question of giving your order. You simply ate what was prepared and were glad to get it. The coffee was good.

There were half a dozen people in the place, and two of them he recognized at once as toughs—or would-be toughs. One of them glanced several times at Val, whispered to the other, and then they both looked at him and laughed.

Val ignored them. He had been in so many towns as a stranger, and he knew the pattern. Most people were friendly enough, but there were always a few who were trouble-hunters, choosing any stranger as fair game.

"I figure he pulled his stakes," one of the men was saying. "All the Mexicans liked him, so I figure he just pulled out for Mexico."

"Naw, he's got him a girl up at Fort Sumner. He'll go thataway. He'll never leave the country 'less she goes with him."

A hard-looking young man with reddish hair, turned to him, leaning his elbows on the bar. Val knew they were about to start something and he was prepared.

"You, over there! Where d' you think Billy the Kid will go?"

Whatever he said they were prepared to make an issue of it. So he merely shrugged. "You can tell by looking at his horse's nose."

"His horse's *nose*? What's that got to do with it?"

"You just look at his horse's nose. Whichever way it's pointing, that's the way he's going."

The waitress giggled, and some of the men chuckled. Val merely looked innocent. The red-haired man's face flushed. "You think you're almighty clever, stranger. Well, maybe we'll see how clever you are. What d'you do for a livin'?"

"I'm an actor," Val said.

The man stared at him. The others in the room seemed to be paying no attention, but Val knew all of them were listening. He wanted to finish his meal in peace.

"You don't look like no actor to me," the redhead declared. "Let's see you act. Get up an' show us."

Here it was . . . well, he intended to finish his meal. Val put down his fork. "Actually," he said, "I'm a magician. I can make things disappear, but you boys will have to help me."

He turned to the waitress. "Have you two buckets? I'd like them full of water, please."

"You goin' to make them disappear?"

"If you boys will help me." A Mexican boy was coming from the back door with two buckets of water. "And two brooms," he added, "or a broom and a mop handle."

He took a broom and handed it to the redhead. "You take this broom and stand right here. And you," he said to the other tough, "stand over here with this broom."

He got up on a chair with a bucket of water and held it against the ceiling, then guided the redhead's broomstick to the exact middle of the bottom of the bucket. "Now hold it tight against the ceiling, tight as you can or it will fall.

"You," he said to the second man, "you hold this one." He placed the second bucket against the ceiling, and the man's broomstick was held against it.

"Now as long as you boys hold those sticks tight, the buckets won't fall. If they fall you'll get mighty wet."

"Hurry up with this disappearin' act," the redhead said, "this is a tirin' position."

Then coolly Val reached over and flipped their guns from their holsters and stepped back to his table.

"What the—"

"No," Val said quietly, gesturing at them with a pistol, "you boys just hold those broomsticks tight unless you want to get wet . . . or shot."

Placing the pistols on the table beside his plate Val calmly returned to eating. He finished the stew, then asked for his coffee cup to be refilled.

"Hey, what is this!" the red-headed man demanded. "Take this bucket off here!"

"Be still," Val said; "these gentlemen want to eat quietly . . . without any trouble from you."

He sat back, sipping his coffee and contemplating them with no expression on his face. The story had already got out, probably from the Mexican boy who had brought the water, and quite a crowd gathered outside. Some even came into the restaurant.

The two would-be toughs stood in the middle of the room, the buckets of water above their heads. If they let go of the broom-handles the heavy buckets would fall, dowsing them with water and probably hitting them a rap on the skull.

"Don't be nervous, boys," Val said. "You wanted to see something disappear. I've made my stew disappear, and three cups of coffee. And now"—he got up and placed a silver dollar on the table—"*I* am going to disappear."

He turned to the others in the room. "They'll get pretty tired after a while, so when you boys get around to it, just take down the buckets for them, will you? . . . but only if you're in the mood."

He stepped to the door. "Good-bye, gentlemen," he said. "I regret leaving such good company, but you understand how it is."

He paused just long enough to shuck the cartridges from their guns, then he dropped the guns on the walk outside. Mounting up, he cantered out of town.

The land lay wide before him, and overhead was the vast arch of the sky. This was what he had missed, the unbelievable distance wherever he looked, the marvelous sweep of rolling hills, the sudden depths of unexpected canyons, the cloud shadows on the desert or the grassland.

Now, topping out on a rise, he could see for sixty or seventy miles across land that shimmered in the sun. He was alone with himself, and he heard only the hoof-falls of his horse, the occasional creak of the saddle, or jingle of a spur.

As he rode, he thought how impossible it was to live in such a land without being aware of it at all times. Even within the narrowed scope of barroom, hotel lobby, bunkhouse, or campfire, much of the talk was of water holes, grass conditions, and Indians.

The Indian was part of the terrain, and travel could not be planned without considering the Indian. Few of them had anything like a permanent home, and they might be expected anywhere. Waterholes were the essentials of all travel, important to wild game, and as important to the Indian as to the white man. Any approach to a waterhole must be undertaken with caution.

In regard to waterholes Val had adopted the practice he had heard Tensleep mention . . . Tensleep, that curious gunman, half an outlaw, half a good citizen, an ignorant man in the way of books, but with a mind crowded with knowledge of which he was scarcely aware, it was so much a part of him and his way of living.

Tensleep would never camp at a water hole, even in country safe from Indians.

"Ain't rightly fair," he had told Val. "Other folks have to get water, too. And if you crowd up a water hole, what about the animals and the birds that have to drink? They're goin' to set out there dry-throated whilst you crowd the water. Get what you need, then make room."

He had learned, too, that it was never safe to drain a canteen until one had actually seen the water hole with water in it, for often there was only cracked mud where water had once been. And he knew that the ancient Indian trails were the safest, for they followed the easy contours of the land, and always led from one water hole to another.

Twice Val stopped at lonely ranches, exchanging news for meals, and listening to the gossip of the country. At the second ranch the rancher offered to sell him a handsome bay mare.

The man leaned on the corral bars, extolling the animal, and Val asked, "What about a bill of sale?"

"Why not?" The rancher grinned at him. "Write it up and I'll sign it."

"But will it be good?"

The rancher chewed his mustache, and then said, "Now, mister, I won't lie to you. If you're riding east I'd say that bill of sale was good; riding west I'd say it wasn't."

"I think one horse is enough," Val said, "but she's a good mare."

He swam the Rio Grande, and pointed across country toward the Pecos, riding easy in the saddle.

# SEVENTEEN

Tascosa was born of a river crossing. It thrived on trail herds; and died, strangled with barbed wire. Its life was brief and bloody, and when it died there were left behind only a few crumbling adobes, the ghosts of dead gunmen slain in its streets, and Frenchy McCormick, the once beautiful girl who had promised never to leave her gambler husband, and who never did, even in death.

But in the 1870's and '80's Tascosa was wild and rough and hard to curry below the knees. The cattle outfits and the rustlers were drifting in, and the ranchers who drove in the big herds wanted the toughest fighting hands they could find.

Billy the Kid was a frequent visitor. The town had its tough ones, and its shady ladies, and some of these were as tough as the men to whom they catered.

Valentine Darrant was headed for Tascosa. He told himself he was not hunting Thurston Pike—he was riding to his ranch, and Tascosa was the only town within a hundred miles or more in any direction. He had stopped one night in Fort Sumner, spending it in a bedroom turned over to him by Pete Maxwell. Pete and his father had been friends to Will Reilly, and Pete remembered Val.

"Quiet around here now," Pete told him. "Pat Garrett comes in

146

hunting Billy the Kid, but the Kid won't come back this way again. If my guess is right, he's headed for Old Mexico. The Mexicans swear by that boy—he's one American who has always treated them right."

"I know Billy," Val said, "I knew him in Silver City when we were boys."

"He's all right," Pete said, "just so's you don't push him. He don't back up worth a damn."

"I saw him a while back," Val commented. "He's riding some rough trails."

Pete Maxwell knew better than to ask where he had seen the Kid, and he knew that Val would not have told him. They parted with a hand-shake after breakfast the next morning.

Now Val was riding into Tascosa toward sunset. He was older, tougher, and stronger than when he had last seen Thurston Pike. He had been a boy then—he was a man now.

Cottonwoods grew along the streets and back of the town. The Canadian River ran close by, and a creek ran right down Water Street. Val rode part way around the town to scout the approaches before actually riding in on the Dodge Trail, which took him in on Main Street. He turned left and rode to Mickey McCormick's livery stable.

After putting up his horse he walked to the corner and went into a saloon. It was near four o'clock and the saloon was nearly empty.

A glance told him he knew nobody there, and he went to the bar, a tall young man in fringed shotgun chaps, boots with Mexican spurs, one tied-down gun, and a spare in his waistband under the edge of his coat. He wore a checkered black and white shirt, and a black hat. His coat was also black, but dusty now.

"Is there a good place around to eat?" he asked, after ordering a beer.

"Yonder," the bartender pointed; "Scotty Wilson's place. It's likely he won't be there himself, but the food's good. Scotty always sets a good table . . . no matter whose beef it is."

Val smiled. "Those might be fighting words in some places."

"Not with Scotty. He's the Justice of the Peace, and I guess he figures the easiest way to settle an argument over beef is for the court to take it. But he won't charge the parties of the first part if they come in his restaurant to eat their beef."

"Sounds like a man I'd like," Val said. After a moment he asked, "What's going on around town? Any excitement?"

"Here? Ain't been a shooting in a week. Or a cutting."

Val idled at the bar. He had not wanted the drink, but he did want the talk, and the western saloon was always a clearing house for trail information—about water holes, Indian troubles, rustlers, and range conditions generally.

A few men drifted in and ranged themselves along the bar. Val listened to the talk, aware of his own vague discontent. What was he doing here, anyway? Why didn't he eat, go to bed early, and be ready for a hard ride the following day? But he did not move, and his soul-searching went on. What did he intend to do with his life? He could hang out a shingle in any of these western towns and gradually build a law practice. He was short of money, and desperately needed some means of income. The ranch had prospered, but the income had been put back into the place.

The thought of Thurston Pike and Henry Sonnenberg lurked in the recesses of his mind, and he felt guilty. He should hunt them down, and do what the law could not do . . . what everyone would expect him to do. But he had no taste for killing.

"Young feller?"

"Yes?" It had been a moment before he realized one of the men was speaking to him.

"Like to take a hand? We're figurin' on a little poker."

He was about to refuse, then said, "All right, but I'm not staying in. I've got some miles to ride tomorrow."

He was a fool, he knew. He hadn't that much money in his pocket, and a man needed money to play well. Two hours later he checked out of the game, a winner by sixteen dollars.

A small, slender man left the game at the same time. "Had supper?" he asked. "I'm going over to Scotty's for a bite."

"All right."

They walked across the street, talking idly. "Win much?" the man asked.

"No."

"Neither did I. About twenty dollars."

The steaks were good at Scotty's. Val had not realized how hungry he was.

Suddenly the other man said, "I think we know each other."

Val studied him. "Where?" he asked. "I've been west and I've been east."

"So have I, but I can't place you. My name is Cates, if that helps. Egen Cates."

Val grinned at him. "You have a bullet scar on your arm, and another one somewhere about you. You got them from the Apaches one time, down Arizona way."

"And you?"

"I was the kid who gave you my seat on the stage. I loaded rifles for you and the others. My name is Valentine Darrant."

"Darrant? Have you been to Colorado lately?"

"No."

"Better go up there. They've been looking for you up at Empire . . . and some of the country around. I think they have news for you."

Val searched his face. "What does that mean?"

"I was a miner . . . remember? Now I'm a mining man. The major difference is that I don't collect wages, I pay them." He grinned. "Although it isn't always as easy as it sounds." He was serious again. "Seems you invested some money up there, some years back. You'd better go see what happened to it."

Colorado . . . he had always liked Colorado. "I knew a pretty little girl up there once, when I was a kid," he said, remembering. "She said she was an actress. Her name was Maude Kiskadden, and she was some relation to Jack Slade."

Cates smiled. "I know the story. She was no blood relation. Her father had been married to Slade's widow after Slade was hung by the Vigilantes . . . which never should have happened."

Cates called for more coffee. "You say you've been east. Did you ever hear of Maude Adams?"

"Who hasn't?"

"Maude Adams, who is about the best-known actress in the country right now, was your little Maude Kiskadden. Her mother used the stage name of Annie Adams."

They were still talking half an hour later when the door opened and Thurston Pike came in.

Val Darrant looked at Pike and then said to Cates, "Mr. Cates, we've known each other quite a spell, but do you remember my uncle?" He had purposely raised his voice a little.

"Your uncle? You mean Will Reilly? Of course I remember him."

Thurston Pike looked across the room at them. He was a tall, thin man with rounded shoulders and a lantern jaw. He had a grizzled beard, and looked dirty and unkempt.

Val returned his look, a faint smile on his lips, and Pike lowered his eyes. He seemed uncertain what to do.

"He was murdered, you know. Shot down from the dark by three men who were afraid to meet him face to face."

Val saw the slow red of anger creeping up Pike's neck. He could think of him only as a killer for hire, undeserving of any consideration or pity.

Cates was unaware of the impending drama. "What happened to them?" he asked.

"One of them is dead," Val replied, "and the others have not long to live."

Egan Cates was looking at him now. "What is it, Val? What's happening?"

"I don't think anything is going to happen," Val replied. "Thurston Pike wouldn't think of shooting a man who is looking at him."

Cates glanced around quickly and got up abruptly. He shifted his chair to one side and sat down again. All eyes were on Pike.

He stared at his plate, knife and fork clutched in his hands. Suddenly, with an oath, he put them down on the table, got up, and lurched to the door, knocking over a chair as he went.

"You might have warned me," Cates said.

"I wasn't expecting him, although I knew he was in Tascosa."

"Well, if he's like you say, you'd best be careful. He'll try to kill you now." Egan Cates ordered fresh coffee. "I'll say this for you. You've got nerve. You had nerve even as a kid."

"I had a good teacher," Val said. "Nobody had more nerve than Will."

"You said one of them was dead. Pike was another . . . who is the third?"

"Henry Sonnenberg."

Cates let out a low whistle. "Leave him alone, Val. You can't get him. Nothing can touch him."

"Maybe."

"Are you going to hunt Pike down now?"

Val thought about that a moment. "No, I'll let him hunt me. He'll do it, because he's worried now. Will had a lot of friends, and some night they might decide to hang Pike."

Cates put his hands on the table. "I have to be getting back to the hotel. Val, why don't you forget this? I like the cut of your jib, and I wish you'd come in with me. I have some excellent properties that need developing, and I have access to the cash . . . come in with me. I think we'd make a team."

"I'll give it some thought."

When Val was alone he sat there considering what he had done, and when he finished his coffee he did not go out the front door. He paid for his supper and went through the kitchen. The cook turned to protest, but Val waved, went on through the storeroom, and out the back door into an alley.

He circled around, moving warily, but he saw no sign of Pike. At the corner he studied the street, then returned to the alley and entered the Exchange Hotel from the back.

Once in his room, he put a chair under the doorknob and drew the curtain down. Then, with water poured into the wash bowl, he took a quick sponge bath. After that he was soon in bed and asleep.

He awoke about daybreak and lay still, listening to the town as it came alive. A rooster crowed, somewhere a door slammed, a pump creaked, water gushed into a bucket. Somebody walked by on the boardwalk, and he heard a low murmur of voices.

Presently he got up, and shaved in front of the flawed mirror, which gave his face a twisted look. After he had dressed he glanced around the room to be sure he was not leaving anything behind. He went out of the room, and moved quietly through the hotel corridor.

The sun was not yet up in the streets of Tascosa. He stepped outside, breathing the fresh morning air, his eyes in one quick glance sweeping the street, then the rooftops and the windows and doors. Such observation had been drilled into him by Will Reilly, and his brief examination now missed nothing.

Scotty Wilson's restaurant was open, and he went in. Two sour-looking cowpunchers, still unshaven and red-eyed from the night before, drank coffee at the counter. They were obviously in no mood to talk. Taking the table at the back of the room, Val ordered breakfast.

He thought of the ride before him. It was unlikely that for some time to come he would have another meal he did not prepare himself. The route he was taking was somewhat roundabout, but water was scarce on the Staked Plains.

Actually, the Palo Duro Canyon offered the best route, but there he would be a sitting duck for anyone shooting from the bluffs. Out on the cap-rock he could see for miles and it would be impossible for anyone to come upon him without warning.

As he sat there, the door from the street suddenly opened and a tall, lean man with frosty eyes came in. He looked at Val, and crossed to his table. "Mind if I sit down?"

"It would be my pleasure," Val said. "What can I do for you?"

"You could leave town." The man smiled as he spoke. "Darrant, your name is?" He held out a hand. "I am Sheriff Willingham. There's a rumor around that you had some words with Thursty Pike last night."

"No, I can't say I did. I was talking with Egan Cates, and Pike was in the room. He got up and left."

"All right. Have it your way. No offense, my friend, but we've had too much shooting here already, and if you and Pike have something to settle, do it outside of town."

"That's agreeable to me, Sheriff. I haven't spoken to Pike, and do not intend to if I can avoid it."

"He's a bad actor, son. He'll give you no fair chance if he can manage it."

Willingham studied him. "Are you planning on locating around here?"

"Not exactly, but I'm a third owner of a ranch southeast of here. Do you know the Bucklin outfit?"

"Yes—good people. I hunted buffalo with the Bucklin boys when they first came west." He gave Val an amused glance. "You a single man?"

"Yes."

Willingham chuckled. "You'll have yourself a time. Pa Bucklin's got two of the prettiest daughters you ever did see, and that Betsy . . . the one they call Western . . . she's something to look at."

"What about Boston?"

"A ring-tailed terror. Beautiful and wild, and she can ride as good as any puncher on the cap-rock. She can shoot and she can rope. At the roundup we had a while back she beat every hand we had at roping and tying calves."

"They aren't married then?"

"No, and they won't be if they stay around here. They scare the boys. Who wants to marry a girl who can do everything you can, and better?"

The wind was picking up when Val Darrant rode from Tascosa, south and a little east. The tumbleweeds rolled along with him, rolled toward a ranch he could call home. Thunder rumbled in the clouds, and when the first drops fell he dug out his slicker. It was going to be a wet ride.

# EIGHTEEN

There was no question of shelter. So far as Val was aware there was nothing nearer than his own ranch, which lay miles away. The country was flat as a billiard table, and it was only after he had ridden several hours in a driving rain that he saw the edge of an arroyo. It was the first break in the level of the cap-rock in all that distance, and he judged it to be a branch of the Palo Duro, long a hide-out for the Comanches.

The rain rattled on his slicker and ran from the brim of his hat. Thunder rolled and lightning stabbed through the sky. His one consolation was that if Thurston Pike was riding in this weather he was doing no better than Val. He figured now that it might be best to ride to the Palo Duro and see if there was some kind of shelter in the canyon. He turned abruptly and headed that way. Riding out here on the cap-rock would make him a target for lightning.

The rain drew a steel curtain across the day. His horse slipped once in the mud, and then he reached the rim of the canyon, but saw no route by which he could descend. He followed along the rim, searching for a way.

Lightning flashed again, and the time between the flash and the roll of thunder was much shorter. Suddenly he saw where the rim was broken and a trail led down to the bottom of the canyon. It was a buffalo trail, and an easy ride.

He started down, but in a moment something struck him a wicked blow on the shoulder. In the moment when he started to turn, believing he had been hit from behind, he heard the report of a rifle and his horse leaped. Val lost his grip and toppled into the mud, while his horse, frightened and perhaps hurt, went racing away down the slope. He realized he ought to move, and lifted his head to look around. He lay on a steep part of the trail. Crawling off it, he found a place under the rim where he would be somewhat protected. He struggled to pull himself to his feet, managed it, and caught hold of a crack in the rock face and worked along it, hunting for a larger crack.

He had been shot, and whoever had shot him had been lying in wait. The chances were good that the unseen marksman, who might be Pike, or might be an Indian or an outlaw, was even now coming closer.

He clung to the rock face, his boots on the steep talus slope that fell away behind him. The rain still hammered against his slicker. He could hold himself up, but though he had been hit he did not believe he was seriously hurt.

His horse, as he saw when he turned his head and looked down, had reached the bottom of the canyon and was cropping grass near the stream, almost half a mile away. His rifle was in the scabbard on the saddle.

He listened, but heard no sound except the rain. Vaguely, he thought he smelled smoke, the smoke of a campfire.

He edged his way along the rock, knowing he had to get himself out of this spot. If the unknown marksman was within sight of him, he would certainly have fired again, but he must be working himself around to get in that final shot.

The rim-rock along here was perhaps fifteen feet high, and was topped by a thin layer of soil and sparse grass. Below him the slope fell away steeply to the bottom, several hundred feet away.

The rim-rock was split in many places, and suddenly he found a crack and eased himself into it. There was no overhang here, but there was a flat sheet of broken-off rock that lay canted across the split, and he backed under it, dried his hands on his shirt under the slicker, and drew his gun.

It was a long wait. Several times he thought he caught the smell of damp wood burning, but a fire in such a place was unlikely; and it was unlikely the killer, whoever he might be, would have a fire.

A slow hour passed, marked by Val's watch. More than once he shifted the gun; at times he was on the verge of crawling out, but the memory of that rifle shot restrained him. There was no chance to check his wound. The shock had worn off, and now it hurt like blazes, but the bleeding seemed to have stopped.

He had almost decided to move out of his shelter when he heard footsteps. He tilted the gun and waited. He had never shot at anything he could not see, and he was not about to begin, but if that was Thurston Pike . . .

"Mister," said a girl's voice, "I can see your tracks and I know you're in there. The geezer who shot you is gone. If you'll let me help you, I will."

"Step out where I can see you," he said.

She hesitated a moment. "That voice is familiar, mister, and I think we know each other. I am stepping out."

She came suddenly into full view, a tall girl in boots and a beaded and fringed buckskin skirt reaching to below her knees. She wore a slicker that was hanging open, giving her hand free access to the belt gun she wore. In her right hand she carried a Winchester. Her blouse was open at the neck and she wore over it, beneath the slicker, a man's coat, cut down to fit her.

He saw that in a glance, but he saw much more. She was young and she was beautiful, with a wild, colorful beauty of dark hair, flashing eyes, bright red lips, and a figure that not even the rough clothes could conceal.

He eased out of his cramped position and stood up. "I thought so," she said. "Val Darrant, isn't it? I'm Boston Bucklin."

"You couldn't be anybody else," he said. "I've heard it said that you were the wildest, most beautiful thing on the Plains. I believe it."

She blushed, but stared back at him. "It won't do, your making up to me. Besides, you've been shot."

"Was that your fire I smelled?"

"Yes."

"You didn't shoot at me?"

"If I'd shot at you, you'd be dead. No, it was a man on a big dapple-gray horse. When he saw me he rode off, mighty fast. He didn't guess that I was alone."

She looked at him as he came away from the crack, watching him move. "You can walk all right. My fire's about two hundred yards down canyon. If you can get yourself to it, I'll round up your horse."

"Thanks," he said.

Her camp, when he reached it, was almost perfect. The rim-rock had caved in underneath, leaving a shelf that overhung a small area within the rim-rock itself. There was room enough for the fire and a bed under the rim shelf, and a place for three or four horses in a sort of pocket not under the shelf. The camp was hidden, with no way it could be seen from above or below until one rode right up to it. Obviously the girl had spent the night here.

She rode back shortly, leading his horse, and when she had tied it, she joined him under the rim, throwing off her slicker. Her wet black hair hung down over her shoulders.

"We've been expectin' you, Val," she said. "Pa, he said you'd be along soon. We've been hopin' you'd come."

"How is your pa?"

"Fair to middlin'. He's packin' a Kiowa bullet picked up last spring. Ails him some when it's wet or cold."

"And the others?"

"They're all right. Cody had him a mite of shootin' over to Fort Griffin. Some fancy gent in a flowered vest had words with him."

"But Cody's all right?"

"Sure."

She had put the coffeepot on, and now she turned to him. "You'd better let me look at that wound. You tenderfeet sicken up almighty fast, seems to me."

"I'm no tenderfoot. I was born in this country."

"I know, but you've been living it high and handsome back east." She helped him off with his coat and shirt. She looked at his powerful muscles with approval. "Well, all that beef hasn't gone soft, anyway."

The wound was not serious. The bullet had struck the top of his shoulder and glanced off, tearing the muscle some, and he had lost blood.

"In those fancy stories a girl always tears her white petticoat and makes a bandage. Well, I haven't got a white petticoat— never had one—and if I did I wouldn't tear it up for no man. Not unless he was in dyin' shape."

"There are a couple of clean white handkerchiefs in the pack behind my saddle," Val suggested.

She got them out. "My, aren't we the fancy one!" She looked critically at the handkerchiefs. "You've become a real dude, I see."

Val watched her. He had never, anywhere, seen so beautiful a girl. She was wild, free, and uninhibited as an animal. "Aren't you a ways from home?" he asked.

"It isn't so far, not across country. I like to ride. I like to see a lot of country, and I'm not worried. I can ride and shoot as good as any man, and better than most. I can also use a knife."

"Pretty dangerous. I'll bet all the men are scared to death of you."

She flushed. "Maybe," she said, lifting her eyes to him, "but it wouldn't do them any good if they weren't. I'm spoken for."

He felt a twinge of disappointment that startled him. "I'm surprised," he said.

Her head came up from the coffee she was pouring. "Oh? You don't think I'm good enough?"

"Oh, you're good enough, all right. Maybe too good. You've got a streak of broncho in you, I think, and you'd need a man who'd bridle you with a Spanish bit."

She gave him another of those straight glances. "I'd handle with a hackamore for the right man," she said, "and no other could do it, Spanish bit or no."

When he had finished his coffee she broke camp quickly and efficiently, brushing aside his efforts to help. "Save it, tenderfoot, you'll need all your strength."

"Not if you're spoken for," he said. She turned on him sharply and seemed about to speak, then swung astride her horse. Only then did he notice that she wore a divided skirt. He had heard of them, but had never seen one. All the women he had known rode sidesaddle. It was considered the only ladylike way.

"If you can sit your saddle," she said, "we can make it tonight . . . late."

"I'll be with you," he said, and she led off at a lope.

The sky was heavily overcast, although the rain had stopped and there was no more thunder and lightning. The ground was soggy and slippery, but they made good time, with Boston leading the way.

So far as he could see, there were no landmarks. The cap-rock was level and seemed to reach to the horizon on all sides. By the time they were a few hundred yards from the canyon they could no longer tell that it was there. Val studied the ground for tracks that might have been left by the would-be-killer, but there were none.

The ranch lay in a hollow among the hills, the spring at the back, a little higher in the notch. That notch was lined with trees, and other trees were growing about the place.

There was a good-sized, two-story ranch house with a balcony, and with a wide veranda all around. There were two large barns for the best riding stock, some milk cows, and the storage of feed, and there were several corrals and a bunkhouse.

Boston drew up on the slope and swept a wide gesture toward the valley. "Well, there she lays. Did we do right by you?"

"You surely did. It's beautiful."

She glanced at him. "I think so. Pa said we'd have to make it so. He said you were the kind of man who would want it to look nice."

Cody Bucklin came up from the corral as they neared the house. "Pa will be pleased," he said. "I knowed it was you when you topped out on the rise. It's the way you set a horse," he said.

Pa rode in with the last light, Tardy and Duke beside him. "We've been makin' a tally," he said. "We'll drive a herd to Kansas this year."

He studied Val thoughtfully. "You've taken on some size, boy, and some beef in the shoulders."

His eyes went to Boston. "So she found you, did she? Boston allowed as how if you didn't come back, she was a-going after you. Be careful, boy."

"Pa!" Boston said. "You're just a-makin' that up!"

When suppertime came they seated themselves about the table, and Pa Bucklin said grace. Val looked around at their faces, and suddenly he felt at home. At home with these people he had known so slightly, yet with whom he had made a business pact that had proved itself, and with whom he felt strangely warm and comfortable.

He felt their easy understanding, their friendship, their sympathy. They were strong, honest people, hard-working, hard-fighting, but simple in their ways.

They knew that not all men are men of good will; they knew there was evil in the world, and stood strong against it. They knew that there were some who would take by force what they would not work to acquire. They knew, as Val did, that outside their windows waited hunger, thirst, and cold; that beyond their doors there were savage men, held in restraint only by a realization of another force ready to oppose them, to preserve the world they had built from savagery into order and peace, where each man might work and build and create without the threat of destruction.

Betsy came into the room, bringing a platter of steak. She was tall, as Boston was, almost queenly. Val glanced again at Pa. How had such women come from this gnarled and hard-shelled man? Yet they were here, slender, shapely, and beautiful.

"We've got four workin' cowhands now, Val," Pa said, "and a grub-line rider who drifted in a few days ago huntin' you."

"Me?"

"Calls himself Tensleep. Said he had word for you." Pa Bucklin paused to chew on his steak, and then added, "Looks like a right tough man."

"He's an outlaw, Pa, but he's been a good friend to me. I met him when I was five," he added, "and I've seen him around since. After supper I'd better hear what he has to say. He isn't given to talking through his hat."

"He's a good hand. He's turned out for work every day since he came, and he works fast and steady. I'd say he's as good a man with stock as I ever did see."

"Does he want a job?"

"Ain't said. I'd say he's been up the trail and over the mountain, and he'd like to light an' keep his feet under the table for a spell."

Then Bucklin looked sharply at him. "You figurin' on stayin' a while? We've made provision. You've got a separate wing of the house for your ownself. The girls furnished it, so if you have complaint, speak to them."

"I . . . I'm not sure." Val looked over at Boston, then turned his eyes away. "I would like to stay, but there is much I have to do. And I don't know yet what I want my life to be. Or where I want to live."

"You got call to be restless, never staying put all your born days."

Val told them then of the places he'd seen, of the men and the women, of the gowns and the wine and the music, and the world beyond the rim of the hills out there, beyond the cap-rock and beyond the Brazos. He told of the work he had done, of the loneliness, and of Van Clevern; and then, of Myra.

After talking a long time he got up from the table, and the girls cleared the dishes away. He said to Pa, "I'd better go see Tensleep."

It was cool out on the dark veranda. He went down the steps to the yard, and he could see the rectangles of light from the bunkhouse windows and the glow of a cigarette from the stoop. He started across the hard-packed earth, listening to the pleasant sound of the horses feeding in the corral, and when he turned once to look back at the big house and its windows, he heard the sound of male voices, then laughter from the girls.

He strolled toward the bunkhouse and said, "Tensleep?"

"He's in yonder, a-waitin' for you. He spotted you the minute you skylined yourself up on the ridge." Then he added, "I'm Waco."

"Val Darrant. Glad to meet you, Waco."

He opened the door and stepped into the bunkhouse. There were bunks for eight men, three of them empty of bedclothes. The men inside looked up, and two of them then returned to their checker game, while another watched. Tensleep was lying on his bunk, but he sat up and swung his boots to the floor.

"Howdy, Val. I come a fur piece, a-huntin' you." He took up his hat, and they went outside, walking to the corral.

Val was thinking: *He's thinner . . . older . . . and if anything, tougher.*

At the corral, Tensleep turned to him. "Boy, you in any kinda trouble? Anything I can take off your back?"

"No. Nothing."

"You sure?" He could feel Tensleep's eyes on him.

"Somebody shot at me. I'm carrying a scratch on my shoulder. Either he figured me for dead, or was scared off when Boston Bucklin rode up. Anyway he ran off. I think it was Thursty Pike."

"Him? He'd be likely to do that. I heard he was in Tascosa."

"I saw him there. He left town."

Tensleep chuckled. "He did if he was smart. Boy, you made yourself a name with Chip Hardesty. They're still talkin' about it."

"I don't want the name. What's on your mind, Tensleep?"

"The Pinks," he said, "they're huntin' you. And when they hunt you they find you."

"The Pinks?" Val's mind was a momentary blank, then it came to him: the Pinkertons. But why would they be hunting *him*?

"Well," he said, "it's not for anything I've done. But somebody must want to find me." He studied the idea, and could think of no one. He had been in touch with Bricker. Van Clevern was dead. There was no one . . . no one at all. He said as much, but Tensleep snorted.

"Don't you believe it. Somebody wants you almighty bad. They've had men a-huntin' you up and down the country, and that costs money. I never knew even Wells Fargo to spend so much. I got wind of it, and put some feelers out." He looked up at Val. "I got friends, you know—I hear things. You done wrong to some woman?"

"No."

"Well, the way the story goes, it's a woman huntin' you."

*Myra* . . .

She had the money, and she might know of him. She might want to find him . . . but for what?

"It might be Myra," he said.

Tensleep stiffened. "Boy, you watch your step. That ain't no woman, that's a rattler. She's pure poison."

He was silent for a moment. "Myra! I never gave a thought to her. I ain't seen or heard of her in years."

"She's been back east," Val said. "She's made a mint of money and a name for herself."

"I bet you," Tensleep muttered. "Watch yourself, boy. I wouldn't trust her a foot." He paused. "Whatever became of that fancy man of hers?"

"He's dead . . . accident."

"I'll bet," Tensleep said cynically. "He knew where the body was buried—all the bodies. If she's big, she can't afford him." Tensleep dug in his pocket for the makings and built himself a smoke. "And she can't afford you, neither. Look, boy, if you saw anything of Van, she'll figure he told you some things about her.

"Van was always a pretty good man," he went on. "He hadn't no more backbone than so much spaghetti, but he always had a ready hand if a man was on his uppers. I figured him for a straight one . . . there was no thief in him . . . trouble was, she had him wrapped around her little finger. He was roped and hog-tied by that woman."

Long after Val was back in the wing of the house the girls had prepared for him, he lay in bed staring at the ceiling.

Of course, Tensleep was right. Van had been murdered. It was all too pat. And now she—or somebody—had the Pinkertons looking for him. The Pinks might be strikebreakers, they might be strong-arm men, but so far as he knew they weren't killers. However, once he was located, there were other men who could handle that.

Perhaps that shot today? No . . . that was Pike. He was sure of that in his own mind. He also knew that Pike would still be around.

His thoughts went back to Tensleep, and the end of their conversation. The old outlaw had said, "Boy, I like this place. I'm riding the grub-line here, but—well—I sure enough care for it. If they'd take me on, I'd hang up my saddle."

"They like you, Tensleep," Val had said, "and they like your work. I'll speak to Pa Bucklin."

"Thanks." Tensleep had thrust out his hand. "Boy, that there cabin in the snow is a long time back, ain't it? An' Will Reilly, and all?"

"And Henry Sonnenberg," Val added.

"Yeah—there's him, all right," Tensleep said. "Boy, you want I should go get him? I could find him. I was never afraid of Henry—he was never up to taking me on. My hand may not be as steady, but if you want—"

"Forget it. He killed Will Reilly . . . he and Thursty Pike are still left. I want them myself. And I want Sonnenberg most of all."

At last his eyes closed, and he slept. On the far ridge above the ranch a lone rider stopped and looked down at the spread below him. He sat there a long time before he rode away . . . but his day would come.

# NINETEEN

At daybreak Boston rode away from the ranch and headed south. It was a sixteen-mile ride she had ahead of her, but when she made up her mind to do something she was not one to waste time.

She was crossing the creek below the ranch when she saw the tracks, and drew up. This was not one of the ranch horses, for she knew every hoof on the place. This was a strange horse, with a long, swinging gait, and the tracks were fresh, probably not more than four or five hours old. She thought of the man who had shot at Val, but at present she would not consider this—she had to go ahead with her errand.

She reached the Winslow place well before noon, and rode into the ranch yard and swung down. Melissa Winslow came out on the porch to greet her. "Boston! Of all people! Do come in!"

Boston went up the steps, spurs jingling. "Mel, I need your help."

"*My* help? *You*?" Melissa smiled. "I would have believed you were the one person in the world who would never need help from anyone."

"I want to be a lady."

165

Melissa glanced at her again. "I never knew you when you weren't. What's all this about?"

"Valentine Darrant. I'm in love with him."

"You mean he's come back? After all this time?"

"He has, and he's . . . he's just wonderful."

"I never thought I'd hear you say that about any man. But do you mean he has complained? He doesn't like you? The man's obviously a fool."

"I think he likes me. I really believe he does; but Mel, I'm too rough. He didn't say that, I'm saying it. I want to know how to act like a lady, how to talk, how to eat the proper way. . . . I want to know it all."

"You *must* be in love," Mel said. "All that for just one man?"

"Yes." Boston sat up eagerly. "Mel, it's got to be fast. I'll work at it. You know I can. He'll be going east again and I wouldn't want him to think he had to be ashamed of me. You've lived in the East. You grew up there. I've never lived anywhere except on a ranch, and Ma died when I was so young. Will you help me?"

"Of course." She looked at Boston again. "But I hate to spoil you. There are a lot of ladies, but I never knew anyone like you. You're the only one of your kind, Boston. I shudder to think what you'd do to the men if you weren't a good girl."

"Don't call me that. It sounds so . . . so prissy."

Before the long day was over, Melissa was sure of two things: Boston was instinctively a lady, and she was also a natural actress, graceful and easy, with an ear attuned to the proper usage of words.

Val had slept late that morning, awakening to a painful shoulder, and a stiffness, especially in his right leg, that hampered his movements. Breakfast time was long past, but Betsy brought his and sat down with him.

"Where's Boston?" he asked.

"She left a note. She rode off this morning before daylight and she'll be gone overnight and tomorrow."

Val had a distinct feeling of disappointment, but he only said, "I hope she hasn't gone far. I think the man who shot at me may still be around."

"She went to Melissa Winslow's place. They have a small outfit about a few hours' ride from here. He's English." She added,

"Mel is a Virginia girl who went to school in London. That was where she met David."

He was in no mood for riding, nor for looking over the ranch. After breakfast he sat on the veranda and looked out over the valley, mentally reviewing his situation. Nothing about it looked particularly favorable.

He should have faced Pike in Tascosa. He should have forced him to draw, and killed him. As it was, the man was free to shoot whenever he chose, and Val must be on guard every hour of the day and night. That Pike would ride on out of the country he did not believe for one moment. The man was vindictive, and dangerous. He would wait. . . . The worst of it was, he might be trapped by one of the Bucklins, forcing them into a shoot-out.

Throughout the day, Val worked the fingers of his right hand. They were limber enough, but the shoulder was stiff, and there was no ease in his movements, and no speed. Meanwhile, he could not help but notice how well kept the ranch was. The buildings had been painted, the gates all worked easily, and what stock he could see was in good shape.

A third of this was his, but though he had provided the money that made the difference, there was here no work of his hands, no planning of his brain. This was the work of others, for which he could take no credit.

He shifted in his chair. He was nothing but an aimless drifter; he was not even as much as Will had been, who was a gambler, admitted it, and enjoyed it—enjoyed it, at least, until he met Princess Louise.

What had become of her? And of Prince Pavel? At the thought of Pavel he felt coldness take hold of him. He would never forget that day on the outskirts of Innsbruck when Pavel had tried to whip Will Reilly.

Yet in the end it was Pavel who had triumphed. His money and his hatred had reached where he could not, dared not. Henry Sonnenberg was only the tool. The killer was Pavel.

"I think I will go to Europe," he said aloud.

"Boston will be disappointed, Val," Betsy said. She had come up to him quietly. "Why to Europe?"

"I've some unfinished business over there," he said. "There's a man I must see."

"You haven't told me how you liked your part of the house," she said. "We spent a lot of time planning it, thinking about it."

He was ashamed. "I've been preoccupied," he said. "Will you show me through?"

He struggled to his feet, swung his stiff leg around and limped after her.

There were three rooms in the east wing of the house—a small but comfortable living room, a bedroom, and a bath. The walls of the living room, which he had not entered until now, were lined with books. He crossed the room to look at them.

"You were always reading," Betsy said, "and you mentioned several of the books you liked, and sometimes when you wrote to us you mentioned what you were doing, so we asked Mel and David to help us."

He saw there Scott's *Marmion*, Volney's *Ruins of Empire*, *The Life of Sir Walter Scott*, by Lockhart, *Hypatia*, by Kingsley . . . and there were works by Plato, Hume, Locke, Berkeley, Spinoza, and Voltaire, and a shelf of the poets.

"You must thank Mrs. Winslow for me," he said. "And I want to thank you and Boston."

It was an easy, comfortable room, unlike the crowded, over-done rooms of so many eastern homes he had seen. It was closer in style to the rather bare rooms of the Spanish ranchos in California.

When Betsy had gone into the other part of the house, Val browsed through the books, taking them one by one from the shelves. A few of them he had read, most of them he had not, but all were books he had wanted to read.

He heard the door from the veranda open, and took a book from the shelf, turning as he did so.

Thurston Pike was standing there, gun in hand. "Got my horse right here," he said, "an' I'm goin' to kill you, mister, an' nobody the wiser."

As he finished speaking, he fired, and the impact of the bullet, fired at a distance of not more than a dozen feet, knocked Val back against the bookshelves, but he drew from his waistband as he fell back, and fired as his shoulders braced against the bookshelves. He felt the impact of another bullet, but Pike was going down as Val shot the second time.

The door burst open and Betsy stood there, a rifle in her

hands. Thurston Pike was on his back in the doorway, half in, and half out.

Val was staring at the book in his hand. He had taken it from a shelf, had turned, and the thick, leather-bound book had taken both bullets, aimed directly at his heart. Neither bullet had gone more than two-thirds of the way through the book.

He glanced at the title. It was Burton's *Anatomy of Melancholy*. "You know, Bets," he said, "I was never able to get through this book myself."

# TWENTY

M yra Fossett sat behind her desk and looked across at Mr.
Pinkerton, "You have news for me?"

"Yes . . . from several sources. First, the young man, Mr.
Valentine Darrant. He is now in Texas, and we discover he is part
owner of a ranch there. It comprises some sixty thousand acres of
range land."

"They own this land?"

"No, ma'am, actually it is government land, but they own the
water holes. You understand this gives them—"

"I do understand. I know all about water holes and water
rights, Mr. Pinkerton. What else?"

"There was an attempt to kill him by a gunman, a notorious
killer named Thurston Pike. He did not succeed."

"What happened? Get to the point, please."

"Young Mr. Darrant was surprised in his library by the killer.
Pike seems to have fired twice, Mr. Darrant also. Mr. Darrant's
bullets found their mark."

Pike, was it? She remembered him, remembered him as a
customer of one of her girls far away in Idaho. He had been a
tough, dangerous man even then. Evidently her son could take
care of himself.

"What led to the fight?"

"We checked into that. It seems Mr. Darrant was reared by a gambler, a man named Will Reilly."

Of course. Will Reilly had been a friend of Van's, but no friend of hers. She felt a little pang when she thought of him, for Will Reilly was the one man who had really interested her. As a matter of fact, she hated men; she used them and got rid of them, but Will had never so much as given her the time of day.

Pinkerton had turned a leaf in his notebook. "This Reilly was the target of a reward offer . . . not by the law, by some private party." Pinkerton looked up at her as he said this, and she smiled cynically.

"Don't worry yourself. I know nothing of that."

"Of course. I did not for the moment—"

"You're a damned liar, Pinkerton. Now get on with it."

"There were three men—Thurston Pike, Chip Hardesty, and Henry Sonnenberg. They ambushed him, caught him coming out of a lighted door."

He paused. "The first two are no longer with us. Mr. Darrant seems to have killed them both."

"And Sonnenberg?"

"I know a good deal of him in another connection, and we have him on our wanted list. He killed a Wells Fargo guard a year or two ago, and there have been other—"

"I know about him. He is an outlaw, a paid killer. Who hired him?"

"That's the odd part. Some jack-leg lawyer from here in town named Avery Simpson offered the money. I don't know who it was who wanted Reilly killed. I suppose it was some gambling trouble. Men who live like that—"

"You have talked to Simpson?"

"No, but—"

"Leave him to me." She stood up, indicating the interview was over.

"There's one thing more . . ."

She waited, impatient to be rid of him.

"That man, Van Clevern. He was killed in a fall from a horse."

"Too bad."

She turned away sharply, her irritation showing, but he remained where he was, his eyes on her face. "I know you told us

you were no longer interested in him, but one of my operatives
. . . well, it tied in with Mr. Darrant—"

"Yes?"

"Van Clevern, shortly before he was killed, directed his family
to mail a certain box—without opening it—to Valentine Darrant."

Myra took up a pen and turned it in her fingers. She was aware
that Pinkerton was watching her, but she had to think. Such a box
would certainly contain papers . . . what else could it be? And
what papers would he be likely to be sending to Val? Something
about Val's mother.

He might have written it all down, there at the last, leaving it
up to Val to do with it as he wished.

"This box . . . Val Darrant has it?"

"No. It has been forwarded to a bank in Colorado to hold for
him. Apparently they expect him soon because of some investments they have been handling for him."

There was still time then. She took the report from Pinkerton
and watched him leave, but her mind was working swiftly. That
box, described as a small metal chest or bond box, undoubtedly
contained Van Clevern's signed statement. With that statement
they would have no trouble finding the evidence needed for a
conviction, and Myra Fossett would be on trial for murder.

Even if, by some chance, she was able to gain an acquittal, her
whole life would have been exposed. She would be ruined. . . .

She picked up the report. The box had been shipped, but only
just now. If she wanted to get the box she must act at once.

A train holdup was too difficult to arrange, but after the train
there would be the stage, and then the bank. She knew a dozen
men who could handle either affair, but the name that came to
her mind at once was Sonnenberg.

Sonnenberg would have reason to want to get Val out of the
way. He was a tough man, and as she knew from the old days, he
was an experienced yeggman who knew all the tricks of cracking
safes.

For a long time she sat at her desk, considering the problem,
but her thoughts returned again and again to Val.

She had a son. What, after all, did that mean? She had given
birth to a child she had never wanted, by a man she had never
loved, and the child had failed to serve its purpose. At the time it
had seemed the quickest road to money, a lot of money. Now she

had the money, from another source, and the child had turned up again and might deprive her of it.

What was he like? She had, of course, no feeling of love for him. Love was not only a matter of blood and flesh, it developed from holding a child, caring for it, answering its need for protection. There had never been any of that. He would have different ideas from hers, different feelings . . . he might even be a weakling, like Van.

She had passed him that day in Bricker's outer office, or so she believed. If that was indeed Val, he was a handsome young man, and anybody who could take Hardesty and Thurston Pike in gun battles was certainly no weakling.

Myra got up and went to the window. It was raining, and she watched a hansom cab go by the door, the lamps thrusting narrow beams of light before them. She remembered nights like this when she was a child . . . remembered her father lighting the carriage lamps and carrying her out so she would not get her slippers wet, nor the hem of her long skirt. How old was she then? Twelve?

She had never gone back, and she had not written. No doubt they believed she was dead, and surely they would never dream that she was *the* Myra Fossett who controlled mills, mines, and railroads.

Of course, if her son got that box and chose to expose her, they would know . . . everyone would know. No doubt he hated her, and once the box was in his hands he could blackmail her for every cent she possessed. That he might not choose to do so never entered her mind.

Avery Simpson had never met Myra Fossett, but he had heard of her, and he smelled money. But he was cautious. He knew who her attorneys were, and he also knew they would not want any dealings with him.

She received him in the library, seated behind her desk. He had grown fat, and was almost unkempt. The woman he saw was not what he expected.

She was very handsome, slender, with a splendid figure, and if there was gray in her hair, he could not see it. She motioned him to a chair and took up a single sheet of paper that lay on the desk.

"You are Avery Simpson. You were involved in the Carnes-Wales business."

He was startled. His connection with that, his hiring of thugs for the company, had never appeared in the papers or the trial proceedings.

Before he could protest, she continued. "You were also concerned with the payoff in the Sterling case."

He jumped up. "Now see here!"

"Sit down!" Her tone was sharp. "You're a cheap, blackleg lawyer, and I could list a dozen cases which, if they were known, could get you disbarred. Now listen to me. If you give me honest answers I will pay you for your time, not as much as you think it is worth, but more than I think it's worth. Are you going to listen, or do I have you thrown out of here and then give all this to the press?"

He sat there, shaking and frightened. Nobody could know all that . . . yet she did. He had best play this very easy.

"You hired the murder of Will Reilly."

He started to protest, but she brushed him aside impatiently. "I suppose you know that Hardesty and Pike are dead?"

He had not known. He dabbed at his face with a handkerchief. Hardesty and Pike dead! "How—?"

"They were killed in gun battles by Reilly's nephew. Do you remember him?"

"But he was only a boy!"

"They grow up very fast out west, they tell me," she said grimly. "He knows about you, doesn't he?"

The boy had been in the room when Will Reilly had forced him to write those letters. Simpson shifted uncomfortably. That was far away in the West. It was true he sometimes worried about Sonnenberg, but—

"That boy was back east a few weeks ago," Myra said, "and he has been asking questions."

Avery Simpson felt as if he was going to be sick. He tried to sit up straighter, his jowls quivering. Back east? Then he was not safe, not even here.

"Who paid for Reilly's murder?" The question was shot at him, suddenly, without warning.

"It was Prince—" He stopped. "I can't tell you that."

Myra Fossett had dealt with men too long and on too intimate terms not to know about such men as Avery Simpson. "Simpson," she said coldly, "and even as I say it I know it is not your true name"—she saw him cringe a little at that—"I did not ask you here to make conversation. You tell me what you know, and no damned nonsense. If you don't," she smiled at him, "I will tell Henry Sonnenberg where to find you."

He stared at her. *Who was she?* How could she know about *him?*

After a moment she said, "Now tell me. And tell me all about it."

Avery Simpson dug into his pocket for a cigar. "Mind if I smoke?"

"Not if it will help your memory," she said; "but get on with it. I have better things to do than sit here talking to you."

Prince Pavel had not told anyone his reasons for wanting Will Reilly killed. He had told neither the go-between who put him in touch with Simpson, nor had he told Simpson; but Avery Simpson, drinking in a pub one night, had mentioned the scars on the face of Prince Pavel, and was told the story of the man he had tried to horsewhip.

After Simpson had gone, Myra Fossett found herself smiling. *The idea,* she said to herself, *of anybody trying to horsewhip Will Reilly!*

She was grimly amused, but her thoughts began to toy with the information she had acquired, and what it might do for her.

Her business was doing well, but there were many doors which were still closed to her, doors that could be opened by such a name as Prince Pavel . . . or by any other prince, she told herself cynically.

He had wanted to make a rich marriage for Princess Louise. Had he succeeded? What, exactly, was his financial situation at the moment? He might be someone she could use.

He was obviously a good hater, and she liked that, but he was also a fool, for no man in his right mind could look into those cool green eyes of Will Reilly's and still fancy they could have him whipped. Killed, perhaps, but not whipped. She had known other men of his kind, men you had to shoot to stop, for their pride and their courage was such that they could not be broken.

She considered the several plans that had been lying in the dark and secret drawers of her mind, plans that awaited the right knowledge of the right people, or their assistance, but all of those people lay beyond walls she had not been able to breach. But with a captive prince . . .

Her thoughts returned to her son. It was with a feeling of irritation that she realized she had thought of him thus. He was a stranger, by accident her son, with whom she had nothing in common. And at this juncture he was an outright danger to her, and to all she had planned and accomplished.

Avery Simpson had provided her with a handle for the manipulation of a prince, or the possibility of it. The first thing was to ascertain the financial standing of Prince Pavel, and of the Princess Louise, if she was still around. If the prince was gambling, as Simpson had implied, he would probably need money.

She glanced at her watch. She had been invited to dinner at the Harcort's, and there was just time to make it. At such times she missed Van.

Though she had no use for men, yet there were times when a woman needed an escort, and Van had always been there; and even when drinking his manners had been perfect. She could have used him now.

At the Harcort's there would be a number of fashionable people, including men with far-reaching business connections. It was at such parties that she had made most of the contacts she had developed and used. Men who were drinking often explained things to a beautiful woman who was a good listener, telling her of stock deals and financial arrangements in which their wives were rarely interested. It was true that some of them had grown cautious after their casual boasting had cost them money. For Myra not only knew how to get information, she knew how to use it.

She rarely worried about meeting anyone who might have known her in the past. The men she had entertained in the mining and cattle towns rarely came east; and she had changed the color of her hair, wore higher heels, and presented a very different appearance. She had never returned to the West, and had no desire to do so. But there remained the chance of encountering some former client, so she restricted her social activities to private parties, rarely going to large hotels or restaurants, or to watering places.

She called for one of her runners and before she left for dinner she had started the movement of events that would have Henry

Sonnenberg checking the arrival of a certain box, and would bring her information as to the financial status of Prince Pavel Pavelovitch.

In a saloon, not more than a dozen blocks away, Avery Simpson stood at the bar and nursed a drink. He needed that drink and those that would follow, for Myra Fossett had scared the daylights out of him.

She knew too much for comfort, but what puzzled him was her familiarity with the identities of Will Reilly, Henry Sonnenberg, and some others. All of which gave rise to the question: Who was Myra Fossett?

# TWENTY-ONE

A few weeks later Prince Pavel was asking himself the same question. He had received through his bank a note written in a small but beautiful hand a suggestion that if he were in a position to come to America on a brief visit it might prove financially interesting to him.

He put the note aside, a bit curious as to this Myra Fossett who had written it. When he went to dinner he noticed an old friend across the room, a man known for his international business affairs, and for his unusual success. It was Robert Fleury. Prince Pavel went over to his table.

"Robert," he said, "do you by any chance know anything of an American woman named Fossett?"

Fleury turned sharply. "*Myra* Fossett? How do you know anything about her?"

"Shouldn't I?"

Fleury shrugged. "It is simply that she is a business woman . . . beautiful, but very shrewd, also."

"A woman? In business?"

Fleury shrugged again. "There are more than you think, but none of them like Madame Fossett."

"She is wealthy?"

"Rolling in it." Fleury studied his friend. "But what do you know of her?"

Pavel's explanation solved nothing. "I do not know what she has in mind," Fleury said, "but be assured there is money in it. She thinks of nothing but money, that one. Be careful, my friend. When she makes any such proposal you can be sure it is for her benefit alone—that much I know of her. She is not only shrewd, she is utterly ruthless, and without a scruple."

Pavel was not impressed. He had no scruples himself; and a woman, a beautiful woman, and very wealthy . . . "I have no idea what she has in mind," he said.

Robert Fleury, whose interests in America were many, was puzzled, because so far as he was aware Madame Fossett had shown no interest in any man that was not casual, nor did she seem very active in a social way. She was not a party-giver, and seemed to ignore most of the social highlights of the season.

"Just be warned," he said again, "but you can be sure whatever it is has money in it."

Prince Pavel, ten years before, had come into a good-sized inheritance which had since dwindled because of his enthusiasm for gambling. It was growing increasingly difficult to borrow, and although he had a small reserve he had kept untouched, it was too small for comfort.

His cousin, the Princess Louise, was single again. Her husband—Pavel had finally been successful in that matter—had died, leaving her a considerable estate, but so far Pavel had been unable to touch it. Louise was careful, and she knew him well enough to distrust him. Nevertheless, they were on friendly terms.

Louise had beauty, she had presence, and there were a lot of millionaires in America, he had heard. If he handled it wisely . . . he did not like the idea of Louise marrying an American, but if the man was rich enough . . .

Prince Pavel was no longer handsome—the scars took care of that—but he had found that scars seemed the utmost in masculinity to some women, and his he represented, without actually saying so, as dueling scars.

He had an idea it would not be difficult to persuade Louise to accompany him. She had always had an interest in everything American . . . at least since she met that damned Reilly.

A few days later he replied to Myra Fossett. *My cousin, the*

*Princess Louise, and I, have been considering a visit to New York.*
*Am I to assume you wish us to come as your guests?*

The response was immediate. Passage was arranged, everything paid for, and there remained nothing but to go.

For three weeks Val Darrant had been working harder than he had ever worked in his life. He had branded calves, cleaned out water holes, repaired corral fences, trapped wolves, pulled steers out of bogs, and helped in the breaking of horses. He had been getting out of bed before daylight, and rarely coming in off the range until well after dark. He had worked as hard as any hand on the ranch, and he had worked with Tensleep beside him, learning from him as they worked.

His shoulder wound had healed rapidly, and he was not one to pamper himself when there was so much to be done. But always, in the back of his mind, there remained the thought that soon he must catch the stage for Colorado.

He was thinking of it now as he topped out on a rise and looked over the wide basin below.

Cody rode up to join him, a lean, wide-shouldered young man with cool eyes and an easy way of moving and talking.

"How you comin' boy? Shoulder botherin' any?"

"No, it's all right now, though I find myself favoring it a little. I just don't like to think about leaving."

"We'll miss you," Cody built a cigarette, touched the paper with his tongue. "You've been doin' more'n your share."

"We need rain," Val commented. "The grass on the high range looks bad."

"Heel flies are gettin' worse, too," Cody said, and he added, "boy, you better let one of us ride along with you. Dube, he's a-rarin' to go."

"It would be company," Val admitted. "How's the work stack up?"

"We got it whupped. You take Dube. I'd admire to go myself, but if trouble shapes up, me an' Tardy ought to be here. Dube is dead fast with a gun, a better than usual tracker, and maybe the best rifle shot amongst us."

"Why all this concern?"

Cody grinned. "Boston said there'd be no foolin' you. Fact is,

Tardy picked up a story. Boston heard talk of it over to Winslows', too. Henry Sonnenberg was in Mobeetie, roundin' up two
or three tough ones."

"So?"

"They taken off, night before last . . . headin' for Colorado."

Far down the valley some cattle were walking toward the
creek, and a thin plume of dust told of a lone rider coming across
the flat. That would be Boston, returning from the Winslows'.

"I can handle Sonnenberg."

"Yeah, I think maybe you can, although there's nobody more
dangerous than him, but what about the others? He's got himself
some tough men."

"You think he's gunning for me?"

"No. I figure there's something else in the wind. So does Pa.
You see, a body don't live long in this country unless he keeps
track of folks, so we got us a little bird over to Mobeetie. Pa, he
gives him eatin' money and this little bird keeps us alive as to
who's comin' and goin'. Seems like one of these men he picked
up, one he asked for special, is just out of prison for blowing the
safe in a bank."

Val turned his horse toward the ranch house, angling across
country to intercept Boston. Cody rode along beside him, and
suddenly he spoke up. "Didn't you tell me one time that you
knew Billy the Kid?"

"Yes."

"He's dead. One of the Turkeytrack boys told me. I met him
yonder, huntin' strays. He was shot by Pat Garrett at Pete Maxwell's
place."

So he had gone there, after all. And now he was dead. He had
known Billy only a short time, but it had been one of the first
times he had been around boys of his own age. He and . . . what
was his name? Dodie . . . Dodie Grant. They had ridden out
with Billy.

Hickok was gone, too, shot in the back up in Deadwood a few
years ago.

He and Cody rode on in silence. Suddenly he felt lost and
lonely . . . old ties were being cut, and so much of the country
seemed to be changing. He said as much to Cody.

"You ain't heard the most of it. This cowhand was tellin' me they've passed a prohibition law up in Kansas. You can't buy a drink nowhere in the state."

"I had heard they were talking of it."

Val stared at the horizon, thinking. He had to belong somewhere, he had to put down some roots. He could not forever be moving. He wanted a *home*.

After all, why should he feel any urge to kill Sonnenberg? Hardesty and Pike were dead, and they had paid their debt for Will. Avery Simpson was somewhere in the East, and Prince Pavel was far away in Europe. Let the course of natural events take care of Sonnenberg.

This was where he belonged, somewhere here in the West. He would marry Boston, if she would have him, and hang out his shingle in some lively western town, in Texas, New Mexico, or Colorado.

Boston came wheeling up then, flashing him a quick smile, her black hair blowing in the wind.

"Do you know what I am going to do, Val? I am going to Denver with you!"

"What?"

"I mean it! We made it up between us this afternoon! Dube, Tensleep, and me. We're all going with you!"

"What is this going to be—a gypsy caravan?"

"I need some clothes, some girl clothes. Dube has never seen a big town and he wants to go, and Tensleep figures he should go along and look after all of us. So there! It's settled!"


The land lay wide before them, under a wider sky—long, slow swells of the grass sea, a grass now tawny with the dryness of a parching summer, streams now scarcely a trickle lost in the width of sandy bed.

A few tracks of buffalo, here and there the trail left by a drifting band of mustangs, and always, lost against the brassy sky, the slow swinging loops of the buzzards. Men may plan, they may dream and struggle, but the buzzard has only to wait, for all things come to him in the end.

They rode due north toward the railroad, coming once upon a covered wagon, standing desolate in a small hollow, its cover blown to shreds, one of the bows broken, and several stacks of buffalo hides standing nearby. The wagon had been looted and left, but there were two grave mounds close by, no marker on either.

"Happened to a man I knew," Tensleep said. "He come upon a trailside grave and rode over to read the marker. It was his brother buried there, alongside the Chisholm Trail, a brother he hadn't seen in ten years because they left home separate. You ever stop to think the number of men who come west and nobody ever hears of again?"

They camped that night near a seep where a tiny trickle of water made a pool the size of your hat and a small area of damp grass where the horses ate and breathed up what little water they could get.

The next creek bed was dry, with cracked mud for a bottom, and digging brought nothing but dust.

They heard the long whistle of the train before they could see the station, four lone buildings huddled together on a flat valley with no trees. Four buildings and a water tank—the station with a few feet of platform, a saloon with a postoffice sign on it, and a general store next to it where the bartender sold supplies between drinks. There was also a stable and some stock corrals.

Several men with drinks in their hands came to the door of the saloon to stare at them as they rode in, and when they reached the stable two of the men in the saloon followed. One was only a boy of seventeen, the other a few years older.

They took sidelong glances at Boston, and approached Val. "Mister," the oldest one said, "meanin' no offense, but is that a woman yonder?"

"Yes, it is. It's his sister." He indicated Dube.

"You reckon I could speak at her? An' maybe look a little closer? Mister, Willie an' me, we ain't seen a woman in nigh onto a year. Nine, ten months, I'd put it."

Val turned. "Boston, these young men haven't looked at a girl in some time. They would like to talk to you."

"Sure!" She walked over. "How are you, boys?"

They stood grinning, the red creeping around their ears.

"Are you ranching out here?" she asked.

The older one nodded. "We went to work for a gent up at Newton, Kansas, and drove some cows down here for him. We been here quite a spell, and a man sure gets hongry to even look at womenfolks."

The hostler came to take their horses. "I'll buy 'em if you're sellin," he said, "or keep 'em for you if you're comin' back."

"We're comin' back," Dube replied, "an' we want these same horses waitin' when we come. I'm Dube Bucklin," he said, "an' you may have heard of our outfit."

"I surely have. That reminds me. Got a letter over to the post office for a gent named Darrant—one of your outfit, I reckon."

Val turned. "I am Val Darrant."

"Pleased . . . This letter, it was misdirected here. Guess those folks back in Boston don't know much about west Texas."

"Are you the postmaster?"

"You could say that. Rightly I am only half of him. Smith Johnson is postmaster and I'm Johnson. Smith is over to the saloon. You see, we couldn't decide which was to be postmaster, so we decided we both would, and we made application for the job as Smith Johnson. You walk over yonder and Smith will give you that letter. Been settin' here nigh onto two weeks."

The saloon-post office was a bare room with a short bar and four or five bottles on the back bar. Smith was a fat, unshaven man in his undershirt, who leaned massive forearms on the bar. A cowhand lounged at the end of the bar, nursing a beer. At a table in the corner two men sat drinking beer.

"Quite a town you've got here," Val said.

"Yep! She's a lollapalooza! Biggest town between here and the next place. Was that really a flesh-and-blood woman you had with you?"

"Yes. That was Miss Bucklin, from down south a ways. Her brother is with her, and we're catching the train for Denver."

"Won't be much trouble, catchin' it. We got a signal here that we hang out and she stops ever' time. You just order yourself a beer, and—"

"I'll have the beer, and the letter for Val Darrant. The other half of the postmaster said you had one for me. Incidentally, which are you? Post or Master?"

Smith chuckled. "First time anybody asked me *that*. Now if I said I was Master I'd have to lick Johnson, and he's a tough old coot, but I wouldn't want to say I was Post, not with all those stray dogs runnin' loose hereabouts."

He drew a beer from the barrel, then took down a letter from a high shelf. "And there's your letter. As for the train, that old busted-down bronc-stomper yonder at the table is what passes for a stationmaster. He'll sell you a ticket. If you ain't got the money he'll trust you for it if you'll buy him a beer."

"Seems like a man can get almost anything around here if he can buy a beer," Val said, smiling.

"Mister, you already have," Smith said. "In this here town when you've put up your horse, bought yourself a ticket and a beer, you've just had about all there is to offer!"

"We pitch horseshoes," the stationmaster said, "and toward evenin' we shoot at jack rabbits or coyotes. Ever' oncet in a while, somebody hits one."

Val drank his beer and waited for the others to come over. The board at one end of the saloon showed a timetable, and the train was due about sundown.

On all sides the brown and slightly rolling plains stretched away to the sky. Nothing changed here but the seasons, and occasionally the cloud formations. Not long ago this had been Comanche country, and some miles away to the south was the site of Adobe Walls, scene of several great Indian fights.

Smith went to the door when Boston crossed the street toward the saloon, accompanied by Tensleep and Dube. "Ma'am," he said, "would you like to come into the post office an' set? It ain't often we have a lady in town."

"Thank you." Boston entered, and went to a table with Val and Dube. Tensleep strolled to the bar.

Smith gave him a sharp glance. "Tensleep, what are you up to? These here folks shape up to mighty nice people."

"I ride for Darrant and Bucklin," Tensleep said. "I'm a *ree*formed man, Smith."

At the table, Val opened his letter. It was from Van's sister.

*Dear Mr. Darrant:*

*As you may know, my brother was killed in a fall from a horse. He had left word that if anything happened to him, this box was to be forwarded to you, unopened. Being unsure of your exact address, we have forwarded the box to Mr. Peck, at his home in Empire, Colorado.*

*Van said Mr. Peck had handled some business matters*
*for you, and would deposit the box at the bank, to await*
*your pleasure.*

A few words followed to say that Van had often talked of him,
and asking him to call on them if he came to Boston. He read the
note twice; then, after reading it to Boston and Dube, put it down
on the table.

When it came right down to it, he knew very little about his
mother, and what he knew he did not like, but Van Clevern had
been with her throughout her bad days, and if anyone knew the
whole story it would be Van.

Now Van was dead, and unless Val was much mistaken, his
death had been anything but accidental. Did Myra know about
this box? He did not see how she could know, but little escaped
her attention if it concerned her. The thought made him uneasy.
Too many had suffered because of her, and if she had the idea
that Mr. Peck or anyone else had a box that contained incriminat-
ing evidence, whoever had the box was in danger.

Suddenly he remembered the account of Henry Sonnenberg
recruiting a safe-cracker . . . and hadn't Will told him that Henry
himself had been a yeggman?

Could there be a connection? Even as he asked himself that
question he realized there easily could be. If Myra knew of the
box, and if it worried her, she would try to gain possession of it.

All right, he told himself, it was a pretty flimsy case, filled with
ifs, but the wise thing to do was to act as if it were a positive fact.
In any event, he was going to Colorado, and this would be part of
the business he would do there.

Sonnenberg . . . Henry Sonnenberg! Val had thought of putting all that out of his mind, of avoiding the man and letting him
come to his own bad end in his own time, but now they were
pointed in the same direction just as if some fate was pulling the
strings.

He thought of Sonnenberg as he remembered him, heavy,
powerful, a man who seemed a composite of rawhide and iron, a
man who seemed indomitable. Even Billy the Kid had looked a
bit wary when he mentioned him. Somewhere ahead he might
meet Henry Sonnenberg, and when they met it would be the last
meeting for one or both of them.

Val Darrant had never wanted a gun battle. He had learned to use a gun just as he had learned to handle cards, or ride a horse, or swim. That he happened to be good with a gun was due to some natural dexterity, some inborn skill, and of course to practice.

He listened to the long drawn-out whistle of the train, and got up with the others and went across to the railroad platform to pick up their tickets. The entire population—all six of them—was there to see them off.

Val escorted Boston to one of the red-plush seats. "Val," she said, "I'm kind of scared. I've never ridden the steam cars before."

"It isn't that hard," Val said. "You just hook your spurs in the bellyband, grab the horn with both hands, and hang on."

He sat down in the seat beside her, while Dube sat across the aisle, facing them. Tensleep, who had held up more trains than most people had ridden on, pulled his hat down over his eyes and went to sleep.

The sun set over the prairie far ahead of them, the night came down, the stars appeared, the whistle echoed across the lonely buffalo lands. The coach rocked pleasantly, and they slept.

# TWENTY-TWO

Prince Pavel was tall and straight, and the scars served to add a somewhat romantic and piratical aspect to his otherwise cold features. Born in St. Petersburg, he had visited the estate from which he drew his income on only three occasions, all of which he remembered with distaste.

His father had been involved in the reform movement of Tsar Alexander II, but father and son had little in common, and disagreed violently on the subject. Pavel had spent most of his life outside of Russia, and like many other Russians of this period who were of the nobility, he spoke French almost exclusively.

Prince Pavel's inheritance was sufficient had he been content to devote part of his time to his estates, and had he not become an obsessive gambler. Unfortunately for him, he had utmost belief in his skill with cards, a faith that was unwarranted.

Moreover, the reform movements of Alexander II had left the nobility politically emasculated; and Pavel, although he served briefly in the cavalry, had no taste for the military life. By one means or another he contrived to maintain himself in the style he preferred, but this had grown increasingly difficult, and nothing remained but to obtain an income somehow, or return to his estates to live the life of a provincial, and to Prince Pavel this was a fate worse than death.

Myra Fossett had opened a way. Where it might lead he had no idea, but a still young woman, worth millions, was a chance not be missed. And for the other barrel of his gun, there was the possibility of a rich marriage for Louise.

Pavel's belief in his own ability with women was equaled only by his contempt for them. Robert Fleury had warned him about Myra Fossett, but the warning merely amused him. If she had that much money, and needed him for some purpose, he intended to have some of that money. Americans, he had heard, were awed by titles, and he was prepared to awe them some more.

"Be careful, cousin," Louise warned him. "This Myra Fossett may cost you more than you can afford to pay."

For the meeting Prince Pavel wore his dress uniform, and the orders on his chest presented an impressive array, especially to someone who did not know what they meant. Confident as he was, he was embarrassed by his position. He needed money, and in a very real way this might be his last chance.

The library was dimly lit, which irritated him. One cannot make a dramatic entrance into a darkened room.

He was announced, and he strode in. Myra Fossett looked at him, asked him to be seated, and returned to the papers on her desk.

He was coldly furious, and was tempted to rise and walk out, but he restrained himself. "Madame—" he began.

She looked up. "I am not called that. I am called Mrs. Fossett."

"You have invited me here to discuss business, I believe. I am here." He glanced at his watch. "I have other engagements."

Myra sat back in her chair and studied him. "Prince Pavel," she said, "you are an attractive man. If you are also intelligent you can be of assistance to me. By being of assistance to me you can make yourself a lot of money, but first we have to understand each other." Suddenly her voice changed. *"So don't give me any God-damned nonsense about other engagements!"*

He could only stare at her. Nobody had ever spoken to him like that in his life; nobody had dared to. But before he could reply, or even rise to walk out, she was speaking again.

"I said you can be useful to me. When I talk about being

useful, I mean, if you will do what I ask, useful to the tune of fifty or perhaps a hundred thousand dollars."

He looked at her. Fifty thousand . . . one hundred thousand dollars! What was that in rubles? In francs?

She moved a sheet of paper under the light on her desk. "Prince Pavel, I have here a list of your debts."

"*What!*" He started to rise. "What kind of impertinence is this?"

"Sit down," she said coldly, "and shut up, or I'll have you thrown out of here, and I'll file charges against you for attempted assault. And"—she smiled—"I will produce witnesses."

He was appalled. He moved again to stand up, then sank back. She had to be joking! This could not be happening to him.

"You are an amazing woman," he said. "Just what was it you had in mind?"

Even as he spoke, he was playing for time. He had to get out of here, he had to go somewhere and have a drink, he had to think this over.

She took up the sheet from her desk and handed it to him. It was, indeed, what she had said—a list of his debts. And they were all there, some even that he had forgotten about, and it came to a very ugly sum. In fact, there were the names of a dozen men there who would sue him immediately if they dreamed he owed as much as this list showed.

"It is rather complete," he admitted, "but I still do not understand what you want of me."

"We are short of princes this season," Myra said, "and the last one was pot-bellied, and his beard smelled of tobacco . . . cheap tobacco. There are a lot of people in this town, people otherwise quite intelligent, who are impressed by titles. I brought you over here to impress them."

Before he could speak, she shook her head. "I am not a social climber, Prince Pavel. Not, at least, in the sense you might think. I am interested in money. Many of the men who own industries or businesses with whom I have no contact are people I do not meet socially. I need to know those people, and I know which ones I want to know, and I know what to do about it when I know them. And that is where you come in."

"Yes?"

"I shall give a party to introduce you. I shall see that there is much in the public press about you, and everyone will come, including the men I wish to meet. Their wives are to come also, and we will in turn be invited to their homes. You can open doors for me that I cannot open by myself."

"And you will pay me for this?"

There was contempt in his tone, but Myra ignored it. She could afford to ignore it because she knew so much more of what was going to happen than he did.

"I will provide expense money," she said quietly, "up to a point. Beyond that point you will have your commissions. I shall require your services for ninety days, no more, no less. If I have not done what I wish to do in that length of time it would be of no use to try any longer. I am prepared to give you five per cent on every deal I make through the meetings I arrange at the affairs where we go in company, or to which your name gives me access. And I will give you my word that such commissions will total not less than fifty thousand dollars, and perhaps several times that."

He searched for the flaw, and could see none. He had merely to pose as this woman's friend . . . the only flaw he could see was the woman herself. She was too cold, too hard—and, he told himself, she was not a lady.

"I might decide to leave," he said. "I might decide simply to take your expense money and go back to Europe."

He looked at her to see what effect that had, but she merely shrugged. "Don't be a fool. If you try that with me you'll carry worse scars then you got from Will Reilly."

His face went white. He felt as if he had been struck in the stomach.

"You were lucky that he only whipped you," Myra said, "obviously you had no idea what kind of a man he was. Will Reilly had killed seven men in gun battles before he ever went to Europe. And they were tough men.

"Of course," she added, "that doesn't count Indians. He survived a dozen Indian fights. I know of some very tough men who would sooner tackle a she grizzly with cubs than Will Reilly."

He was silent at first, hating every word she had said, but then he had his triumph. "You are right. I did know nothing of him." He paused, then added ever so gently, "He is dead now, I believe?"

"You should know. You arranged for his killing. Of course, you had more money then than now. Avery Simpson found the right men for you, didn't he? I wonder if you know the sequel?"

"What sequel?"

"Two of the men who killed Will Reilly are dead . . . There were three."

He stared at her. This woman must be the devil in person. Did she know everything?

"That's another reason," she said, smiling slightly, "why you had better be a nice boy. Avery Simpson, in turn for a lighter sentence, could give evidence against you. And they hang men for murder in this country."

"I think," he said, "you do not understand my position. In my own country—"

"But you are not in your country," Myra interrupted, "and you will find little sympathy here. On the other hand, since we like titles over here, and with those scars and all those medals—oh, don't worry! I'll not tell anybody how you got the scars—that you were horsewhipped by a gambler."

She looked at him, still smiling. "And you may even find it amusing here. The women will idolize you, especially the older ones, or those with daughters who are single. You can make a lot of money; and if you are interested you might marry one of the daughters and get a substantial settlement."

Pavel's mind was reaching for a solution that would save him, but he was realizing that there was none. From now on, until he had money enough to escape from this situation, he was practically a prisoner.

She was hard—he admired her for that even while resenting it that any woman could outgeneral him. He was, he admitted, a little afraid of her. She had told him a good deal. She had, as these Americans would say, "laid it on the line," but what worried him were the things she had not told him, the further plans she preferred to keep to herself.

"I shall need money," he said, "as long as we are talking money. If this is to be your operation, it is only correct that you should finance it."

"Of course." She opened a drawer and took out a packet of bills. "There are five thousand dollars."

Then she said, "There is to be a performance at the opera tonight. We will go . . . You and your cousin are to be house guests of mine. You are to accept no invitations that do not include me; however, I doubt if anyone would go to that extreme.

"If anyone inquires as to how we met, say simply that we have mutual friends." She took another list from a desk drawer. "I want you to memorize these names. The three men on the left are the men with whom I wish to do business. They operate on a very large scale, they make excellent profits, and no outsider has ever participated in their operations.

"The names on the right are those of men who belong to clubs to which the men on the left also belong. They are occasional associates of yachting, gambling, hunting, and at social events. Any one of those on the right might introduce you to those on the left.

"Don't gamble with them. They are very shrewd, tough gamblers, and any one of them can win or lose enough in an evening to support you for a year—I mean that—and there is no sentiment in their gambling. It is all-out war.

"If I succeed in what I have planned," she added, "your share might even come to a quarter of a million dollars. You could return to Europe a modestly wealthy man."

"It seems simple enough," he said at last. "Those people will be at the opera?"

"They will. They will see you, and they will be curious. I shall see that they know who you are. The rest will follow."

He stood up now. "And my cousin, the Princess Louise?" he asked.

Myra got to her feet also. She was almost as tall as he. "She need know nothing of all this. You have some land in Siberia, I believe?"

He was no longer surprised, but he had almost forgotten that land himself.

"You can tell her I am interested in hydraulic mining, and wanted to discuss a deal whereby one of my companies would dredge for gold there. In fact, you can mention this to anyone, if you like. The people with whom we are concerned know that I am a business woman."

"These arrangements . . . they will be here? In New York?"

"Yes." She hesitated. "There is a possibility we may have to travel to San Francisco. One of the men in whom I am most interested lives there."

When Prince Pavel was out on the street he stood on the curb for a moment, waiting for the carriage to come around.

Ninety days, she had said. Three months—and then a rich man. He doubted many things about Myra Fossett, but he did not doubt the genuineness of her intentions. She wanted to make money and she would; and after all, was not that what he came over for?

# TWENTY-THREE

The Windsor, in Denver, opened in June of 1880, was the height of elegance, with three hundred rooms and sixty bath-tubs, gaslights, and Brussels carpets. The backbone of its business was furnished by mining men and cattlemen, the latter coming from half a dozen states, for Denver was considered by many to be the only city worth visiting between Chicago and San Francisco.

Denver had the name of being a wide-open sporting town, but Valentine Darrant had no desire to gamble or to visit any of the tough joints on Blake or Holliday streets. He was in town on business, and he was wary of trouble.

It was a gun-toting town, but the guns were usually kept out of sight, worn in the waistband or elsewhere not visible to the immediate glance. Bat Masterson was in town, and so was Doc Holliday. They were only two of the best-known of the forty or fifty known gun-handlers in town.

Val was in his room, dressed in a gray suit, with black tie. His black hat lay on the bed. Dube came in, uneasy in his store-bought clothes.

"Where you goin' to meet this gent?" he asked.

"Peck? He should be here now . . . In Denver, I mean. He was coming down from Empire to meet me here."

"He the man you left your money with?"

"His father, actually."

"Lot of eastern folks down in the lobby. Seems like some big mining deal is about to be pulled off. You know anything about it?"

"No."

"Well, those eastern folks do. Come up all of a sudden, they say, and there's a scramble on."

Val was concerned only with Peck. Once their business was completed, he could relax and show Boston some of the town. Dube and Tensleep probably had plans of their own, but there were several places in Denver noted for their good food. Although he had not been in the city for several years, he remembered the City Hotel where Charles Geleichman was chef, he who had been chef for the King of Denmark, or so it was said. There was also Charpiot's.

He was combing his hair before the mirror and debating whether he should wake Boston, if she was not awake, when there was a sudden tap on his door.

His pistol lay on the table, and habit made him pick it up as he moved to the door. Opening it, the gun concealed but ready, he was surprised to see Stephen Bricker standing there.

"Val!" Bricker stepped in quickly and closed the door. "Have you heard the news?"

"What news?"

Bricker glanced at the pistol. "Thank God, you're armed!"

Bricker was older, a little heavier, but still a fine-looking man. He looked at the lean, powerful-shouldered young man before him with pleasure. The boy he had known had become a man.

"Val, we've been trying to get hold of you for weeks! Peck told me what he believed was happening, and I did a little discreet investigating, and whether you like it or not you are right in the middle of one of the biggest railroad-mining fights this country has ever seen!"

"How could that be?"

"Look," Bricker explained, "when you were a youngster you left some money with Peck, senior, to be invested. Am I right?"

"Of course. It wasn't much, but—"

"Val, Peck turned that money over to a banker and he and his son have since acted in a sort of unofficial supervisory capacity.

Right at the beginning they bought a piece of some mining claims—the discoverer needed money—and then because there seemed to be an effort developing to close off access to the upper end of the canyon, they went down below and bought about half a mile of the canyon right where it opened out. Today that half-mile of canyon is worth almost any price you want to ask for it."

"What's happened?"

"The railroads want it. They want a branch line in there to bring out coal. Nobody dreamed that stretch was anything but government or state land, because it was just about useless for anything but a right-of-way. We hoped to let you know what was happening before anyone talked you into signing anything."

Val chuckled. "Me? Mr. Bricker, you know I never sign anything. Will Reilly was a born skeptic, and I guess I developed into one."

Steve Bricker lit the cigar he had in his fingers. "Forgive me, Val, if I talk like a Dutch uncle. We've been friends for a good long time now, and I tell you you are going to have to move fast, very fast."

"Why? There seems to be something going on here that I don't know about."

"Val, if anything should happen to you, who would inherit?"

Val realized, with a kind of startled wonder, that he had never given the idea a moment's thought. Will Reilly had been his family, and they had been uniquely close, drifting continually as they had, and having no one but themselves to consider.

"I haven't given the idea much thought. Of course I'd want it to go to Boston."

"But you have not made a will? Is that right?"

"No, but—"

"Then who would inherit, Val? Have you stopped to think of that? Who would suddenly find herself the owner of the hottest piece of property in the country? And believe me, Val, it is worth millions."

"Myra . . ."

Myra was next of kin. If anything happened to him, whatever he had at the time would be hers.

"Does she know about this?" he asked.

"*Know* about it? Why do you think she's coming to Colorado?"

"Myra is coming out here? She told Van once she would never come west again . . . never as long as she lived!"

Bricker brushed the idea away with a gesture. "When she said that she didn't know how much returning could mean; and after all, she won't be here more than a day or two. If the Sante Fe doesn't get that stretch, the Denver & Rio Grande will. She and that prince of hers can arrive here one day and go back the next if she likes."

Val thrust his pistol into his waistband and put on his coat. "Have you had breakfast?" he asked.

"I had some coffee. I can't spare the time now, Val, but promise me you'll keep your eyes open."

They went down to the lobby together and Val went in to breakfast. His thoughts were confused, and he needed to think clearly, to decide what he wanted to do. If Myra was coming west, the chances were good that they would meet. The idea of meeting her after so many years was disturbing. Yet, why should it be? To him she was a stranger, a woman whose wish it had been to have him left to die in the snow.

What Bricker had said was right, of course, and he should have a will drawn up at the earliest possible moment. He wanted nothing of his ever to fall into the greedy hands of Myra Fossett.

He ordered breakfast and sat staring out of the window, wondering what his next move should be. He should prepare a list of his assets, and then find a reputable attorney. He might draw up the will himself, but he was not experienced in such things, and he wanted a will that was fool-proof.

He considered his situation. If possible, he wished to avoid trouble. Nothing was to be gained by meeting Myra. What he ought to do was to get the best offers of the companies concerned and settle quickly.

Once the deal was made, the reason for Myra's presence here would be gone, and he himself need stay no longer. He should have asked Bricker just who the men were with whom he should deal; it was likely that some were living right here in the hotel.

Of course, even if Myra were kept out of the right-of-way deal she would still be his heir, in the event of his death. There was a solution to that which would not require the writing of a will. He could marry Boston.

As he sat there the door of the dining room suddenly opened

and Dube came in. He looked exactly what he was, a cowhand in off the range, and Denver knew that a cowhand in run-down heels and faded Levis might be a grub-line rider, but that on the other hand he might own five thousand head of stock.

Dube glanced around the room, where only a few people were eating at this early hour. Then he went across to Val and dropped into the chair opposite him. "You packin' iron, boy?" he asked.

"Yes."

"Well, watch yourself. Sonnenberg is in town. I run into him down on Blake Street, and he's walkin' wide and mean. He's a big one, ain't he?"

"He's pretty big, all right. Weighs about two-fifty, I'd say, and he carries no more fat than a jay-bird."

Val let the waiter fill his cup again, and then he said, "Dube, I want to marry Boston."

Dube grinned at him. "You figger that's news? If it's news to you, it sure ain't to Boston."

"I haven't said a word to her. Not exactly, that is. I think she understands, all right, but the point is, it may have to be here . . . now . . . if she'll have me."

"Why so sudden? Pa an' them would sure be put out."

Val explained, as briefly as possible, and then he added, "I am going to make a will, but that won't be enough, if I know Myra Fossett. She would try every trick in the book to break the will, and as she's a blood relative she could probably do it."

"Can she prove she's your kin?"

"There may be records up north, but anyway she would find a way."

Dube was quiet, and looked his name, which was Dubious. After a while he said, "Val, why don't you just cut and run?"

When Val started to protest, Dube interrupted. "Look, you got this friend Bricker. Now, if he ain't in on the deal himself, he knows who is. Let him handle it for you, subject to your okay, and you just duck out. You don't check out of the hotel, you just walk out one evenin' in your fancy duds, but you have yourself a horse staked out, and you run. You make it to Leadville or Walsenberg, or even Durango. Then you just hide out there under another name, an' let this Bricker handle it for you. Me and Tensleep could keep an eye on 'em for you, and we could keep you in touch.

"It ain't that I'm agin' you marryin' Boston," he went on. "That's up to her, but we folks set a sight of store by marryin', and Pa an' Bets, they'd be almighty put out if you an' Boston tied the knot without them handy. I mean it."

Val stared out the window at the street, considering the idea. It appealed to him, and that disturbed him. Would he be avoiding responsibility if he ran? Did he want to dodge the issue? Would it be an act of cowardice?

Mulling over the idea, he had to admit Dube had come up with a solution. If he stayed in town there was every likelihood there would be violence. He was not prepared to guess what Myra might plan or attempt; but he was sure that sooner or later he would come face to face with Sonnenberg, which would surely mean a gun battle.

Denver was no longer the frontier town it had been, but a city with law and order, and some very definite ideas about men shooting at each other to settle personal quarrels.

To leave would seem to be the wise thing. Stephen Bricker was a trustworthy man, but there were ways in which Val could learn of the prices to be offered other than through Bricker.

"Maybe you've got the right idea," he agreed, "and if I can bring this thing to a head by nightfall, I'll do it."

"All right," Dube said, "I'll stake out a horse for you."

Dube got to his feet and Val stood up with him. He had eaten almost nothing, and his food had grown cold as he talked with Dube.

Suddenly the door opened again and Boston came in, but a different Boston, a Boston he had never seen before.

# TWENTY-FOUR

V al was startled, and so was Dube. Val could only stare.
Her black, wild hair had been drawn back and parted in the
center; the corwn of her head was covered with curls and there
were ringlets down the nape of her neck. The dress she wore was
floor length, cut almost like a coat, of black wool rep over black
and gray striped satin. The black skirt was draped back over a
bustle to expose the pleated flounces of the silk skirt underneath.
The waistcoat front was held by a strap of mother-of-pearl buttons. The sleeves were tight, with a silk facing.

She started toward them, and they stood, while Boston walked
up to them and held out her hand, obviously pleased at the effect
she was creating—not only on them, but on the entire room.

Val held her chair for her, and when she was seated he sat
down abruptly. Dube hesitated, then sat down.

"Boss, where did you get that riggin'? I never seen the like!"

"I bought it." Her chin went up. "You aren't the only one who
can maverick calves, Dube Bucklin! And this isn't all," she added.
"I've got more! I've got six new dresses, just like the ones they
wear in Paris and Vienna!"

"You're beautiful!" Val exclaimed. "Boston, I want to marry
you! I've just been talking to Dube about it."

"Dube! What's he got to say about what I do?" She gave him a straight, frank look from her dark eyes. "When you ask me that, don't be looking at the girl in this dress. There's a lot more to a girl than clothes."

"I'm quite sure of that," Val said.

She flushed slightly. "I mean, I'm not just a girl who is wearing these clothes, nor just a girl who can rope and brand calves, either."

"At this moment," Val said honestly, "you look as if you'd stepped right out of a fashionable shop in Vienna. Where did you get the dress?"

"Mel Winslow measured me, and she sent the measurements to a lady right here in Denver. She sews for Mel. She came over from Austria about two years ago and her husband was killed in a mine accident, so she's had to sew."

Boston turned to him eagerly. "Oh, Val! Do I look all right? I mean . . . I never wore clothes like these before!"

"You look as if you had never worn anything else," he said. "If I hadn't been in love with you for a long time, I'd fall in love with you right now. I couldn't help myself."

She laughed at him. "That's blarney—I know it when I hear it. But Val! There's the most beautiful woman here! I just met her in the lobby. There she is now!"

It was Myra . . . and she was both beautiful and smartly gotten up, and the tall man beside her was an impossibly handsome man but for the three scars. . . .

Val was suddenly cold.

"Val?" Boston caught his sleeve. She looked frightened. "Val, what's the matter?"

"That's my mother," he said quietly, "and the man with her is Prince Pavel Pavelovitch."

He sat very still, looking at Myra. She was, he admitted, a very striking-looking woman. She was slender and tall, and looked not within ten years of what her age must be. When she looked across the room at them, her eyes met his.

This was his mother, but she was also the woman who had him taken out to be left to die in the snow. This was a woman that even such a man as Tensleep feared. If all he had heard was true, men had died at her hand, yet looking at her now as she came toward them it was hard to believe.

For only a moment she hesitated. Then she walked straight to him and held out her hand. "Val! You've grown into a very handsome man."

She turned slightly. "Val, I want you to meet Prince Pavel Pavelovitch. Pavel, this is my son, Valentine Darrant."

"How do you do?" Val's tone was cold, and the Prince looked at him in surprise.

Val turned and introduced Boston . . . Dube had disappeared.

"May we join you?" Myra asked, and she seated herself without waiting for any word from Val.

Myra ordered tea, as did Prince Pavel. As he was still hungry, Val ordered something more, wondering how he could escape from this situation. Only Boston seemed completely at ease. She chatted gaily with the Prince about Denver, the mountains, and the hotel. When the tea arrived she poured for them all.

During a momentary lull Myra said, "You're in a very fortunate position, Valentine. They tell me that you own the land needed for the right-of-way."

He shrugged. "It isn't important."

"But it is. If the situation is handled correctly, it can make you independent . . . even a wealthy young man."

"I really don't need very much. I prefer the simple life, except" —he paused—"that I do like to play cards occasionally."

Boston gave him a quick glance. This was something new.

"We all like to risk a little something occasionally," Prince Pavel said.

"And in doing so, sometimes one risks too much," Val replied. "Sometimes one underestimates those with whom he plays."

"I dare say," Pavel said, and he looked thoughtfully at Val. Why did the fellow look so damned familiar? And what had he meant by that, exactly?

"You have a chance for a real coup, Valentine," Myra said, "and if you'd like, I'd enjoy helping you. After all, you are my son."

"It must be nice," Boston said brightly, "to discover that you have a son."

Myra glanced at Boston without expression, then she said to Val, "Or if you don't want to bother with the details, I would buy you out for a hundred thousand dollars—in cash."

"It is a nice sum," Val agreed.

"Then it is a deal?"

"I only said it was a nice sum, and don't worry about the business part of it, Myra." He discovered he could not call her mother. "I served an apprenticeship with Stephen Bricker."

"I heard you had been admitted to the bar," she commented.

Myra was searching for an opening. She had not believed it would be easy, but she would have expected her son to react in a rather different way. Val seemed in no way impressed.

"I might be able to make a better price," she suggested.

Val gave her a direct look. "You would have to, Myra. Many times better. I haven't discovered yet what that property is worth, but I do know it is worth in excess of a million dollars."

Before she could reply, Val turned his attention to Pavel. "Are you staying with us long, Prince Pavel? The hunting in Colorado is excellent."

"Mrs. Fossett and I have some business to take care of," he said. "I doubt if I shall remain longer than necessary. In any event, I am not a hunter."

"But there are times when hunting can be quite interesting, especially when circumstances contrive to bring the game to the hunter."

Pavel was puzzled. What exactly did he mean, this American? He asked the question.

Val shrugged. "With deer, it is a bit of cloth on a stick that will bring them near. With men, I suspect that money would do it. Have you ever played poker, Prince?"

"Very often. In fact, it is a favorite game of mine. I learned at Salzburg from an Englishman who had lived in America. It is an exciting game."

"Then you should enjoy Colorado. They play an exciting brand of poker here."

Myra was puzzled even more than Pavel. The conversation seemed to have no point, yet she seemed to detect an undercurrent of hidden meanings. But that was absurd. It would have been directed at her, not at Pavel.

There had been little chance to utilize the Prince's name in New York. They had appeared at the opera, and they had attracted attention, just as she wished. Several invitations had arrived, at least one of them from one of the men close to those with whom she wished to do business. It was from this man that she received the first inkling of something impending in Colorado.

To travel in the West was the last thing she wanted, but when she discovered that it was her own son who held the property needed for the right-of-way, she decided to accept the risk of recognition in that part of the country. After all, years had passed, and she knew that she had changed. When she had worked on the Line she had been considerably plumper. Men who paid for their women liked them well rounded and full. She was fifteen pounds lighter now . . . everything was different.

It would be only a few days—a meeting with Val, a quick deal, and then a return to the East. The Prince would serve as wonderful window-dressing, and there was also the possibility that he would prove valuable in any subsequent negotiations. Ostensibly, she would be showing the West to the Prince and his cousin.

She had no doubts about success. Even if Val was skeptical of her good wishes, she could always appeal to sentiment. And if all else failed there was always the other way, and whatever he had would automatically become hers.

She was not without contacts in the Rocky Mountain area, though none of them knew who she was, but she had arranged to gather information on mines, railroads, and cattle through them, and to make it worth their whole.

Myra studied Val's face as he talked to Pavel. Was there any of her in him? If so, she could not see it. He looked like a taller, more handsome version of his father; and something, she had to admit it, of her own father was in his jawline and nose.

She supposed she should feel proud of him, but she did not. Suddenly she felt a pang of jealousy. It was Will Reilly who could feel proud, for after all, Will had raised him, and he seemed to have done quite a job of it.

Val had mentioned poker . . . was he a gambler, too? But her Pinkerton reports had made no mention of that, and it was something they would not have missed. So if he gambled at all, it was very little. No doubt Will had tried to keep him away from all that.

"If we could talk alone, Val," she suggested.

"He has promised to go shopping with me," Boston said.

Myra was growing irritated. The girl annoyed her, and she sensed a like feeling from Boston. "Please"—there was just an edge of sarcasm in her tone—"he can buy you pretty dresses any time. This is business. It is important."

"You misunderstand," Boston said very politely. "I buy my own dresses, with my own money. Some girls do, you know."

Myra stiffened as if she had been slapped. For an instant everything within her was still. Then she felt a shock of cold anger. She started to retort, but cut the words off and forced herself to speak with care.

"That's very nice, I'm sure." Then she added, "I suppose you have your own ways of earning money."

"Yes," Boston said, smiling, "I mavericked calves, if you want to know, out on the range with a branding iron and a rope."

Myra looked at her in frank disbelief, and Pavel said, "I don't understand . . . what is it . . . maverick?"

"It's a Texas name for an unbranded calf, or whatever," Val said. "It got its name from a Texan who didn't take the time to have his cattle branded, and when he sold the herd, riders moved in and branded every one as one of Maverick's.

"There are a lot of loose, unbranded cattle around, and although the practice is beginning to be frowned on, it is still the fastest way to build an outfit of your own. Boston is one of the best riders, male or female, I've ever seen, and she's good with a rope and fast with a branding iron, so she has done very well."

"It is difficult to believe," the Prince said. "You do not seem the type, somehow."

"We all work in this country," Val replied, "and Boston rides like one of your Cossacks."

Myra sat waiting, fighting down her impatience. The conversation kept wandering away from the subject, and this room would be filling with people at any moment now. Already a few had come in, and she was expecting Masters and Cope.

"We must settle this, Val. If you are going to sell the property, why not sell it to me, your mother?"

Val stifled the sharp answer that came to his lips. "I shall have to think about it. In the meantime, you might decide what is your best offer and make it to Bricker. . . . But don't waste time returning to the fact that you are my mother. I haven't had much of an example of that, Myra."

He got to his feet. "Prince Pavel, if you are interested, there are usually some good poker games around. Don't bother with Blake Street. You can find a good one right here in the hotel."

Myra sat very still as he walked out, but her mind was working rapidly. She was going to lose this deal unless she acted swiftly. There was also the matter of the box . . . she had forgotten about the box temporarily.

Had Val received it? If not, he must be prevented from receiving it. His room must be searched, and then she must get word to Sonnenberg. She had come west so quickly there had been no chance of waiting to learn if they had obtained the box.

"Your son," Pavel asked, "has he ever been to Europe?"

Her thoughts were elsewhere. "Europe? Of course not. How could he have been in Europe?"

Myra was frustrated and bitter. The breakfast conversation had been inconclusive, to say the least. Valentine seemed in no mood to do business with her, and she dreaded his receiving an offer from Cope or Masters.

First the box. She must have it, or at least examine its contents. . . . And then Val. For Myra Cord, now Fossett, killing had come to be simply a solution to a problem.

She got up, waited for Pavel to receive his change, and then left him in the lobby, and went to her room.

She had already taken care to find out which room was occupied by her son.

# TWENTY-FIVE

In the lobby, Val paused and took Boston's hand. "I was proud of you, but be careful. She's not like ordinary people, and she has been pretty successful in what she has done. By now she probably believes that she cannot make a mistake.

"Her entire life has been a struggle for money, for power. She doesn't have to have a reason for killing other than that you are in the way, and I am sure she feels you are, as I am."

"I'm not afraid of her, Val. I think she is more afraid of me."

"I've got to find Bricker, and tonight I must have a meeting with Pavel."

"What are you going to do?"

He hesitated. "Boston, I am going to play poker. I am going to play for blood, using everything I have except the ranch. I am going to twist him and break him."

"Can you do it?"

"I've got to try. He had Uncle Will murdered, but there is no way I can prove that here and now, so this will be my way to make him pay."

"All right, Val. Only be careful. I do not like him."

Dube met him outside. "Val, you better do as we planned. You grab yourself a horse and light a shuck."

"I've got to see Bricker, then Pavel."

"I looked him over. I don't care for that Russky. I've known some good ones, but he's got a mean look under all of that polish."

"I can't go now. I've got to stay in town."

"Val, don't you do it. Light out for Durango. You've got business there, anyway. Make 'em follow you—I mean those gents who want you to sell to 'em. But you get away from that woman . . . and from Sonnenberg. I meant to tell you about him. He ain't alone. He's got three men trailin' him around. One's a kind of crazy galoot they call Tom, then there's—"

"Tom?" His thoughts went back to the cold winter day when Will and he had driven up to that lonely hide-out in the snow, the hide-out where Tensleep, Sonnenberg, and . . . wasn't the other one named Tom?

"That's what they called him. Odd-lookin' crittur. Eyes never stop, one shoulder hangin' lower than the other, sunken chest, hollow cheeks."

"Who are the others?"

"There's a breed called Pagosa, and a long, lean slat of a man named Marcus Kiley. They're bad ones."

Dube was silent for a moment. "Well, I told you. That's all I can do except to have that horse where I planned. It will be there, come midnight, but you do whatever you're of a mind to."

By noon Val had located Stephen Bricker, and had made arrangements with him to open negotiations with Cope, Masters, or anyone else interested in the right-of-way.

When Val emerged on the street he paused to take stock of the street and of the windows all around before moving on. He was wary, and he liked the feel of the Smith & Wesson in his waistband. Every bit of common sense he had told him he should do just what Dube had wanted him to do . . . leave town, leave fast, and by back trails.

He had never been a man who hunted trouble, and as he had not faced Sonnenberg, nobody could ever call him a coward for quietly dropping out of sight. Moreover, he had business in Durango and the vicinity. But the memory of Pavel and how he had bought the death of Will Reilly held him in Denver.

There would be a big poker game in the Windsor that night, and if Pavel entered, Val would. And from that moment on, it would be war.

Myra had wasted no time. Val's room was not far from her own. And she had long possessed five skeleton keys that would open almost any lock. If seen by anyone in the hotel, she had only to say what was true—that she was going to her son's room.

She opened the door and stepped inside quickly. She stood still for a moment, sweeping the room with her eyes.

There were half a dozen suits in the closet, shirts and underwear in the drawers. Her son, she decided, after a glance at the clothes, had good taste. She went through the room working with the skill of a professional. If the box was in the room at all, she was quite sure it would be hidden, and she knew the places where things are usually hidden. She had hidden things many times herself, and she had a devious mind, given to quick apprehension of trick or device. Within a matter of minutes, she was sure the box was not in the room.

Where, then, was it?

She had had no word from Sonnenberg; if he had the box he had not notified her. If he had not been able to get it, the box must be at the bank, in which case the bank must be entered and the box obtained. This part of the affair was in Sonnenberg's hands.

But what if Val already had the box? If not in his room, where was it likely to be?

In the room of Boston Bucklin.

Myra paused, considering that. To enter the girl's room was dangerous, too dangerous unless she definitely knew the box was there and the girl was out.

The solution, then, was to get into the room by invitation, and then look around. If she could not see the box, she could, at least, eliminate all but a few hiding places, which could be examined later.

What her son would do with that box and its contents she had no idea, but without it nobody could do anything. Men had died, and by now worms had eaten them, and only Van could name dates and places. Only Van could know or guess where the bodies were buried.

She was positive, judging by his attitude, that he had not yet obtained the box—at least, he had not opened it and studied the contents. She must move quickly.

She listened a moment at the door, heard nothing, then slipped out. As she pulled the door shut behind her she thought she heard the click of a closing door an instant before Val's closed.

Quickly, she glanced around, but the hall was empty. She walked back to her room, fumbled with the lock long enough for a quick look around again, then stepped inside.

There were five doors along that hall. Surely, Boston's room was one of them. Had she been watching? Had Boston seen her leaving Val's room? Or was it that cowhand brother of hers who had come to Denver with them?

For several minutes she watched from a crack of her door, wondering if anyone would come to check Val's room, but no one did. Whoever had opened and closed the door might have been a stranger . . . or it might have been her imagination.

After a few minutes she went down to the lobby, inquired for Miss Bucklin, and learned that she was in her room. From a writing desk in the lobby Myra sent out several notes, one to Stephen Bricker, others to Cope and Masters. Another note went to a man on Blake Street.


Cheyenne Dawson did not look the way his name sounded. He should have been a cowhand or a bad man, the "bad" used in the western sense, meaning a bad man to tangle with. Cheyenne was all of that, only he made no show of being tough or mean, or good with a gun.

Cheyenne Dawson held forth in a saloon or two along Blake Street, and was known in all the less savory spots in Denver. He was a huge, sloppy man, wide in the hips, narrow in the shoulders, the tail of his shirt nearly always hanging out on one side or the other.

He had large, soulful blue eyes, was partly bald, and wore a coat that was too big, even for him. He was five inches over six feet, and was said to weigh three hundred pounds.

The years that lay behind him had covered about everything

dishonest that a man could do, but his activities usually were those that demanded the least activity. After a spell of smuggling over the border and of rustling cattle, he had decided it was easier to make a living by selling whiskey and guns to the Indians. As the country built up and the Army became more active, he decided there was too much risk in that, so he opened a saloon with a couple of barrels of "Indian" whiskey.

One day he was approached by a cattleman who was having nester trouble. Did Cheyenne know of a man who was discreet, good with a gun, and who could keep himself out of trouble?

Cheyenne did, and the man proved to be just as good as Cheyenne promised, and he also kept out of trouble. Soon Cheyenne became known as a reliable source for hired gunmen, or anyone who was needed to do anything at all, and Cheyenne got a satisfactory payment without moving more than a city block or two from one of his accustomed chairs.

For some time now Cheyenne had been getting notes, accompanied by cash, for various errands, mostly for information he acquired simply by listening, or through minor thefts.

The first time it was connected with assays on gold from a certain mining property, and after his report the property's source of eastern capital dried up. Cheyenne noted the cause and effect with considerable interest, and over the years he learned that whoever was asking for the information had considerable money, and furthermore seemed to have a wide knowledge of the West and its people.

Often when that person asked for a man to do a job, the man was asked for by name, as in the case of Henry Sonnenberg. In every case that mysterious person in the East had known exactly whom to ask for, and the person requested was the best at his job.

Cheyenne Dawson owned a part of a saloon, a part of a livery stable, and had more than a passing interest in several cribs in the red-light districts, but during the past ten years the income from that person back east had been so substantial that he had roped in, through women or drink, bookkeepers or shift bosses from various mining and railroad ventures to keep him supplied with the information he needed.

The notes that came to him were invariably written on a

typewriter, until one day he received a hastily written note in long-hand.

Interrupted in the reading of it, he had started to get up when Lila Marsh, one of the older girls, indicated the note. "Haven't seen hide nor hair of her in years. What's she want . . . a job?"

Cheyenne's scalp prickled, but he merely folded the note. "Who? Who ya talkin' about?"

"Myra Cord. I'd know that handwriting anywhere. We worked in the same house in Pioche one time . . . and again in Ogalala."

Cheyenne fished the stub of a cigar from his capacious coat pocket and lit it. "How was she?" he asked.

"Good . . . maybe the best I ever saw at taking them for money, but cold . . . all she ever cared about was money. Even her man—Van Clevern, his name was—didn't seem to mean a whole lot to her. She owned her own place in Deadwood for a while, then she sold out and I haven't heard a thing of her since."

"How old would she be then?"

Lila hesitated. That was cutting closer to her own age than she liked. "Oh, she was older than most of us! I guess she'd be forty-odd now, but she'd look good. She always kept herself well."

Cheyenne started for the door. "Are you going to bring her down here?" she asked.

"I'll think on it. I doubt it," he said.

Outside on the street, he rolled the cigar in his fat lips and considered. Of course, Lila had had only a glimpse of the handwriting and she could be wrong. On the other hand, a woman who'd been on the line would know the people she had mentioned. Cheyenne went on up the street, stuffing in his shirt-tail.

During the year that followed he had pieced together quite a dossier on Myra Cord, without any idea of how he expected to use it . . . or if he intended to.

There were a couple of rumors . . . a trail-drive foreman had sold a large herd, paid off his men and headed for the station with the bulk of the cash, some sixty thousand dollars. He dropped the comment to one of the hands that he had found himself a girl and was going to stop in Kansas City for a wild time.

He had disappeared, and investigation brought nothing to light except that he was said to have visited Myra at least twice after the herd arrived in town.

Now, nearly five years after he had received that first hand-written note he received another. Only this one was written on Windsor Hotel stationery. Not that the printed heading had been left on, for in fact it had been neatly creased and torn off, but Cheyenne Dawson knew that paper, and knew the watermark. Nobody else in town used it.

This woman then, Myra Cord or whoever, was in Denver and staying at the Windsor.

Cheyenne Dawson, like a lot of people before him, had tired of the petty day-to-day deals he was making. He wanted a big killing and retirement. This looked like it. He tucked his shirt-tail into his pants, rubbed out his cigar and put it in his coat pocket, donned his narrow-brimmed hat, and walked to the Windsor.

He leaned his heavy forearms on the desk and stared at the desk clerk from watery blue eyes. "Woman here . . . stayin' here. Wanted to buy a horse. Forgot her last name . . . Myra . . . Myra something-or-other."

"You must mean Mrs. Fossett. However, I did not know she wished to buy a horse. If you would leave your name, Mr.—?"

He shook his head. "I'll come back," he said, and padded away through the lobby. He was just going out of the door when Myra Fossett came in from the dining room.

She caught a glimpse of him, and then the clerk said, "Oh, Mrs. Fossett, I didn't know you were in the dining room. There was a man here . . . said you wished to buy a horse."

"I had thought of it," she replied. "Did he ask for me by name?"

"Well, as a matter of fact, no. He wasn't sure about your last name."

"I see. Well, thank you very much."

In her room Myra Fossett sat down quickly, for suddenly her legs were trembling. She had been a fool to come west! A triple-dyed fool!

Yet how could he have traced her? Even if she had written from here in the city . . .

Now she was in trouble, in real trouble.

# TWENTY-SIX

V al knotted his tie before the mirror. It was time to leave. He should not be going to the game, but to that horse that Dube had for him. He should be riding out of here, for his every instinct told him he was heading for trouble.

His room was somehow different. Not that anything was disturbed, but there was a vague, troubling suspicion of perfume in the air, as though a woman had been here. It was the perfume his mother wore, but no, that could not have been.

He looked at himself. It was for the first time, it seemed, that he truly saw himself as he was. He was two inches over six feet, and he weighed a hundred and ninety pounds, though he looked less. His clothes were well tailored, his general appearance perfect. Even the pistol under his waistband made no bulge.

He knew what it was—he looked like Will Reilly.

He was as tall as Will, a little heavier, and perhaps broader and heavier in the shoulders. He looked like Will and he could do a lot worse, for Will had been a handsome man. And tonight, if all went well, he could pay Will's debt to Pavel.

For it was Pavel, after all, who was to blame. Avery Simpson and Henry Sonnenberg were only tools. The man who had pointed the gun was Pavel.

Once free of that burden, he would marry Boston and they could make a life for themselves here in the West. But first there was Pavel.

Suddenly he was uneasy. He had that cold chill, that quick shudder that comes when, as the saying is, somebody has stepped on your grave.

He had the feeling that he was caught fast in a web, and the strings were drawing tighter and tighter. For an instant he felt panic, the desire to get away. He did not want to be killed, and he did not want to kill.

It was all very well to have faith in himself, and he had it. He knew he was good with a gun, but many men had died who were good with their guns. Billy was dead, and Hickok was dead . . . it could happen to anyone. There was no divine providence that would watch over him.

Yet while he was thinking these things, he was straightening his tie, buttoning his vest, and drawing it down . . . but not over his gun.

He checked the room one last time, then stepped out into the hall.

Before him, not fifty feet away along the passage walked a woman alone. He felt his mouth go dry . . . he knew that back, those shoulders, that carriage. He started to speak, then turned and went back. He unlocked his door, entered the room and rummaged among his things. He found the book where he kept it, at the bottom of his trunk. He had stored it there after he repacked his clothes in the trunk after his arrival in Denver.

Then he turned and went down to the lobby. It was early, but dinner time still. He walked into the dining room.

She sat across the room, her back toward him. He motioned to a waiter, handed him the book and a coin. "Take it to the lady," he said.

He waited, his heart pounding. He saw her take the book, and he was walking toward her when she turned.

"Val!" She held out both her hands to him. She was a beautiful, a truly beautiful woman. "Val!" she said again. "Can it be!"

For a moment she looked at him. "Val, you have become quite a man. Will would have been proud of you."

"I hope so." He seated her, then rounded the table and sat

down opposite her. "He loved you, you know. You were the only woman he ever loved."

"Thank you, Val. I believe that. I always wanted to believe that. And I loved him . . . I still do, I think."

"He was not a man it was easy to forget."

"Val, how did he die? I heard it was a shooting of some sort."

"You don't know then?" Val hesitated, but this was no time to hesitate. "He was murdered, shot down in cold blood as he walked out of a door in a town not very far from here. There were three men . . . they were paid to do it."

"*Paid?*" There was something like fear in her eyes.

"Paid through an American attorney, a cheap lawyer called Simpson . . . it wasn't even his real name."

"Who paid him, Val?"

"Who could it have been but Pavel? Avery Simpson confessed that. I am sorry, for your sake."

"You needn't be, Val. For a long time I felt sorry for him. He was always borrowing money from me, but his mother had been good to me, and I always liked her, and Pavel seemed harmless enough. When I began to see that he was using me, that he was interfering in my life . . . I tried to get rid of him, and for a few years I did.

"That was when he had money. He inherited a little, won some gambling, then lost it all. I had not seen him in a long time when he came to suggest this trip to America. I don't know why I came. Maybe I was hoping just to see where Will had lived, what his country was like."

Suddenly, she looked at him. "Val, you're not going to—"

"In a way. He is gambling tonight, I think. I am going to play in the game. I play very well. I am going to bring up the question of Will Reilly."

"Val! He will kill you—in those rages of his he is terrible!"

"I have a debt to pay. I must pay it the way Will would have done. I do not want to kill him, only to face him with it."

"Don't do it. Please."

"One of the men who actually killed him is here in town, too."

"You said there were three."

"Two of them are dead . . . I killed them in gun battles. I did not really look for them. They came to me."

He changed the subject deliberately. After a few moments, he got to his feet. "I will keep my *Faust*, if you do not mind. I have treasured it. You were very kind to a boy who was often lonely. I never saw much of women in those days, and it meant a lot to me."

"I am glad."

"Will is buried at Empire. It is a little town not far from here. When this is over I will take you there, if you wish."

The game had been in progress for at least an hour when Val arrived. Pavel was winning. He was flushed and excited, and he was pushing. Val watched the game for a few minutes. Stephen Bricker was one of the men, the only one except Pavel whom he knew.

Bricker nodded when he entered, and continued playing. After a while he looked up. "Would you like to sit in, Val? That is, if these gentlemen do not mind."

Bricker introduced them. "Valentine Darrant—Jim Cope, Quentin Masters, Clyde Murray. I believe you know Prince Pavel."

Val seated himself and received his cards. Cope glanced at him. "Darrant? Are you the man we're looking for?"

Val smiled. "That's a dangerous way to put it, out here, but I guess I am if you're referring to the right-of-way business."

They played, and did not talk then about the right-of-way. Val's cards were nothing to speak of, but he passed or went along for the sake of staying in the game and seeing how the others played.

He lost fifty . . . a hundred . . . thirty . . . He won a little, lost a little more. Then bucking Pavel, he drew two pair and on a hunch stayed with it and added a third queen for a full house. He won sixty dollars, then won again.

"You have been doing all right," he commented to Pavel. "You're a lucky man."

Pavel shrugged. "Sometimes."

An hour later Pavel was sweating. His run of luck had failed him and he lost three hands running, at least two of them when he was obviously beaten.

Bricker had been losing, Masters had won a little. Murray cashed in and left the game. Cope was watching Val with some curiosity and a little puzzlement. He had become aware that Val was playing against Pavel, that it was only when Pavel was raising that Val pushed his luck.

Val was taking his time. He had played poker since he was a child, and he had been coached by a master, and had watched many games. Moreover, he knew that Pavel was a compulsive gambler as well as a complete egotist.

He picked up his hand to find three nines. Pavel was staring at his hand, trying to compose himself. Pavel took one card, Cope threw in his hand, and Masters took two cards. Val hesitated, seemed uncertain, then asked for two cards. He drew a trey and a nine . . . four nines.

Pavel was raising, Masters stayed, and Val saw Pavel's raise and boosted it five hundred dollars. Masters threw in his cards, Pavel saw the five hundred and raised another five.

"It's been a long time, Pavel," Val said, "but for old times' sake I am going to raise you one thousand dollars . . . if you aren't afraid."

Pavel stared at him, his irritation obvious. "What do you mean . . . afraid?" He counted one thousand dollars from the stack before him and shoved it to the middle of the table.

Val glanced at him. "Are you going to boost the price a little bit? You must have six or seven hundred on the table."

Pavel stared at him. "All right, if you have money to lose." He shoved the money to the middle of the table. When Pavel spread out his cards he had a full house—aces and kings.

Val took his time placing his four nines on the table; then he reached for the pot.

Pavel flushed as he watched the money drawn in and stacked. "I have had enough," he said lurching to his feet.

Val remained where he was. "As I said a few minutes ago, it has been a long time."

"What does that mean?"

"You don't lose well," Val said, "but you never did." Val tucked a sheaf of bills into his inside coat pocket, and gathered the coins into a sack. "I think you had better get on the train and go back to New York, and from there back to Russia, and be glad you're getting there alive."

"I don't know what you mean," Pavel said. "Are you trying to quarrel with me?"

"You aren't a man with whom one quarrels," Val replied. "You hire your killing done."

Several other men had come into the room, and all were standing about, watching.

Pavel's face had turned pale. "That's a lie!"

"I could kill you for that," Val said, "but I don't intend to. I think you will suffer more from staying alive."

He pushed back in his chair. "You gentlemen deserve an explanation," he said. "The Prince here does not remember me. I was only a child then." Coolly, in a quiet voice he told them the story. The attempted whipping, the escape over the mountains, the final murder of Will Reilly.

"Three men performed that killing, using shotguns on an unsuspecting man. I should kill him, but I decided that taking his money would cause him more grief."

He stood up. "Gentlemen, I understand that you may wish to talk business with me. Tomorrow morning I am leaving for the new town of Durango. If you still wish to talk business, I can see you there."

Deliberately they walked out, and no one looked back at Pavel. He stood there for several minutes, his face gray and sick-looking. Then he went out into the night and started for the hotel. Why had he been such a fool? He might have known he would lose, lose to that, that . . .

He stumbled once, then walked on. When he reached the hotel he went at once to his room. He had six dollars and a handful of rubles.

Myra was not in, and he went to Louise's room. There was no one there, but a maid walking along the hall paused and said, "The lady that was in that room left about an hour ago. She said she was going to Empire or Georgetown or somewhere."

Louise *gone?* He couldn't believe it, but at the desk they confirmed what the maid had said.

There was nothing to do but wait for Myra. After a few minutes Masters entered and walked past him, ignoring him completely. Pavel swore, but he remained where he was.

He had to get out of this town. He had to get back east. He began to pace back and forth, then went outside. If only Myra . . . but suddenly he became uneasy. If Myra knew, if she even guessed, he would no longer have any bargaining position with her at all. The first moment he could get he had best cable for some cash . . . cable to whom? He owed everybody.

Cheyenne Dawson was sitting at his usual table when Henry Sonnenberg strode through the door. "Hi, Henry! Come an' set!"

Sonnenberg strolled across the room and dropped down at the table. "Where's the bar-keep?"

"I let him off. Things're slack today. Here"—Dawson pushed the bottle toward him—"this here's better'n bar whiskey."

When Sonnenberg had filled a glass, Dawson spoke up. "Hank, I been keepin' an ear to the ground. There's more goin' on around here than a body would figure. Me, I got me an idee how we can make some money."

"I got a job."

"Now, see here. You been gettin' work through me. Don't you figure you should ought to split with me?"

Sonnenberg chuckled, without humor. "Now that would be somethin', wouldn't it? No, I got me two jobs, Cheyenne—one of them right here in town, the other one in Durango."

He paused for a drink. "Cheyenne, this here's a job I'm going to like. I'm going after Val Darrant."

Dawson sat up slowly. Val Darrant was living at the same hotel as Myra Fossett, and he was the one they said owned all that property.

"Ain't he the one who got Hardesty?"

"Uh-huh . . . and Pike, later. I never figured that kid would get old Thursty."

Cheyenne was drawing wet circles on the table top with his glass. He was scarcely listening to what Henry was saying. "You know," he said, "there's money in this. Not just a few dollars . . . there's real money in it, but we got to act fast."

"I told you I got a job. I got one right here in town."

"In town?" Cheyenne looked at him. "Who is it, Hank?"

Henry Sonnenberg wiped his mustache. He smiled suddenly, his small eyes almost closing.

"It was this woman," he said. "She gave me five thousand for Darrant's scalp, and a thousand for the other job."

"Who is it? You can tell me, Henry."

Henry grinned at him. "Sure I can, Cheyenne. It's you."

Cheyenne Dawson stared at Sonnenberg, not grasping what he had said. Then slowly the idea got through to him, but even then it was not real. It could not happen to him, not to Cheyenne Dawson.

"You got to be joking," he said. "That ain't funny."

"This woman, she gave me a thousand for you. I never figured to make that much so easy, but she wants you done in, Cheyenne, and tonight. So I taken the money."

"Why, that don't make sense. Look at all the money we made together."

"After I done the work," Sonnenberg said. "No, she paid me for the job. That Val, he might be good with a gun. He might give me trouble, but not you. Seems you've been getting nosey in the wrong places, Cheyenne. You've been askin' questions."

"Look, Henry, this is real money. You forget this deal and work with me. You'll make twice as much—"

The gun sound was muffled by the table, but it still seemed loud. Cheyenne felt the blow in his stomach, and he tried to cling to the table as he slid off his chair and fell to the floor.

For a moment he was there on his knees, his fingers on the edge of the table as he stared across at Henry, who picked up the bottle, took a long drink, and got to his feet. Cheyenne slid down from the table and sprawled on the floor.

Henry Sonnenberg nudged him with his foot, then taking the bottle with him, he went out the back door into the alley, through the stable, and out on the street on the other side where his horse waited.

Within twenty minutes he was out of town and riding west.

# TWENTY-SEVEN

Nobody slept in Durango unless lulled to sleep by the sound of pistol shots. The town was not quite two years old and was still celebrating. The grand opening of the West End Hotel had to be postponed when it was badly shot up by the Stockton-Simmons bands of outlaws and gunmen.

The Stockton gang, from the Durango area, had a going feud with the Simmons outfit of Farmington, down in New Mexico. The West End Hotel happened to be caught in the middle.

Some of the pistol shots in Durango were fired in sheer exuberance of spirits, others were fired with intent to kill, and a good many of them were fired erratically, and often as not it was the bystanders who suffered.

Val Darrant rode into town, coming up the trail from Pagosa Springs. Purposely he had chosen the longest and less traveled route from Denver, for he had a hunch that somewhere along the way he was supposed to be met by Henry Sonnenberg, or somebody like him.

Dube caught up with him thirty miles out, and Boston, not to be left out, had taken the stage.

Animas City had been the town of the locality until the railroad came . . . but did not come to Animas; so the bulk of the

223

population promptly packed up bag and baggage and moved to
Durango, two miles or so to the south. Animas City had been
alive for twenty years, and it died in the space of a day.

Val Darrant was riding a line-back dun when he came into
Durango, Dube Bucklin beside him on a dapple gray. They rode
to the livery stable and left their horses, and packing their Winchesters they walked along the street to the West End Hotel.

Boston met them in the door. "Val, there's a man here named
Cates. He knows you, and has a box for you."

"Thanks." He paused before the hotel, sweeping the street
with sharp attention. He saw nobody with the bulky body of a
Sonnenberg.

He did not know the men who had been reported to be
traveling with Sonnenberg, except by name. The half-breed Pagosa,
Marcus Kiley, and Tom . . . he might know Tom.

He would surely know him. Tall, lank, ill-smelling because he
rarely bathed, a strange, mentally disturbed man. As Will had
said so long ago, nobody ever knew about Tom . . . and it was
something to remember.

He said as much to Dube. "Don't worry," Dube replied.
"Tensleep is in town. He rode west right behind Boston's stage,
sort of keepin' an eye on her. She'd throw a fit if she knew . . .
says she can care for herself, and likely she can, but a body never
knows. But Tensleep knows them all, especially Tom."

"I remember him," Val said. "As a matter of fact, I remember
that he knew my grandparents—Myra's folks. He came from the
same town, or somewhere near. He said they were good people."

It was cool and pleasant here. A few thunderheads showed in
the north, over Animas Mountain.

Val went into the hotel, and looked down the street from the
lobby window. A man had gotten up from a seat on the edge of
the boardwalk and gone into the saloon.

"Val," Boston said, close behind him, "be careful."

They heard a door close, and turned to see a man coming up
the dark hall from the back of the hotel. It was Tensleep.

Suddenly Val realized that Tensleep was an old man. He had
never thought of him that way, for the outlaw-cowhand-gunfighter
had never seemed to change.

"They're all here, Val. I don't think they saw me, but I seen

ever' last one of them. And they're loaded for bear. Pagosa's got
him a buffalo gun, and Kiley is packin' a double-barrel shotgun."

"Thanks. Stay out of the way, Tensleep."

"You kiddin'? This here's my party as much as yours. I never
did like that Sonnenberg, and he knows it."

"How about Tom?"

Tensleep shrugged. "He's with them, ain't he?"

Egan Cates came into the room. "Val, we've got to talk. There's
this box—"

"I know about it."

"Yes," said Cates, "and so does everybody else. I've had two
flat cash offers for it in the last twenty-four hours. Masters wants
to buy it because of what he could do to Myra if she starts
trouble. Myra herself wants it . . . and Lord knows who else."

"Where is it?"

"Under my bed . . . and it isn't easy to sleep with it there."

"I'll take it off your hands. Tensleep"—he turned to him—"you
go with Cates. Move that box to my room and you sit on it, do
you hear?"

"And miss out on the fight?"

"No, just until Boston can get there. She will take care of it."

Dube had been leaning on the door jamb, watching down the
street. "It's quiet," he said, "but that's normal, this time of day.
This here's a Saturday-night town, and by day most folks are
about their business, whatever it is."

"Your canyon is right out of town," Cates said, "if you want to
look at it."

"I'm selling it," Val said, "that's all." He was cold inside, and
he felt oddly on edge, and did not want to talk.

Boston was quiet, and he liked it that way. Just having her here
was important. They moved into the dining room. The waitress
was apologetic. "They hadn't really planned to serve meals, and
they may not continue the practice, so we're really not set up for
it."

"Just anything," Val said. He was not hungry, but he wanted to
be busy.

"You hadn't better eat," Cates said. "It makes it worse if you
get shot in the stomach."

But they ate, and Val gradually began to simmer down, some of
the tenseness going out of him as he drank the coffee.

"Boston," he said then, "you go back and stay in my room or yours, but watch that box."

"Is it so important?"

"To me it isn't important at all, but it is important to her. Everything she's done goes right down the drain if that box is opened and the contents get known."

"What about you? And her people?" Boston said. "Val, her people probably believe she's dead. It would ruin them if all this came out now. Don't do it, Val."

"Why should I? She hasn't anything I want. The one thing she could have given me was just to be a mother to me, but that's long ago and far away."

The street was empty except for a dark man who leaned on a horse as if he were sick. He had just come from a saloon and he had his head down against the saddle, one hand gripping the horn as he stood there.

It was quiet in the room. Somebody had put a grandfather's clock in the lobby when they began fitting the hotel for operation, and they could hear its ticking. Val pushed back from the table and stood up. "I never was much for waiting," he said. "I'm going down there."

"That's taking too much of a chance," Dube said. "You might get drilled when you walk out on the street."

"I don't think so. I think Henry would like to let me have it close up."

"Even so," Cates protested, "you're forted up here. Make them bring it to you."

Val was wearing a holster, had been wearing one since riding out of Denver. He eased it into position on his leg, dropped his hand to the butt. "You can do me a favor, Cates, by keeping an eye on Boston and that box."

"All right." Cates hesitated a moment, started to speak, and then went out.

"Well," Dube said, "there's three of us, and four o' them . . . so far as we know."

"That Sonnenberg," Tensleep said, "is an army all by himself. I've seen him work."

The sick man leaning against the horse was no longer visible, for the horse had turned broadside to the door of the hotel, and the man was behind it now. How old had he been when Will

taught him that trick? If he walked out of the hotel there would
be a rifle peering at him from over that saddle.

"Sonnenberg is the one I want," Val said, "I don't care about
the others."

The rifle muzzle had appeared over the horse's back now.

Val took up his rifle, and then put it down. He did not want
anybody to get hurt helping him. "Dube, there's a man behind
that horse down there with a rifle trained on this door. I can't
take a step if he's there. Why don't you go upstairs where you'll
have a better view of him. Just give him a shot to get him out of
there . . . shoot at his feet or whatever you like, but move him."

Val poised at the door, waiting. Suddenly a rifle's sharp crack
cut the stillness of the afternoon. The horse sprang away, and the
suddenly exposed rifleman raced for the door. He had taken no
more than two steps when a second shot ripped splinters from the
boardwalk. He fell, got up, and a second bullet struck his boot
heel and knocked him sprawling.

Val left the door running, reached the back of the buildings,
raced along them to the saloon, stopped suddenly, and stepped
inside.

At the sound of his step Sonnenberg, Kiley, and Tom turned as
one man. They were spread out badly, but that could not be
helped.

"Well, Henry," Val said quietly, "it's been a long time since
that time on the mountain in the snow. I never figured you'd live
this long."

Sonnenberg was smiling. He looked huge, invulnerable. His
body seemed like the side of a battleship. "You come to get it, kid?
We're goin' to kill you, you know."

Val was smiling and easy. All the tenseness seemed gone from
him. He heard himself talking as if he were another person.

"Howdy, Tom. You're the one I'm not likely to forget. You
knew my grandparents once, Tom."

"They were good people," Tom said, "not like their daughter."

"But she's the one who is paying to have me killed—or did
Henry tell you?"

"No, sir, he never told us that. You never told us any of that,
Hank."

"Hell, who cares?" Kiley said. "Her money's as good as
anybody's."

"But she's his mother! She's blood kin to 'im! Why, I used to deliver milk to that house when I was a boy, I—"

"Shut up, old man!" Kiley said. "We got us a job to do."

"I remember you, Tom," Val said. "I was a mighty lonely, frightened kid then, and when I left in the sleigh with Will Reilly, it was you who tucked the blanket in."

"What is this?" Sonnenberg said. "Old home week?"

"No," Val said, "I just wanted Tom to know I wasn't going to shoot at him," and he drew.

Henry Sonnenberg was fast and sure, but that split second of reaction time cost him his speed. Val's gun slid out as if it was greased.

The speed of it shocked Sonnenberg, and something clicked in his brain. *I couldn't have beaten him anyway!* it said.

The bullet slammed into him, but he never moved his body, only his gun came up like the arm of a well-oiled machine. The gun muzzle dropped into line and the hammer slid off his thumb just as the second and third bullets jolted him. He took a step back then, his arm swinging wide.

Guns were hammering in the room, but Val Darrant knew the man he had to kill was Henry Sonnenberg. He took a step to one side, so that Sonnenberg would have to swing his gun into line, and he shot the big man again.

Four bullets . . . one more.

Sonnenberg turned and shot and the bullet knocked Val around and to his knees. He felt another bullet cut through the hair at the side of his head, a sure hit had he not been knocked down.

He lunged up and dived into Sonnenberg, who took a cut at his skull with his gun barrel, but Val had ducked in close and stabbed the muzzle of his gun into the big man's belly. He held it tight and squeezed the trigger and felt the man's body jolt into his arms. Their faces were only inches apart.

"Hello, Henry," he said, and then, "Good-bye, Henry."

The man sagged against him, his gun going off into the floor, and Val stepped back, letting him fall heavily as Tensleep and Dube came bursting through the door.

Marcus Kiley was down, shot to doll rags by Tom, who was sitting wide-legged, his back against the bar.

"They were good folks," Tom said. "Used to let me warm

before their fire on cold mornings. They never deserved a girl like Myra . . . even then she was a mean one."

Blood was staining his shirt. "You got him, boy. You killed ol' Henry. He never believed the bullet was made that could kill him."

Val dropped to his knee beside him. "Thanks, Tom. Will Reilly always said you were a good man."

"But a little crazy. Just a little crazy in the head, that was what they always said about me—but Myra's folks, Will Reilly, and you . . . it never made no difference to you all."

"Tom, I—"

"Val," Tensleep said, "he's dead. He died right there."

Val was feeding shells into his empty gun. "What about the breed?"

"He was dead before we got to him. One of those bullets of mine or Dube's must have ricocheted into him—we were both shootin'."

They started back up the street together, walking side by side.

Boston came out of the door to meet him, running into his arms.

"There's a train through here tomorrow," Val said. "Let's go home on the Denver & Rio Grande."

The stage came in just before sundown, and with the crimson and pink of the sunset coloring the sky and the rims of the mountains around, Val closed his deal with Cope, a clear sale for cash and stock.

"Myra's gone east," Cope told him. "She could only make money with the right-of-way if she sold to one of us, and we wouldn't do business with her."

Cope glanced around at Dube, Tensleep, and Cates. "Son," he said, "it looks to me as if you've made some friends, some really good friends."

"I hope I can always be as good a friend to them as they have been to me," Val said, "and I think I can. I had a man who taught me how."